LORD MOIRA'S ECHO

A Novel

Stuart Bennett

Longbourn Press

ISBN: 1494475197
ISBN-13: 9781494475192
Library of Congress Control Number: 2013923460
Longbourn Press, Belmont, Massachusetts

PREFATORY NOTE

J ane Austen's family destroyed much of her correspondence, although enough records survive to piece together a fairly detailed chronology of her life. But there is one notable gap. All primary sources for June 1801 through September 1804 have disappeared.

Jane was rumored to have had a love affair during this time. With whom? What happened to him? Jane's sister reported that the man had died, but Jane's recent biographer David Nokes is skeptical of the whole story, lover and all.

One largely unremarked but historically important figure made a shadowy appearance in the lives of Jane Austen's family during this period. He was Francis Rawdon-Hastings, second Earl of Moira and, after 1816, first Marquess of Hastings. Jane's brother Henry spoke of him bitterly even after Jane's death in 1817, and he figures in Austen family correspondence as late as the 1820s.

Lord Moira had distinguished himself as a young officer fighting American rebels, from Bunker Hill in 1775 to the bitter closing months of the war in the Carolinas. Later Moira became a parliamentarian and close friend of the young Prince of Wales, afterwards George IV. But the Prince demanded loans from his friends, loans which were never repaid. Moira parted with more than £100,000 – at least £7,000,000 in modern money. Some of this was money Moira didn't have. By 1801 he was all but bankrupt.

This novel, which takes place in 1823 and shifts back and forth to 1801 and 1802, imagines what might have happened if Lord Moira had cast more than a shadow upon the Austens. Almost everyone who appears is real, with two notable exceptions. Readers of my previous novel, *The Perfect Visit*, will recognize Vanessa Horwood as a young Canadian musician from the 21st century stranded by a failed time-travel experiment. Her companion, the Honourable William Lonsdale, is captain in an imaginary regiment of the British army. I have also created a largely fictional character in Sir William Clifton and an imaginary office and employees of Hoare's Bank in Hampshire. I should add, however, that the location of the bank is real and that it previously belonged to Jane Austen's brother Henry until its collapse in 1815. With one or two minor exceptions, there is nothing in the historical record to prevent any of the real characters being where and when this story puts them.

CHAPTER I
1823

It was the cigar smoke Vanessa hated most. That and the heat which made her perspire and threatened to dissolve the gum aspic holding her blond moustache and side-whiskers.

She regretted being back in London. London was a reminder of hard times, six years earlier when she was struggling to make a living as a piano instructor and dismissed as a worthless colonial by the middle class and aristocracy alike.

It was Will Lonsdale's dare – the Honourable Captain Lonsdale of the Twelfth Sussex Foot – that had brought her both to London and into this shroud of smoke. He was a daring fellow, and had recognized Vanessa as the sort of woman likely to rise to a challenge.

She looked at him across the baize-covered circular table, intent upon his betting. Vanessa had thrown in her cards, disappointed at her losing hand but well aware how much she'd already won that evening. The hundred pounds she'd taken from her small savings wouldn't normally have got her through the door of White's Club, St. James's on a busy summer night in 1823.

But of course she'd never have got in at all if she hadn't dressed as a man, in her sporty blue nankeen jacket and cream-colored breeches. And been in the company of the Hon. Captain Lonsdale.

She'd won enough in the public rooms downstairs to tuck her original stake into a pocket of her jacket. Playing with other people's money was much less nerve-wracking.

And she had quite a bit of it, mostly banknotes, stacked on the table in front of her, along with enough gold in another pocket to live in luxury for a month. But she knew she'd keep her tiny room at the Bell Inn by St. Paul's Cathedral, and in due course go home to Bath in the least expensive post-coach.

"Home to Bath" felt almost natural to her now. She'd moved with a friend almost five years ago. But Vanessa would never be quite at home there, or anywhere in this time. She'd always be a stranger, stranded by a twenty-first century time-travel experiment that had failed.

She thought of that failure every day, sometimes every hour, always with bitterness. What had happened to the man who was supposed to have been her fellow time-traveller, a man she had begun to love? And why hadn't he and the rest of them rescued her? Her mind told her they were bound to have tried, but her heart said she'd been abandoned. Maybe, she wondered – and was surprised she hadn't thought of it before – that's why she was so quick to take a dare. She felt she had nothing to lose.

One of Captain Lonsdale's acquaintances had invited them upstairs to a private room, where games were played for higher stakes. It had been vingt-un for nearly two hours and she was longing to leave. She felt like a fool in her men's clothing and artificial whiskers. The evening had seemed such a lark when Lonsdale proposed it, but now she was in the thick of it she kept thinking of women who'd come to grief by cross-dressing. Especially Lady Caroline Lamb, subject to fits of insanity ever since she'd dressed as a page for her assignations with Lord Byron, assignations which had come to a notorious conclusion. And women who dressed as men seldom fared well in fiction either, as the novels of Frances Burney and Maria Edgeworth could attest.

Even Vanessa's satisfaction in winning couldn't compensate for the way Lonsdale was looking at her across the table. As though she were already a conquest, as though he could do with her whatever he would.

He'd been dealer for a long stretch of the game, and because the dealer was the last to turn over his cards he had a slight edge over the other players. But a few hands earlier two opposing players had been dealt natural twenty-ones. Lonsdale had been required to pay out double stakes to both and to hand the deal over to the one with the higher honors.

Once again Vanessa looked around the table. There had been ten players at first. Now there were six. She looked at Will Lonsdale again, compelling him to meet her eyes, impatient for him to throw in his cards. She'd never seen his mood so dark, his temper so edgy.

She'd known him for three months. He'd attended one of her piano recitals in Bath and then sought her out at the next ball. He'd seemed quite the military rake in his elegant red uniform, its facings so perfectly white, its buttons and boots so brightly polished.

But he'd spoken of her recital with an appreciation that made clear he'd actually listened, and proved himself educated, witty, and adventurous in ways Vanessa couldn't help but admire. He taught her to drive his curricle, took her to musical events in Cheltenham, and gave her entrée into literary circles in Oxford she'd never have seen without his companionship. He'd been charming, undemanding. Now he seemed dangerous.

Lonsdale had lost every round since he'd transferred the deal, betting heavily on each. And although he held his liquor well Vanessa could tell he was drunk. She'd never seen him like this, and she didn't like it.

He and the dealer were the last players in this hand. All the others, including Vanessa, had overdrawn – gone over twenty-one. It would be easy for Lonsdale to be cautious, to show his two cards and challenge the dealer, who had to draw on a sixteen.

Lonsdale looked once more at the concealed card in his hand. He was showing a ten. If he'd been counting the cards, as she had, he'd know that the last hand had seen a run of low cards. The final player had taken four to reach sixteen and gone over with a final, foolishly-taken six. If Lonsdale's two cards totaled fifteen the odds were normally only slightly against him. But Vanessa calculated there was now a better-than-even chance he'd draw a ten or a face card, which would make him overdrawn even if he held only a twelve or thirteen.

"Two hundred," he called, pushing the last of his banknotes towards the centre and tapping the table for a card.

The dealer turned it over. Another six.

Vanessa heaved a sigh of relief. But Lonsdale flipped his concealed card: the last six in the pack. He'd bet on sixteen, just as his predecessor had, and his twenty-two likewise put him over. He'd lost.

He looked at Vanessa.

"One more hand, Horwood. I'll give you my note for five hundred."

She shook her head, not wanting to speak.

Another player, more visibly drunk, started to laugh.

"Is your catamite holding out on you, Lonsdale?"

"Take care, sir," Lonsdale answered coldly. "Horwood is a fighting man, whom you insult at your peril."

"Are you so, my lad?"

Vanessa swallowed. "I do not seek it."

"Well said, young sir," came a deep voice from across the table. "Our friend means no harm. He is drunk as an owl, and speaks without thinking."

Vanessa had been watching this last speaker throughout the game. Obviously another aristocrat, he was lean and tall, surely closer to seventy than sixty, with receding gray hair above a sun-blackened face and just a hint of an Irish accent. He had a habit of holding himself ramrod-straight without apparent effort, radiating authority in spite of his age.

He smiled at Vanessa, and turned to his companion.

"You're no better off than Captain Lonsdale, Clifton. I hope you've some banknotes up your sleeve."

Clifton was a pleasant-looking, medium-sized younger man, with wavy brown hair and no single prominent feature. He forced a smile but didn't reply.

Vanessa glanced at the last two players. Another military man had the dealer's card-shoe. He'd been the one to invite them upstairs. The other was the civilian who'd insulted her, now blinking, just as the old aristocrat had said, like an owl. Vanessa, in her mid-twenties, was the youngest in the room.

The dealer smiled. "Perhaps Clifton needs a banker too."

Clifton glared across the table, but the lean old man laughed, tipping back in his chair and raising thick, bushy eyebrows.

"Clifton has me."

"But you are soon to leave England again, are you not, my lord?"

"Likely so," said the old man. "And Clifton will come as well, will you not, sir?"

"I must consult my wife, my lord."

"Your wife," replied the old man. "Of course you must."

Vanessa tried to stay relaxed, but similar banter had gone on throughout the game. She was tired of it. Come *on*, Lonsdale.

"Well, Horwood?" came Lonsdale's voice, more insistently.

"Of course I shall take your note," Vanessa snapped, pushing banknotes across the table. "But haven't you lost enough? You need not play another hand."

"He knows that," said the dealer. "Give the boy your note, Lonsdale, and let's get on with it."

Lonsdale took his cards and bet the two hundred pound limit once again. He won that hand, but still refused to leave. Vanessa, shaking with anger, withdrew, bowing to the other players. It was less smoky outside, and a little cooler. She scanned the corridor to be sure she was not observed, and then nudged her moustache back into what she hoped was its proper place.

Ten minutes later Lonsdale emerged, empty-handed.

"It's over," he said. "Hastings has won."

The four other players joined them in the hallway. The dealer shook Lonsdale's hand and departed, helping his civilian friend negotiate the stairs. The two others remained.

At close quarters the old man was even taller than Vanessa had expected, unpretentious in a dark frock coat over fawn breeches. His waistcoat was simply embroidered, his white neck-cloth loosely tied. He was still vigorous, his military bearing even more obvious now he was standing.

Vanessa almost curtseyed before she caught herself and bowed.

Lonsdale did likewise. "My lord Hastings," he murmured.

"I surmise, Captain Lonsdale," said the old man, "that your friend intends to tear up the note you wrote just now."

"Surely not," replied Lonsdale.

Lord Hastings turned to Vanessa. He was smiling, but she was startled at the sadness in his eyes. "Are you not?" he asked.

Vanessa hadn't expected to like him, and surprised herself when she smiled back.

"Perhaps, my lord."

"Quite," said Hastings. "I have a proposal for you, young – ah – sir. I shall purchase Lonsdale's note from you for the sum of two hundred and fifty pounds. We shall share his losses equally."

"Done," said Vanessa instantly.

"But your lordship can collect upon the note, surely," Clifton interposed.

"Indeed he can," said Lonsdale ruefully.

Lord Hastings was counting out banknotes, and after a moment exchanged them for Vanessa's slip of paper, which he promptly tore up.

"Since when have I ever collected on a debt?" he demanded. "But, Lonsdale, you must repay me by bringing your young friend to Campden Hill tomorrow afternoon for whist." He turned to Vanessa. "I assume you play whist?"

"Yes, my lord."

Hastings smiled again. "You may unpin your pretty blonde hair and wear a gown if you choose. I expect my wife and daughters would take it kindly."

He turned back to Lonsdale. "We dine at five o'clock, Captain." Then he nodded to Clifton, who accompanied him down the stairs.

Vanessa and Lonsdale followed. She shivered as the night air of St. James's Street struck them. It was past midnight on a mild summer evening, but much chillier outside than in the stifling upstairs game-rooms of White's Club. There were still lights in many of the surrounding buildings, and revelers staggering towards them from Piccadilly. To their left, down St. James's Street, some well-dressed whores were confronting a group of young officers.

"I know them," said Lonsdale.

Vanessa couldn't resist. "The ladies?"

Lonsdale snorted, turning to her with a smile and taking her arm. His mood had recovered. Vanessa knew she was being uncharitable, but she couldn't help wondering if it was because Lord Moira had forgiven his debt.

"You know better than that. Let's avoid them all and go along Jermyn Street instead."

"I shall take a hackney-coach to St. Paul's," she replied. "Shall I drop you at your brother's house?"

"Yes, please," said Lonsdale, drawing her closer. "And you should stay too. There is no one at the house but servants, and they are souls of discretion."

She went on tiptoe to kiss his cheek. "You know I shall not, love. But you may share as far as the Strand."

They found a carriage in Haymarket and were soon on their way. Vanessa waited, knowing Lonsdale would speak in his own time.

"I was a fool," he said, "to take your money."

"I don't deny it," she replied.

"And now the Marquess of Hastings has forgiven the debt."

"How do you know him? All I've heard is that he's just resigned as Governor-General of India."

"My father tried to form a ministry with him when I was a child. And my regiment served under him in the Nepal campaign in 1816." He gave a reminiscent sigh. "After Wellington he is the finest commander I've ever known. I cannot imagine how he managed to remember a young lieutenant from seven years ago."

Lonsdale's voice, slurred only half an hour earlier, was once again sharp. The carriage struck a pothole and he took the opportunity to put an arm around Vanessa, smiling down at her.

"You are none the worse for the evening, I believe."

"No, sir, I am not, in spite of your taking my money. I shall stand your breakfast and coach fare to Bath, if you like."

She reached up, tugging at her moustache. It came away easily, but the false side-whiskers were stuck to some of her own hair, at the temple.

"Ow," she cried, pulling away from his arm with an imploring look. "Can you cut them off for me, Will?"

He smiled. "Yes," he said, pulling a clasp knife from inside his uniform tunic. "But first. . . ." He leaned across to kiss her, but Vanessa retreated further. She'd watched him all night, and knew where this was leading.

Lonsdale's older brother, heir to the family title, had a townhouse near the Royal Society of Arts, close to the Strand. Vanessa had never been inside, and was not about to make her first visit at midnight, now only half-disguised as a man. As their carriage made its right turn after Charing Cross, she asked Lonsdale one last question.

"Who was the man with Lord Hastings?"

Lonsdale turned. "Clifton?"

Vanessa nodded. "He didn't seem to like the joke about his lordship never collecting on debts."

"He wouldn't. His wife is Hastings's ward, and Hastings has encumbered her dowry. I don't suppose Sir William Clifton is his largest creditor, but there must be a good deal of money involved."

The carriage stopped. Lonsdale held out an arm in one last invitation, and when she shook her head he leaped out, striding to the house without a backward look.

CHAPTER II
1823

Francis Rawdon-Hastings, Marquess of Hastings, Viscount Loudon, Earl of Rawdon and second Earl of Moira, sat in the old phaeton carriage he'd owned for thirty years, since the time of his extravagant renovation of a newly-inherited house in Leicestershire. His extravagant days were over, but it nevertheless pleased him that he'd been able to tear up young Lonsdale's promissory note.

The act hadn't pleased his protégé, Sir William Clifton, but there was little Hastings could do that pleased Clifton. Clifton and his lady, along with Hastings himself, were paying the price of King George IV's ruination of the family fortunes.

George IV had been Prince of Wales back then, of course, and the Marquess of Hastings had been Earl of Moira in the Irish peerage and Baron Rawdon in the English. "Two brothers," the Prince had said, all those years ago. "When one wants money he puts his hand in the other's pocket." But the only pocket ever invaded had been Hastings's own.

He bitterly regretted it all. He was fond of Lady Clifton, who'd been a child when she became his ward, and he'd mortgaged her inheritance along with every-thing else to satisfy the Prince's vanity and carnal appetites.

Clifton was making his own way home from White's. Hastings was able to stretch his long legs as he sat beside his Indian driver in the run-down but still jaunty old carriage, now making its way west towards Kensington and the Marquess's rented house at Campden Hill. This had been his first night out since he'd arrived home from India. He supposed his wife had dispatched Clifton to prevent too much betting.

But he'd confounded them all. Even after redeeming Lonsdale's note he had won more than two thousand pounds. His wife and daughters could go shopping in Bond Street tomorrow morning, and his creditors be hanged.

He knew his good cheer would not last. What was left of his world was too full of gloom and intrigue for that. The Hyderabad banking fraud which had clouded his last years in India would not go away, and it seemed that, for all the man's protestations to the contrary, Clifton had been involved in some questionable transactions using Hastings's name and position as security. Lady Clifton deserved better, even if the scandal would taint the rest of Hastings's life.

As the phaeton passed the southeast corner of Hyde Park, Hastings's thoughts returned to the evening just past. It was the girl who'd pleased him most. Had anyone at the table truly believed her a man? Her voice was too high and clear to manage a convincing gruffness, and her complexion – brown though it was (though by no means brown as his own) – too pure ever to have grown a beard. Nor had whatever padding she'd used in her jacket done much to conceal her natural curves, slender though she was.

Her wide blue eyes had captivated him throughout the game. Their spirit reminded him of another young woman long ago. She'd been about the same age then, and was now dead.

They'd met at Bath's Assembly Rooms in 1801. His career had been more hopeful then, as if there'd been a chance of his winning better treatment for the Irish, and for poor debtors. He'd even imagined extracting himself from the financial disasters surrounding the Prince of Wales.

Tonight's young woman had blue eyes and blonde hair; the one he'd fallen in love with in Bath had hazel and auburn. He leaned back against the phaeton's seat and allowed himself to reminisce.

It had been a close, unseasonably hot week in May 1801 when he'd gone to the Assembly Rooms, wearing an old-fashioned powdered wig and keeping his head down for the short walk. Hastings hadn't been a marquess then, but his portrait as Earl of Moira had been in some recent journals – not to mention caricatures – since he'd spoken out on Irish and military matters in the Lords. All too often strangers would accost him in the street and insist that he hear their opinions. It had happened again that morning and he was tired of it. Bath was supposed to be an escape from his duties in London, not an extension of them.

He'd gone to the Assembly Rooms for whist, but the game-rooms had been even hotter than White's on tonight's July evening, and his companions more dreary. He'd put on his powdered wig once more, and drifted out to watch the dancers.

She'd been gossiping with Mrs. Chamberlayne.

"Oh yes," she had said. "I have a very good eye for an adulteress, and that is certainly she."

He'd followed the young woman's gaze across the room. She'd been exactly right: the adulteress was Miss Twistleton, whom he'd seen in London on the arm of a member of the House of Commons.

Unable to stop himself, Moira gave a snort of laughter, catching Mrs. Chamberlayne's eye. She knew who he was, of course, and began to speak, curtseying deeply. But Moira cut her off.

"My dear madam," he said. "Pray forgive the intrusion and permit me to introduce myself to your companion." And before she could say another word he'd bowed, searching his memory for a name that wouldn't give away his rank. His mind went blank. Damn and blast, he thought. Fire and smoke. And then it came to him.

"John Evelyn, at your service." John Evelyn, he recalled triumphantly. Author of *Fumifugium: or, The Inconvenience of the Aer and Smoak of London Dissipated.*

He'd almost missed Mrs. Chamberlayne's response, ". . . Miss Jane Austen, recently arrived with her family from Hampshire."

Moira nodded. "Welcome to Bath, Miss Austen. I expect you share the common misery of visitors, which is finding suitable accommodation."

The girl had dropped her eyes, but when she raised them their hazel had the same spark as Miss Horwood's blue. Humor and defiance mixed.

"Indeed, Mr. Evelyn, although surely you are spared such misery. I presume you are a relation of my father's cousin Mr. William Glanvill-Evelyn, who has a fine house in Queen's Parade."

"Related, perhaps, at some considerable remove," replied Moira, giving a sidelong and he hoped forbidding glance at Mrs. Chamberlayne, who appeared to be choking. "My own family is Irish."

"Oh sir," cried Jane. "We know nothing of the Irish manners in Hampshire. We must cease to speak at once, before one or the other of us unwittingly gives offence."

"I believe you are safe with Mr. Evelyn, my dear," Mrs. Chamberlayne managed to say. "He has lived amongst the English for some considerable time now."

Moira bowed. "Thank you, ma'am. And now, Miss Austen, I believe you were about to speak of your own residence here."

Jane looked at him directly then, all humor gone.

"My family is temporarily spared the town's worst by the hospitality of my uncle, Mr. Leigh-Perrot."

She had to believe he would recognize the Leigh-Perrot name as one blackened by scandal. Only a year earlier Mrs. Leigh-Perrot had appeared at the Taunton Assizes on a charge of shoplifting from a Bath merchant. She'd been found not guilty, but the accusation lingered.

In fact Moira had heard the story only by chance, as it was hardly one to signify in the greater calendar of national crime. Evidently Miss Austen was offering him the opportunity to avoid her acquaintance.

But he chose not to. It wasn't that she was a great beauty – she certainly was not – but there was something intriguing, almost contradictory, about her looks. One would have expected meanness from such a small mouth, but her smile was gentle, even inviting. Her large, liquid, hazel eyes seemed designed for melting, come-hither glances, but he'd already seen a hard, ironic glint in them. She was tall, a blessing for one as overgrown as Moira. And she had a wonderful figure, complemented tonight by her simple gown, high-waisted and cut straight across the bosom, with a topaz cross sparkling above.

Moira bowed. "Would you grant me the honor of a dance, Miss Austen?"

From the side of an eye Moira perceived Mrs. Chamberlayne, apparently now in danger of fainting. He turned to her at once. "With your permission, ma'am, of course."

"Pray continue, my l -- . . . Mr. Evelyn. I shall undertake to revive myself by the time you return."

The little orchestra struck up 'The Pleasures of the Town,' an allemande. If Miss Austen was puzzled why so many of the other dancers made room for them so readily, she gave no sign of it. They joined a group that was one couple short, and were soon parading with the best of them. Moira's hard looks quelled those few of the other dancers who attempted to speak, and he and Jane remained on the dance floor for two further rounds.

Afterwards he bowed again. "You dance beautifully, Miss Austen, and I greatly regret that I must take my leave. You were much admired, however, and I do not doubt there will be a siege of prospective partners as soon as I am out the door."

"Never believe it, Mr. Evelyn," she cried. "The other young women will not allow it, even were their gentlemen so inclined, which I doubt."

"Surely you cannot know them so well, having just arrived in town?"

"I know them scarcely at all, sir. But I have learned to recognize the characteristics."

Moira decided this was too good to abandon. "And may I ask what *are* those characteristics?"

"You will note from the eleven other couples sharing the dance floor, that all but three of the women were short. The shorter the lady, the more determinedly exposed the bosom, and the more steadfast she clings to her gentleman, with what I conceive my nautical brothers might call 'grappling-hooks.'"

"Indeed," replied Moira, preserving a straight face. "And the taller ladies?"

Jane met his eyes again. He almost recoiled at the strength in her gaze.

"I perceive you are teasing me, sir."

Directness called for directness. "Never in life, Miss Austen. I cannot recall when I have more enjoyed a conversation."

Her mouth scarcely twitched, but he decided it could be counted a smile.

"You wish me to continue?"

"In the same manner, I beg."

"I shall not comment on those with the misfortune to be as tall as I, lest you think I attempt to excuse myself."

"What of the two sisters opposite?"

"Oh no, sir, I may speak ill in generalities, but I shall not say unkind things of any young women in *particular*."

"Indeed you must not, or at least not in public. Perhaps you will walk with me in Sydney Gardens tomorrow?"

She curtseyed in reply. "I may walk in the morning, sir. In the afternoon I am promised to my father for another tour of Bath's putrefying houses."

Moira bowed. "I shall be at the Gardens' west entrance at ten o'clock."

"Unless it rains."

"Just so, Miss Austen."

And so it had begun, all those years ago. There must have been something more than the eyes of the young woman at White's for her to remind him so forcibly of Jane. He sometimes went for days without thinking of her. Was it returning to London after ten years in India that had brought Jane back? He felt himself shaking his head. No, it was tonight's young woman, Miss Horwood herself. As he climbed out of the carriage he knew he was glad she and Captain Lonsdale were coming to his house tomorrow.

CHAPTER III
1823

Vanessa woke up worrying. Usually the familiar warmth of the ancient, half-timbered Bell Inn was reassuring. But today its age only made her feel further from her home and friends in Bath and more awkwardly aware of her status as someone out of her own time, in danger of making a fool of herself, or worse, at any moment.

She felt intimidated by the old aristocrat whose invitation last night had seemed more like a command. Not to mention perplexed by her relationship — romance — whatever it was she had with Will Lonsdale.

Until this week he'd never hinted that the time had come for more than kisses. She couldn't really protest that he'd started to push his luck, not even last night when she'd rejected his invitation to spend the night at his brother's townhouse. It was obvious that Lonsdale wanted to sleep with her, and she knew that by his standards — and perhaps even those of London at large — she'd encouraged him to believe that she would.

What did *she* want? Love, she supposed. And she wasn't getting it from the Honourable Captain Lonsdale. Lust he certainly exuded, which in itself was a fine compliment from a man as good-looking as he was. But she didn't want to be an officer's concubine. She knew well enough where that led: half the whores in St. James's had been kept by an officer at one time or another.

Could Lonsdale have assumed that her coming to London with him, and attending White's Club disguised as a young man, was itself so ruinous of her

17

reputation that the next step – having his way with her – had to be a foregone conclusion?

"Of course," she whispered, pulling herself from the bed.

She splashed her face with water from the basin and put on her best walking-dress. It was navy muslin with very little trim and that plain white, long enough to conceal her half boots. She wore no make-up, but a silk floral shawl from France brought out the blush under her unfashionably-tanned skin.

She decided she was presentable as she could ever be, and tried to let go of her cares. She'd find a piano and practice the morning away. Two brothers had engaged her to perform Mozart and Beethoven trios in Winchester later in the month. If Lonsdale wanted to make his own way to the Marquess of Hastings's house, he knew he could leave word at the Bell Inn.

Vanessa had spent two years in London as a piano-teacher before moving to Bath. She'd given lessons in Dean Street off Holborn, an easy walk from St. Paul's Cathedral and the Bell. She knew an instrument would be available there at short notice, although she would probably have to spend much of her first hour tuning it.

She took the long way around via Hoare's Bank in Fleet Street. Last night's gambling gains more than doubled her savings, something years of scrimping had never managed, and she wanted her money safely deposited. She went on to Dean Street with a mixed sense of accomplishment: happy to be so much richer but certain she never wanted to gamble again. For two hours she lost herself in her music, returning to the Bell shortly before one o'clock.

Lonsdale had not left word. He was waiting for her in person, impatient at the delay. He was freshly shaved and pomaded, even in his civilian clothes looking every inch the military man. Two of the hotel maids hovered in the doorway of the public bar, trying not to be seen casting longing looks in his direction.

Vanessa smiled. He was absurdly handsome, in the Byronic way that had become even more fashionable since the poet had gone into exile. But – perhaps this was part of her problem with him – he'd be more attractive if he were a little less sure of himself. Lonsdale knew how well he looked. He *cultivated* it.

"We should have eaten an hour ago," he snapped. "The Marquess will serve dinner at five."

"I'm happy to wait," Vanessa replied mildly.

Lonsdale moved his head sideways, as though allowing her words to fly past. "And how are you to get to Kensington? *My* horse is in the stable."

Vanessa stiffened at his rudeness, but she kept her voice even.

"You are surprisingly ill-tempered, sir. If you are determined to ride, I shall make my own way."

"Four miles, at least. And the last of it uphill."

"I live in Bath, sir. London hills are no trial."

"Damn it, Vanessa. . . ."

All eyes in the public bar were upon them now. She stepped closer and touched his face. Her voice was almost a whisper.

"Don't act like a child, Will. Are you regretting you didn't have one of the street-ladies last night?"

"Yes!" he cried. And then, abashed. "Of course not." He smiled ruefully. "Besides, I had not the means, whatever I might have wished."

She took a step back, and her voice, though quiet, became hard.

"You preferred to try me for nothing?"

"That is *not* what I meant. I've wanted you ever since I saw you."

Vanessa smiled, taking his arm and speaking naturally.

"Enough, sir. I intend no more than a sandwich before I cross London. In honor of the Marquess of Hastings and my ill-gotten winnings – which are now in the bank, in case you were wondering – I shall hire a chaise there and back. You may accompany me if you choose, and collect your horse upon our return."

"The Marquess's card-parties may have high stakes, Vanessa. If you have left your money behind how will you play?"

"And what about *you*, after last night?"

"Touché," he replied. Then he surprised her by laughing out loud. All at once he was the easy-going Lonsdale she thought she knew, charming and attentive. He took her arm and walked her towards the lounge.

"I lost more than I could afford," he said quietly.

"Then the Marquess must moderate the stakes. I have twenty-five pounds, and the chaise will get at least one of them."

Lonsdale guided her towards the dining room. "If you're paying for our transport, I shall buy our sandwiches. And I'm not *quite* so indigent that you couldn't have collected on last night's note. I can cover us up to five pounds a point this evening, if need be."

She smiled up at him. "Thank you, Will. But you must promise not to say so to the Marquess."

There were four large houses at the top of Campden Hill. Fortunately their driver knew which one belonged to the Hastings family. The Marchioness and her children had lived there since 1817 while the Marquess completed his tour of duty in India. The house was on a narrow plot of land, although Vanessa could see a deep garden behind it. There was a gate and gravel forecourt, and she was sure the upper rooms must have splendid views across London. But she admitted to herself that she had expected something more grand.

As a dark-skinned servant took their cloaks they were confronted by Sir William Clifton, the Marquess of Hastings's companion at White's. He spoke quietly, but with determination.

"You are here at my lord's invitation, but against my better judgment. I require your assurances that you will not encourage him to venture large sums upon the cards."

Vanessa caught Lonsdale's eye and smiled. "I have twenty pounds with me, sir, and I believe Captain Lonsdale has a little more. Is it too much?"

Clifton drew himself up. "You are toying with me."

Before either of them could answer, Lord Hastings entered the hallway.

"Ah, there you are Clifton. You've cornered our guests."

Once again he smiled at Vanessa, his face softening. His spirit infected her once again, and she grinned as she replied.

"He wished to make a request, my lord."

Hastings shook his big head, bushy eyebrows rising.

"No, my dear, if you will forgive my manner, for I must say you make a very creditable young lady. Clifton was not making anything so polite as a request. He would not believe that a 'Captain' anyone, and most particularly a captain who looks like young Lonsdale, could be anything other than a professional gambler."

It was Lonsdale's turn to smile.

"Surely, my lord, he must have been persuaded by my disastrous performance last night."

Hastings turned to Clifton, who declined to share the joke.

"I assumed, my lord, that Captain Lonsdale deliberately lost last night in anticipation of higher stakes this afternoon."

Hastings gave a deep chuckle. "I propose a shilling a point. My daughters will not play for more – or for less. And I may not play without them."

Vanessa caught Lonsdale's eye, but she managed to remain solemn.

"This is serious, my lord. In a truly unlucky session your daughters and I might lose as much as two pounds each, might we not?"

"Oh, no," came an earnest female voice from the end of the hallway. "On the worst night of my life I scarcely lost a guinea."

Lord Hastings turned and swept a bow. "My eldest daughter, Lady Flora. Flora, I present Miss Horwood and Captain Lonsdale."

Three more children followed: George, Selina, and Sophia. They made their bow and curtseys, and to Vanessa's surprise joined the adults at dinner, along with the Marchioness of Hastings, Sir William and Lady Clifton, and another couple.

Instead of the gentlemen retiring for port, the three whist tables assembled immediately after the meal. Lord Hastings did Vanessa and Lonsdale the honor of insisting that they join him and his lady for the first two rubbers, which meant that Vanessa was the Marquess's first partner.

No amount of careful play could compensate for her poor cards, and she and the Marquess lost two games in a row. In one respect Vanessa was grateful: she wasn't sure she could ever have concentrated with the children's table resounding with called tricks and honors, and howls of protest as each point was disputed.

After an especially loud shriek the children were advised that further noise would lead to instant dismissal, with no prospect of play at the adult tables. In the ensuing calm the Marquess began to ask questions.

"I was not informed you were Canadian, Miss Horwood, but now I am able to hear it in your accent. It is softer than the voices of the Americans I was obliged to fight near fifty years ago."

"Thank you, my lord."

The Marchioness spoke for the first time since play began.

"What brought you to this country, Miss Horwood?"

Vanessa turned to her hostess. She was much younger than her husband – she had to be to have such young children – but what had once been a round and possibly pretty face was now lined with care and, Vanessa thought, sorrow. It was full of kindness, however, and her voice was gentle, with a hint of Scottish burr.

"I shall make a long story short, my lady," Vanessa replied, smiling. She knew she could not tell the accident of her time-travel – some quirk of time itself prevented her speaking of such things even if she tried. She glanced across the table at Lonsdale. He knew one of her more recent secrets, and made a silencing gesture, which she ignored.

"I achieved a small reputation in Montreal playing the piano-forte, and my family decided to send me to England to study. But a bank in Hampshire declared my draft from the Hudson's Bay Company a forgery. I spent my first three months in gaol."

The Marchioness gasped and Lonsdale heaved a sigh. Out of the corner of her eye Vanessa saw the Marquess sit up straighter.

"Indeed, Miss Horwood. But forgery is a hanging offence, and you describe your sentence as though it were a misdemeanor."

"It was no sentence at all, my lord, simply detention as I awaited trial. An officer of Hoare's Bank identified his own signature on the draft, and I was released."

"Do you hear that, Clifton?" cried Hastings. "Another banking scandal, however trifling. Is there no end to such things?"

Young Lady Flora had approached the table and was gazing at Vanessa, wide-eyed.

"It wasn't trifling for Miss Horwood, Papa. You just said she might have hanged."

Vanessa smiled at the girl, who seemed to be imagining all that might have been, and was becoming pale.

"Thank you, Lady Flora," she said softly. "In fact I was fortunate enough in that gaol to meet the kindest person I have ever known, an Irishwoman my own age."

Lord Hastings rose, putting an arm around his daughter.

"I am pleased to hear your friend is Irish, Miss Horwood, as am I. Less pleased that you met her in gaol. Was she a forger too?"

"No, my lord, a debtor. She co-signed a note for the man she hoped to marry, and never saw him again."

"All too often the fate of my people. But" – he cast a significant look at Lonsdale before turning back to Vanessa – "you are not sharing lodgings with your Irishwoman now."

Flora, shocked, pulled away from her father. Vanessa smiled again.

"No, my lord. Nor am I with Captain Lonsdale. I am on my way to Hampshire for another friend's lying-in."

"And you took a small diversion along the way," remarked Hastings.

"Yester-night's was small. This afternoon's is not."

"Oh, well said," cried Hastings. "Let no-one declare that Canadians have no manners. You must speak to me of Canada one day, Miss Horwood. A man in the colonial service never knows where he may be posted next.

"Now, Flora," he continued. "Perhaps you will join your father for a second rubber, while your mother takes the children upstairs."

"I am *not* a child," called George from across the room.

"No," said the Marchioness firmly, "but you have been ill, and any more excitement will keep you from sleep. Come along, the three of you."

The adult tables switched partners as well. Vanessa saw the other players staring at her, obviously in a new, less complimentary light. She gave them all what she hoped was a carefree smile.

"May I partner with Miss Horwood, Papa?" asked Flora. "And may she play our pianoforte afterwards? We have just had it tuned."

"We shall not ask Miss Horwood to sing for her supper, my dear."

Flora blushed, but held her head high. "*I* could sing, if Miss Horwood would play."

"Brava," said Lonsdale, taking his seat opposite Lord Hastings. "And Miss Horwood can play anything on sight, if you have the music."

Flora gave Vanessa a shy smile. "We'll discuss the music later, shall we?"

Vanessa nodded, as Hastings spread the deck to cut for dealer.

Lonsdale had the high card, and as he dealt Hastings spoke again.

"Do you read poetry, Miss Horwood?"

"Oh, yes," cried Flora. "Byron, perhaps?"

"I dined with him in Italy not long ago," said Hastings with a smile. "And knew him a little before. He gave a fine maiden speech in the Lords, and then seemed to lose interest."

"I do admire Byron," Vanessa replied, "but I believe if I were to choose just one modern poet it would be John Keats."

Flora clapped her hands. "You see, Papa. Miss Horwood is a woman of taste, and admires him just as I do."

Hastings started to laugh, and Flora became indignant.

"You are *not* to repeat that story to Miss Horwood."

"May I not?" cried Hastings. "Watch me. You see, Miss Horwood, I also dined with Byron's bookseller only day before yesterday. He quoted from memory a letter Byron had written to him."

"You speak of John Murray, my lord?" asked Vanessa.

"Just so. Murray sent Byron a volume of Keats, and Byron wrote asking him to desist. Called it 'Johnny Ketch's piss-a-bed poetry,' and worse." He glanced at Flora and smiled. "Much worse. Murray said Byron was the most entertaining correspondent he's ever known. As I left he invited me to return and read more letters. Only when I reached home did I remember that I'd spoke not a word of Byron's news."

"It's rumored he's going to Greece."

"His preparations are now complete."

"So you may return to Mr. Murray's?"

"If time permits. I shall not be long in England."

Hastings's face darkened as he spoke, and Vanessa almost lost courage for her next question. Then he smiled at her, and she dared.

"Do you suppose he would let you read correspondence by his other authors?"

"I don't doubt it. Of whom are you thinking?"

"A lady novelist," said Vanessa. "Miss Jane Austen."

"Oh!" cried Flora. "I have read all of her books."

Hastings was silent, subdued and thoughtful. He took his time sorting the cards in his hand. Finally he spoke, looking straight across the room, over Lonsdale's head.

"I did not recollect that Murray published Miss Jane Austen. I shall make enquiries." Then he turned to Vanessa. "What is your interest in this author, Miss Horwood?"

"I came to know her a few months before she died. It is her family that expects me tomorrow in Hampshire."

For an instant Hastings met her eyes. Vanessa could not remember ever before seeing so much concentrated grief as he raised his cards to cover his face. When he lowered them it was as though he'd put on a mask.

He remained impassive, preoccupied for the rest of the evening. He played his cards competently but without enthusiasm, and applauded when his daughter sang a Mozart aria with Vanessa at the piano. Flora insisted that Vanessa play at least one piece unaccompanied as well, and she chose a couple of short sonatas by Pleyel. They had a special place in Vanessa's heart, as she'd played them on her first visit to Jane Austen's Hampshire cottage in the spring of 1817. Lord Hastings listened intently, but Vanessa could tell he was relieved when he could bid his guests goodnight.

CHAPTER IV
1823 AND 1801

Hastings was still reeling from this talk of Jane when he went to bed. How could this Canadian girl, who'd reminded him so much of Jane, turn out to have known her? And to echo some of the very music that Jane herself had played on the same pianoforte more than twenty years ago?

What had Jane become in the years since he'd loved her? Of course he'd read her novels, smiling at their dismissive treatment of titled aristocrats. He'd learned of her death more than a year after the event, from reading her brother's introduction to *Northanger Abbey and Persuasion*, published in 1818. Hastings had picked up the book by sheer chance, at his Calcutta bookseller's that summer. . . .

**

In May of 1801 his younger self, the Earl of Moira, had been at the entrance to Bath's Sydney Gardens the morning after the Assembly Room ball. Jane arrived in the hazy sunlight with a white-haired clergyman who introduced himself as her father.

"Jane asserted she needed no escort, sir. She claimed you were a relation of my own cousin William Evelyn, that you were a man as old as I, and that you could pose no possible threat to a young lady's virtue. I see she has once again composed a fiction."

Moira came to full attention. Jane had alerted him to this family connection the night before, when he'd unthinkingly introduced himself with the first alias that came to mind. He'd never imagined the name could matter. But now this old man might be about to challenge it. He chose his words carefully.

"No fiction, at least as far as being a threat is concerned. I am honored by both your companies, sir, but if you have other engagements you may see that the gardens are well-populated, and that help is close at hand should your daughter feel endangered."

"Just so," said Mr. Austen. "But I may add that Mrs. Chamberlayne wrote this morning to vouch for your honor. I daresay that is sufficient."

Moira glanced at Jane, radiant in the morning light, or perhaps simply blushing with embarrassment. She was also struggling not to smile.

"Has Miss Austen anything to add?" asked Moira. "She appears to be biting her lip to keep from speaking."

Jane curtseyed. "Well-bred young ladies never contradict their fathers, sir."

Mr. Austen gave a mild snort. "You thus declare yourself ill-bred, my dear, and so dishonor your family." He bowed to them both. "Do not over-tire yourself, Jane. You know I shall rely upon your judgment during our house tour this afternoon."

"Might I enquire what you propose to see?" asked Moira.

"I shall not tire you with the list. I believe our best prospect is at Green Park Buildings, but Jane tells me the kitchen is impossibly damp."

"Philips owns the terrace, if I am not mistaken," replied Moira. "I shall speak to him, but not in such way as to place you under any obligation."

"You are uncommonly generous to strangers, Mr. Evelyn. If you are able, sir, I should take it as a kindness if you would join us for tea at Mollands in Milsom Street after our labors. We shall be there no later than three o'clock. And with that I believe I shall take my leave."

Jane curtseyed once more, and her father retired with a bow. Then she took Moira's arm, and for what seemed the first time in his life he was speechless. They crossed the first of the garden bridges before Jane took matters in hand.

"Have you left a family in London, Mr. Evelyn? I assume you are here to take the waters."

Moira laughed. "Do I appear so infirm, Miss Austen?"

"Indeed not, sir. You are the picture of health, which is why I infer illness. If you appeared any stronger, I should assume your disease was fatal."

"I shall disappoint you. As far as I know I have no diseases and, apart from more brothers and sisters than I care to count, no family."

Jane stopped short, letting go his arm and turning to face him.

"Surely, Mr. Evelyn, you do not mean to inform me you are a bachelor?"

He knew she was mocking him. But this was 1801, when far too many men of her age and class were at war with Bonaparte. Under the mockery lay a harsh reality.

In the end he only bowed, sharing the joke. She took his arm once again.

"Just as I was beginning to think I might enjoy your company, I find I must treat you as a prospective suitor."

"You need not, Miss Austen. I might tell you I am betrothed, or disinclined towards women."

"It would have been a kindness, sir, but now it is too late."

"Then we shall speak of other things. Your father accuses you of composing fictions. Are you a writer?"

"In the humblest way, sir. I attempted novels and found I had insufficient invention. Then I undertook a play, with the same result."

"You abandoned them?"

"Oh, no. I stole the story of the play entirely from Mr. Richardson, as my brothers and sister will attest. All have performed in it, a play from his novel *Sir Charles Grandison*."

"Did these brothers include the nautical ones you spoke of?"

She looked up at him, eyes sparkling. By now they were in the centre of the gardens, surrounded by flowers. The lavender and lilacs were in bloom, along with a few forward roses. Perhaps it was the scent, and the suddenly brighter sunshine, but he recognized that what he saw in her face was love – even if, as he must assume, it was the love she bore her brothers.

"Where to begin," she said, touching the same topaz cross on her breast that she'd worn at the Assembly Rooms.

She saw him watching and smiled. "This," she said, holding it up, "is from my brother Charles, bought with his prize money from the capture of a privateer."

Moira smiled. "It is very fine, is it not?"

"Unbearably fine, sir." She tried to look stern and failed, beginning to laugh as she continued. "And an intolerable extravagance for a young lieutenant."

"And your other brother?"

"Poor Frank," she sighed. "He was made post captain last autumn, only to be visited, collared, and thrust out of his sloop by her new commander. He awaits his next appointment. And I have yet another brother in the military, Henry, who is captain in the Oxford militia, but threatens to resign to become a banker."

"I advise against it," said Moira earnestly. "Your other brothers will bespeak the dangers of inshore sailing, I am certain. Your Henry will be in uncharted waters, with shoals on all sides."

Jane's smile vanished. "You are serious, sir. Have you no love for bankers?"

"When they suit my purposes. But I fear I suit theirs better."

"And what of *your* life, and your brothers and sisters?"

"All but one of my sisters are married, and my brother has made his way to the House of Commons."

Jane was insistent. "This is all very well, sir, but what of *you*?"

Moira was usually quick-witted, but this simple question went to his essence. Did he mean to lie in order to keep up pretences? And how long would those pretences survive? He'd danced with the girl on a lark, and walked this morning for the pleasure of her company. But she was no flibbertigibbet. He could see the strength of her feeling for her family, and he perceived that her question for him came from no idle curiosity. He could tell the truth, swallow his shame and disappear, or continue the lie and stay, knowing she would never forgive him for it. Or he could stall.

"I mentioned I am Irish, Miss Austen, and I confess my family affairs are complicated. Far too complicated to begin explaining so near the end of our promenade. May I come for you in my phaeton next Wednesday? It arrives in Bath on Tuesday, and we can make first use of it together. I believe there are fine views to the east, along Kingsdown."

"So I am told, sir." She blushed. "I am content to wait till Wednesday."

"Oh, no," he replied. "I shall see you this afternoon at Mollands, faithful to your father's command. And I shall walk again here come Monday morning. Perhaps I may see you then?"

She smiled. "Perhaps, sir. That would make the outing in your phaeton our fifth meeting. I am quite certain a young woman should never accompany a gentleman in such a manner on shorter acquaintance."

"Ten o'clock Wednesday, then," he declared. "I shall send my sister with the invitation, to give comfort to your mother and aunt. No. 1, The Paragon, I believe."

She curtseyed. "You have the memory of a politician, Mr. Evelyn."

CHAPTER V
1801

Moira woke early that Wednesday morning. The sunny weather had given way to one of Bath's misty, rainy days. Good for gardens and gardeners, he thought. Not so much for sight-seers.

The afternoon meeting at Molland's tea-rooms had been brief. Jane had been with her aunt and uncle as well as her father. Mrs. Leigh-Perrot had been so full of foolishness, and Mr. Leigh-Perrot so full of gout, that real conversation had been impossible.

At least he and Jane would be in the phaeton today, and on their own. From the hills around Kingsdown they could look down on a kaleidoscope of small farms and green pastures, if they weren't altogether obscured by the mist. And there was an inn at Kingsdown, his coachman had said, with good food, and excellent stone fireplaces in the private dining rooms.

Go to it, Moira thought, pulling himself from his bed. One of the house-cats was asleep on the second pillow, and he had a vision of Jane's head there instead.

What would *that* be like? he wondered. He was forty-six and a bachelor. Women were occasional visitors to his beds and he to theirs, but as far as he could remember not one had ever slept through the night with him. He'd never been attracted to that kind of companionship before, and now he was wondering what it would be like with a young woman he'd scarcely met. And wondering what she might be like as a lover.

Enough, he decided. It was time to shave and he rang for his man. Under the lather he planned his morning. Usually he rode for an hour or more, but soon enough he'd be driving the phaeton. He decided on a leisurely breakfast.

Groomed and dressed, Moira gathered up a manuscript he'd received from an Irishman and his daughter, supposedly sent in honor of Moira's advocacy for the Act of Union which had bound Ireland to Great Britain the previous year. Something in the authors' letter made Moira wonder if their regard was altogether genuine, but it piqued his interest.

An hour later he was still at the breakfast-table. The manuscript was called *An Essay on Irish Bulls* and he'd begun laughing after the first couple of pages. The "bulls," he was told, were "vulgar Irish blunders," exemplified in one Irishman who, upon being told that a shout would echo around the lake of Killarney no less than forty times, replied "'Faith that's nothing at all to the echo around my father's garden, in the county of Galway; if you say to it 'How do you do?' it will answer 'Pretty well I thank you, sir.'"

Moira wondered how Jane would take to Irish blunders were he to quote them to her. She certainly had a satiric turn of her own, that pleased him uncommonly. So far, however, her strongest sallies seemed always accompanied by a blush.

Not that he minded. Her blushes were becoming, even alluring.

The mist had lifted a little when Moira went out to take the phaeton's reins from his coachman. The four horses were skittish in the drizzle and the phaeton's hood was up.

"Any hope?" Moira asked.

His man smiled. "Clearing by mid-day, my lord."

At the last moment Moira remembered to tell the coachman to put the black side-panels over the coats-of-arms on the carriage doors. The man raised his eyebrows: such concealment was normal at times of political upheaval in London, but almost unheard of elsewhere. Moira had no intention of explaining himself, however, and the deed was done in a couple of minutes.

Old Mr. Austen saw Jane to the carriage as soon as Moira arrived. No fashionable nonsense about making a gentleman wait: it seemed Jane had been anticipating the outing, and perhaps been ready to go as early as Moira.

They reached the Somerset hills before noon and with the coachman's prediction accomplished. The rain had all but ceased, and shafts of sunlight were beginning to part the clouds.

From one vantage point they could see a good-sized house, with a circular path winding to an opposite hilltop and back again by the other side. The house had smoke coming from no fewer than four chimneys.

"I am told that's the Swan Inn," said Moira. "We could leave the phaeton there, and if you did not mind some mud upon your boots we could walk along that path until dinner?"

Jane gave her assent. By the time they had finished their long walk Moira knew himself to be in love. And the looks Jane had given him, and him alone, had something of the radiance she'd shown in Sydney Gardens when she'd spoken of her brothers.

Their dinner was light, their wine scarcely touched. After the plates were cleared he knew it was time to speak. The table was small, and as he reached for her hand their knees touched. He felt an electric shock, like something from the erotic accounts of Dr. Graham's celestial electrical bed. He almost smiled, remembering his early-morning vision of Jane in his own bed.

"I told you I was Irish, and my affairs were complicated. Will I tell you more, now that I believe you may take an interest in them? And" – he took a deep breath – "in me?"

She blushed deeply. "You are right upon both counts, sir. I take a passing interest in the affairs of Mr. Evelyn. But I am not so entirely foolish as to ignore my own – shall I call it *fate*, my lord Moira?"

Now it was his turn to color. He had considered himself so dark-complexioned an Irishman as to be incapable of blushing, but the blood he felt in his face and the smile he saw upon Jane's gave him the lie.

"Ah," he said. "It is everyone's favorite play upon my title." He paused, gathering his thoughts. "I had been reading of Irish bulls – blunders of language – this morning, and now I find myself wallowing in one of my own making."

Her smile was gentle. "I am not so certain, my lord. You have behaved in a perfect, gentlemanlike manner all the time I have known you, a manner consistent with the Mr. Evelyn you pretended to be. But if you choose to speak differently, you must become yourself. Or so I conceive it."

"How long have you known?"

"I walked with Mrs. Chamberlayne yesterday, to Lyncombe and Widcombe. It was a longish walk, and she was about to leave Bath. She said she could not go without discharging the responsibility she felt for introducing me to you."

Jane smiled. "She produced an engraving from the *Universal Magazine*, published on the occasion of your speech calling for relief to insolvent debtors."

"I am one myself, you must know."

Jane nodded. "How not?" she asked softly. "The Prince of Wales is reported to have said that you and he are like two brothers. When one wants money he puts his hand in the other's pocket. Have you ever asked to put your hand in his?"

Moira shook his head, unable to speak. Finally, throat tight, he continued.

"I must go to London tomorrow, and do not know when I shall return to Bath. The consequences of the Act of Union with Ireland are not yet entirely clear, and there is also a chance of peace with France. Both require my presence in the Lords."

"I understand." He'd lost the pressure of her knee, and now she retracted her hand. She was sitting very straight. "You owe me no explanation, my lord."

"I do," he choked out. Then, more steadily, "I do if I want your promise, and want you to accept mine that when I have put my finances in order I shall ask you to be my wife."

Tears were rolling down her cheeks, which had gone crimson. But her eyes were bright, and looked directly into his as she replied.

"If that is what you have in mind, you are indeed obliged to explain yourself."

Moira took a deep breath. Once more he leaned across the table, this time taking both her hands.

"May I tell you the first Irish bull I read in my manuscript this morning?"

Her eyes were puzzled, but as her lips opened to speak he rushed on.

"It is pertinent, I believe, to our present concerns."

She leaned closer. "Go on."

He was reveling in the scent of her, wondering how long he could prolong this closeness. He made the story of the "How do you do?" echo last as long as he dared, and when she laughed, gently and appreciatively, he went on.

"There is a French version better still, sworn to be true by our own philosopher Lord Bacon. The echo at Port Charenton will never reply to anyone calling upon Satan."

"What does it say instead?"

"'Va t'en,'" said Moira.

"Get away," Jane whispered in confirmation.

"And so I must."

"From the Prince," she said softly. "How?"

He shook his head. "I have yet to find a way."

They left the inn then, not wanting to stay in the private room so long as to invite comment. The hood of the phaeton was still up. Moira longed to kiss her in the privacy it offered, but would not risk the presumption.

Once on the road he kept the horses in check, intent upon making the journey back to town last as long as possible.

"There will be days I may drive down, perhaps staying a single night. Can you meet me at short notice?"

Jane smiled. "I shall meet you whenever you come, although I may have to bring my sister for the sake of decency. She will soon arrive in Bath."

She hesitated. "And. . . my brother Henry is in London, and I sometimes stay over on my way to see yet another brother in Kent. It is not impossible for me to linger if it means" – she blushed again – "I might see you."

Moira nodded. "You know, of course, of the Prince's circle, and that being seen with me could ruin your reputation."

Jane's head went up. "I rely upon you to preserve it, my lord."

The phaeton was in the London Road now, approaching the Paragon. They passed a group of pedestrians and Moira realized that for a moment at least there was no one in sight, either on the pavements or approaching on the other side of the road.

In defiance of his earlier judgment he leaned sideways, keeping in place his arm with the reins and turning his head to kiss her. As their lips met, the front wheel on Moira's side struck a pothole. He lurched away, nearly losing control of the horses and struggling to keep from falling out. After he saw her to the door of the Leigh-Perrot house he returned to the phaeton, which still seemed to echo with the sound of her laughter.

Va t'en, he thought. Get thee behind me, Satan. And away from the Prince.

CHAPTER VI
1801

Moira's first letter to Jane was circumspect. He referred to their several meetings in Bath, gave an address in London where she could send her reply, and signed himself "Jno. Evelyn."

The address belonged to Moira's confidential man of business, Captain Charles James, who delivered Jane's reply without so much as a raised eyebrow. James was in his mid-thirties, thick-set but fit, with a shock of curly fair hair above wide, expressive eyes. As a boy he had studied in a Catholic seminary in Bruges, and later served under Moira against the French in the 1790s. He'd published poetry and political pamphlets and, more to Moira's purpose, kept meticulous, discreet, accounts. They shared a sense of humor, allegiance to the Whig party, and indignation at the government's treatment of the Irish.

Moira felt he should explain himself, but James cut him off.

"You wish a private correspondence, my lord. If you tell me what it is, it ceases to be private."

Moira's next letter to Jane offered a musical evening and a carriage tour of Hyde Park at such time as Jane and her family were able to visit London. He explained that the formal invitation would come from his spinster sister Charlotte, to whom Jane could refer as another acquaintance from Bath's Assembly Rooms.

Jane responded admirably, suggesting she might soon visit her brother Henry, now living with his wife in Upper Berkeley Street, a quarter-hour's walk from Henry's office in St. James's.

Moira looked up from the letter and smiled, realizing that Jane had gone further than looking at his portrait. "St. James's" was underlined in her letter, making it clear that she knew Moira's own house was in St. James's Place.

A week later Jane reported that her first visit was scheduled for the end of June. She planned two days with Henry and was then expected at her brother Edward's country estate not far from Canterbury.

Moira plotted carefully, inviting his spinster sister Charlotte to stay. In his book-strewn study, upstairs and well out of servants' earshot, he let her know his secret.

At first she was horrified. "My dear brother, you cannot think of marrying a young woman of no family."

"They are perfectly respectable. One brother has married a general's daughter. Another has an estate in Kent."

Charlotte waved a handkerchief at him. "Do not trifle with me, sir. Two of *your* sisters are married to earls."

"Yes, and our brother John has married a penniless girl from Crazy Castle in Yorkshire, who does no more at dinner than tell stories out of *Tristram Shandy*."

"John is a poor example for his elder brother."

Moira bit back an angry reply. He took a deep breath and spoke softly.

"At least send her an invitation, and promise you'll be kind. She may give me up herself when she realizes how complicated my life is."

Charlotte relented, leaning forward to pat his hand.

"No woman who comes to know you will give you up. And I suppose after all these years we should be grateful you have found someone you like. Of course I shall be kind to her."

Moira made certain that Charlotte did not stray from the house on the morning Jane arrived. A footman ushered her to the large drawing room on the first floor.

Moira stood, nervously watching her entrance. Her eyes first met his, then took in his sister as she rose from the sofa. He wondered if Jane would be intimidated by the house, especially the oversized room she'd just entered, its walls hung with yellow silk and overlaid with family portraits. The matching tables along the far wall were Chippendale, with silver candelabra. Next to the window overlooking the garden was a large piano-forte, and at right angles to the fireplace were facing settees, overstuffed and damask-covered.

Jane held steady, smiling and murmuring a compliment on the room, and regret that the foggy morning prevented her better appreciating the views across Green Park.

Charlotte took Jane's arm, settling the two of them side-by-side and asking polite questions about travel from Bath and Jane's brother's house in Upper Berkeley Street.

Moira was on tenterhooks. Would Charlotte be as kind as she'd promised? Would Jane be comfortable with a peer's sister? Would *he* remain as infatuated as he'd been after a few days' acquaintance in Bath?

He strode to the front window, looking out over the park. Shafts of sunlight began to penetrate the fog. As he listened to the conversation behind him he knew the answer was yes to all three questions. Charlotte and Jane seemed delighted with each other, and were soon exchanging more intimate family details and tracing links to mutual acquaintances.

Moira, still looking out the window, reveled in Jane's conversation. Even on trivial subjects there was an underlay of observant humor and – or was this wishful thinking? – something sensuous in her voice, something that said 'This is for you, dear Moira.'

Then Charlotte caught his attention.

"Married to General Mathew's daughter, indeed."

Moira knew this referred to Jane's eldest brother. As he turned, Charlotte continued.

"My brother knows the general, I believe."

"I did not serve directly under him during the American rebellion, but he distinguished himself there and in the Leeward Islands afterwards. I am not alone in regretting he is too old for service against Bonaparte."

"Would you bring him under your own command?" asked Charlotte.

Moira smiled. "I should be under his, sister. He is a full general, and I a lieutenant-general."

"In your last promotion," said Charlotte proudly. "You will go further."

Moira smiled at Jane. "Sisters are a soldier's most effective partisans."

"So they should be," said Jane firmly. "If I had my way I should promote my two brothers admiral at once."

Moira raised his big eyebrows, grinning. "No promotion for your brother in the Oxford militia?"

"Henry," replied Jane, her voice cooler.

Moira turned to Charlotte. "This is the one in London."

Charlotte nodded as Jane continued.

"I gave Henry your advice about the dangers of banking. But without being able to mention your name it carried no authority" – she smiled – "and so he paid no attention. He has set up his office here in St. James's, with our uncle Leigh-Perrot providing the surety for his army agency."

Moira shook his head. "If he is indeed without experience, as you say, he may come to grief. I have seen bankers treat other people's money as their own plaything, never conceiving that lives, including their own, hang in the balance."

Jane was watching him closely. "My cousin Eliza," she began. "I should say my brother Henry's wife Eliza. . . ."

Charlotte rose. "Will you take coffee, Miss Austen? My brother rides in the park at dawn and takes breakfast early. But I often have mine as late as eleven. Your joining me would be a kindness."

Moira was on his feet as well, silently willing his sister's departure.

"Coffee for us all, Charlotte. Perhaps in half an hour?"

Charlotte smiled back. "And then we shall drive in Hyde Park, and Miss Austen will stay to dinner."

"Forgive me, but I may not," replied Jane, also rising.

"Indeed?"

Jane blushed. "My brother expects me. When he asked we had not spoken, and I dared not presume."

Charlotte nodded. "Tomorrow, perhaps?"

Jane curtseyed. "With the greatest pleasure."

"We shall rely upon it," said Charlotte. And with that she retired.

"Now," said Moira, stepping close and taking Jane's hands. "You mentioned your brother's wife Eliza. Let us dispose of her at once so we may speak of other things. She was formerly married to the Comte de Feuillide, I believe, who lost his head to the guillotine."

"Yes," said Jane. "Eliza spoke this morning of your house in Leicestershire, and that you opened it to the French princes during the Terror. She says some of them are still there."

There was an edge to this inquiry.

"You give me the French princes as an example of how easily people can dispose of money not their own, do you not?"

"I do, but also of the generosity of the man I have come to love."

"They have been at my house for eight years now. The time for their departure has long since passed, but where will they go?"

"Another reason for you to achieve peace, my lord."

Moira led Jane back to the settee, shaking his head slowly. "You must not call me that."

Jane smiled as they sat side-by-side. "Have you been to the Tower Menagerie?"
He shook his head again. "I have not."

She laughed out loud this time, though softly. "You must go. When you shake
your head you are the image of its great lion."

"Am I so ugly? There are many who say so."

Jane blushed, indignant. "By no means! I have never seen a nobler beast."

"Or a shaggier one, I expect. In that the lion and I are surely alike. But you are
avoiding my request. Will you not call me by name, as my sisters do?"

Jane touched his cheek, her first physical overture, and he put his own hand
over hers, holding it close as she replied.

"Why, dear Moira, should I presume the acquaintance of a sister, when you
have encouraged me to hope for the love of a husband?"

He paused. "On your lips I almost believe my father's title is my salvation
instead of my doom."

"'Moira' need not mean 'doom.' Can it not be 'destiny,' our destiny together?"

"Let us hope so." He longed to kiss her. She had a way of sitting, tall and
straight, head up and eyes bright – were those eyes mocking him now? – that half
invited, half defied him to take her in his arms.

Another day, he told himself. Soldiers must live to fight another day.

He changed the subject. "Have you said anything about us to your brothers?"

"I could scarcely breathe when Eliza began to speak of your French princes
this morning. But *she* must not know of us, and for that reason I dare not speak to
Henry. He would certainly tell her, and our story would be across town in an instant. I have spoken only to my brother Frank, and my sister Cassandra, in neither
case revealing who you truly are. Both are sworn to secrecy. "

"Good," said Moira. "Now speak to me of this brother Henry. Upon what
basis does he establish his bank?"

"He's taken what little savings we have, and a great deal from my brother
Edward in Kent who is rich enough to offer £5,000. As far as I understand it, my
uncle's surety establishes Henry with the army, and allows him to collect money in
the counties and then lend it at interest before he must remit to the government."

"Exactly so," replied Moira. "It's a risky business, but your brother is by no
means alone in it. I can, I believe, patronize him to some modest degree, and
where I go, others will follow."

Jane's small mouth pursed in disapproval.

"I know what you're thinking," he said. "I am already a notorious debtor,
and the only clients I could possibly bring your brother would be more notorious

still. Will you believe me when I say I have no intention of borrowing from him myself, and that I shall encourage only those I consider reliable to communicate with him?"

"Thank you," she said.

"Now let us speak of you. You told me in Bath you had written novels."

"Yes. But you will also recall that I told you they lacked invention."

"I do not believe it."

"It's true. My *First Impressions* is not fit to be seen till I have finished revising. The only fair copy I have is *Susan*, and she could not fill even three volumes, let alone five like Miss Burney's *Cecilia*, or seven like Mrs. Bennett's *Beggar Girl*. I cannot imagine anyone will publish it."

"May I read it?"

Jane's hazel eyes flashed. "Upon one undertaking, sir. You must be true to your destiny and speak your opinion frankly. And you must *not* recommend it to any of the booksellers. They would never gainsay you, and I should never know whether my book appeared because of its own merit, or because of your patronage."

Moira spread his arms in a gesture of helplessness. "Agreed, my dear lady. And now, before Charlotte rejoins us. . . ."

He moved closer to her on the settee, with its view across the drawing room and into Green Park. The fog had lifted and a distant rose-hedge was in full bloom. He contemplated it, content for the moment. He could feel Jane settle herself too, following his gaze. Their shoulders touched as she spoke.

"The park is very beautiful. This is as fine a town prospect as anyone could wish."

Moira had hoped for something more personal, praise for Charlotte if he could have none himself. But Jane was being careful. He couldn't blame her if she was not yet at ease with him. And he was certain his grand townhouse didn't help.

"Another day I shall show you the rose-garden Repton planted for me at my house in Donington Park. We shall decide which of their colors is closest to your blush."

Jane was forthright in many ways, but sometimes a man had to take the initiative. He'd already waited too long.

"But for now," he continued.

"Yes, dear Moira?"

He did not reply, except to kiss her.

CHAPTER VII
1823

Vanessa returned to the Bell Inn from the Marquess of Hastings's whist-party in her chaise, just as she'd planned. Lonsdale kept her company, and as he took his leave at the inn he announced that he would also accompany her on the morning coach to Alton in Hampshire, where he had an invitation to join a cricket match.

"Bachelors against married men," he said cheerfully. "The old marrieds don't stand a chance, harried as they are by wives and children."

"Will you call upon the Austens at Chawton House?"

"I think not," he replied. "I have only once met your friend Miss Lloyd, and the Austen sister – what is her name?"

"Cassandra," replied Vanessa.

"Just so," he said. "You became a different person altogether with them, and I expect it would only get worse with the rest of the family present. I liked you as a gambler better."

He called for her at eight o'clock the next morning. The weather was fine, and they had time for the walk to Charing Cross. What luggage they had would reach the coach before they did, on the Bell Inn's cart.

They were silent for the first half-mile, companionably arm-in-arm, enjoying the bustle of the street vendors and the tradespeople opening their shops. As they passed Temple Bar Lonsdale finally spoke.

"I had a note from my colonel this morning. We're to go to India once more, in mid-August, and I must recruit another dozen men for my company."

"Less than a month," replied Vanessa. "Do I congratulate you?"

He laughed. "You are supposed to say you'll miss me. It will be ferociously hot, and there are rumors of another Nepalese war. But war is how I earn my pay, and how captains become majors."

Vanessa smiled up at him. This was the Lonsdale she liked best, good-humored and resolute. Then his expression changed.

"I don't know how the colonel heard so soon, but he knew about our visit to Lord Hastings. 'A word to the wise,' his note said. 'Officers seen in the company of the Marquess of Hastings should not expect preferment.'"

"What's that supposed to mean?"

"The Marquess resigned his governorship of India under a cloud. No-one is quite sure *what* that means, except for some kind of banking scandal in Hyderabad."

"He spoke of scandal last night, didn't he?"

"Yes," said Lonsdale. "I think you might observe the colonel's wisdom too."

"*I* don't expect preferment. And Lady Hastings invited me to stay with them on my way back to Bath. I've already accepted."

Lonsdale shrugged. "Don't say I didn't warn you."

Their coach to Alton was an express, stopping only at Guildford and Farnham. Lonsdale, in spite of what Vanessa thought were sometimes over-masculine affectations, was sensitive enough to recognize that she hated conversation on coaches. He helped her to a corner seat where she could look out the window.

As the other passengers climbed aboard, a dark-skinned young man took the seat opposite her. He immediately began to talk in a vaguely foreign accent, asking her opinion of Hampshire and commenting on her own accent when she briefly replied.

Something about the man caught her attention. He seemed out-of-place even for a foreigner. Could he possibly, like her, be out of his own time as well, perhaps even trying to identify her before a rescue?

She was about to speak when Lonsdale intervened, leaning across the gap between the seats.

"The lady plans to enjoy the view, not conversation. I suggest you exchange seats with the gentleman at the other window."

To Vanessa's surprise the young man bristled. She had never seen anyone challenge Lonsdale. Even in casual clothes he looked dangerous, his reputation in the army as a swordsman and pugilist well-earned.

There was a general intake of breath. Vanessa kept still, watching out of the corner of her eye as the two men glared at each other.

After a long pause the young man acted upon Lonsdale's suggestion, his counterpart at the far window quickly agreeing to the exchange. Gradually the tension in the coach eased. Lonsdale nodded to Vanessa, and neither spoke again until they reached Alton, where they and the belligerent young man were the only passengers to depart.

The July afternoon was glorious, with just a few fleecy clouds on the horizon. Lonsdale said the cricket would begin at four o'clock and continue till dusk, resuming the next morning. They had an hour before the start, and Vanessa accepted his invitation to join the players for tea.

The first man they saw at the pavilion was Jane Austen's brother Henry. He'd claimed a place as an umpire, declaring that his holy orders disqualified him from playing on either the married or the bachelor side, that his wife was away, and that he was staying at Chawton House for the next few days. He promised a cart to Chawton when the match ended, if she would care to stay and watch.

"Mrs. Francis Austen is in no danger of delivering the child in your absence, Miss Horwood. The midwife says it could be another week or more, else my brothers might have been here to play for the married men. Instead they are in Portsmouth on navy business."

Henry bowed and turned away. Vanessa thought of Lonsdale's remark that morning, how she became a different person around the Austens. She didn't agree, but could appreciate his reluctance to visit them.

They were a formidably close-knit family. Vanessa knew she would never have been accepted had not Martha Lloyd – Jane's closest friend, now living with the Austens in Chawton – welcomed Vanessa's company in the six years since Jane's death. Jane's two sailor brothers, Francis and Charles, had been quick to follow Martha's lead, as had Francis's wife Mary, soon to give birth to her eleventh child. Martha, along with Jane's sister Cassandra, cared for the elderly Austen matriarch, now well into her eighties.

Henry and Cassandra had been the most distant of the Austens, rarely speaking more than politeness demanded. Vanessa had never understood their coldness, and could only suppose that the two sea-captains were more accepting of foreigners than their brother and sister. Unless Henry and Cassandra were influenced by Vanessa's stay in Winchester gaol? Or somehow jealous of the brief friendship with their sister she had enjoyed?

As Vanessa joined Lonsdale for tea she decided that if she wasn't needed at the manor house this evening, she might as well relax and enjoy the cricket. The players, most like Lonsdale in their twenties, made a handsome sight in their loose white blouses and snug breeches. Some wore waistcoats, unbuttoned in the summer warmth; others had bright sashes around their waists or collared neck-cloths. And a few of the married men had handkerchiefs tied around one knee.

When Vanessa asked why, Lonsdale smiled. "Their wives make them choose only one – for kneeling to trap the ball. Grass stains are less troublesome in hand-kerchiefs than in breeches."

The cricket was more expert than Vanessa expected. Most of the players were military men and showed high competitive spirit. Henry, frock coat, clerical collar and all, held a spare bat as a badge of authority and hovered behind the nearer wicket.

The bachelors won a coin toss and elected to bat first. The first player Henry called out, for leg before wicket, raised a loud complaint and both Henry and the second umpire raised their bats in an attempt to enforce silence. Order returned slowly, in part due to Lonsdale's intervention, and not without a round of sympathetic cursing from his and the batsman's teammates. Not all begged the clergyman's pardon.

The rest of the evening proceeded without incident, with the bachelors scoring more than a hundred runs and with only two more batsmen out. The umpires called a halt as the light began to wane. Within a few moments a little donkey-driven cart appeared from the lane leading to Chawton, an old man guiding the animal by the halter. Vanessa refused to ride, but was pleased not to have to carry her portmanteau on the more than a mile-long walk to Chawton House. She and Henry followed the cart, and were about a hundred yards down the tree-shaded and darkened lane when a voice called Vanessa's name.

She turned to see the dark young man from the coach hurrying to catch up.

"Move along, sir," he called to Henry. "I must speak with the lady."

"I shall not," replied Henry. "Miss Horwood is in my care."

Vanessa turned to face her pursuer, noting the sheathed knife visible where his jacket had fallen open. He was about twenty feet away when the sound of running footsteps from behind made him whirl.

Lonsdale tackled the man full on, sending both of them to the ground. The young man was quicker to regain his feet, and had his knife in hand as the two faced each other.

It was almost full dark now. Vanessa could see the whites of their eyes, and the blotchy white of Lonsdale's cricketing clothes, now marred by dirt as well as grass. Both men were in a half crouch, but Lonsdale was unarmed.

"Come on then," he called softly.

"No!" Vanessa cried.

For an instant the young man was distracted. Lonsdale attacked at once, knocking the knife hand to one side and smashing his fist into the man's windpipe.

Vanessa could hear the sound of collapsing sinew, and a horrible choking as the man began to gasp for air. She ran towards him as he fell, his face contorted with shock, eyes bulging. He turned his head towards her, trying to speak, and then his entire body began to shudder. A moment later it was over.

Vanessa took a step back. "You've killed him."

Henry Austen took her arm. "The young man was armed, and Captain Lonsdale was not. I do not perceive he had a choice."

"You did though," said Vanessa softly, looking into Lonsdale's still-feral eyes. "I know you did, Will."

Lonsdale was brushing dirt from his clothes. "I'd like to know what he was doing on our coach this morning. And where he got the knife. It's a Lascar knife, probably Bengalese."

Vanessa was shaking with anger. "That's not an explanation."

"I've nothing to explain." He took a single step back and bowed. "Good night to you both. I shall report to the constables and have the body removed. They will require your statements in the morning."

Lonsdale returned the way he came, disappearing in the gloom before he reached the main road.

The donkey had become skittish, but the old driver remained impassive.

"Deaf," said Henry. "I expect he never saw it. But the donkey knows the smell of death. Animals always do."

Vanessa was numb. Shocked by Lonsdale's cold-blooded killing, but unable to escape the thought – selfish as it was – that if her instinct had been right the young man might have been her only hope of returning to her own time. She started to shiver, and Henry pulled a blanket from the cart, wrapping it around her shoulders.

"There may be fleas, my dear, but they are preferable to your catching cold."

"We can't just leave that man's body lying there."

"We must," said Henry. "The constables will require Captain Lonsdale's statement, and will wish to see the body where it fell."

He paused, composing his features. "We must accept God's will as it manifests, and content ourselves with our own capacities."

This was such nonsense that Vanessa almost laughed. But she knew if she started to laugh she might not be able to stop. Hysterical, she told herself. She bit her lip, allowed her arm to be taken, and accepted Henry's promise of a hot posset when they reached Chawton House.

CHAPTER VIII
1823

Two constables came to the door next morning, as Vanessa was about to sit down to breakfast. She hadn't slept much, and when she had she'd dreamt of the fight the night before. She knew Lonsdale had been defending her, and that the man had drawn a large and dangerous knife. But Lonsdale had moved so quickly, so decisively, that it had almost seemed like murder.

She had assumed the constables would take her and Henry's statements separately, but they did not. The four of them sat in a small withdrawing room next to the library, and Henry spoke of "the gallant Captain," his determination to protect a defenseless young woman, and the unfortunate result for the young attacker. He stated he had never seen the man before, at which the older of the two constables turned to Vanessa.

"You had seen him before, Miss Horwood, had you not?"

Vanessa nodded, swallowing hard as the vision of him choking his life out on the path from Alton came to mind once again. With an effort she recalled her first sight of him.

"On. . . on the coach from London."

"But not before?"

"No, sir," Vanessa replied.

"Captain Lonsdale said you appeared to recognize him."

"I recognized him when he accosted Mr. Austen and me on the path. I had not seen him before he spoke to me on the coach yesterday morning."

The constable made a note before continuing.

"And you concur with Mr. Austen's account of the incident last night?"

"I do, sir."

The older constable nodded, and both rose. "That will be all, sir and madam. We regret the incident extremely."

Henry seemed entirely unruffled by the constables' visit.

"I must return to the cricket, Miss Horwood. We begin at eleven, intending our full fifty overs a side. My fellow umpire and I may have a long day of it. Shall we see you there?"

"Only if I have a companion," said Vanessa. "First I must see how Mary is feeling."

Henry nodded and took his leave, nodding to Martha Lloyd who was waiting for Vanessa in the hallway. She took Vanessa's arm at once, leading her into the library.

"We've scarcely spoken since you had your terrible fright. Did you sleep, at all?"

There was an old leather settee where they could sit side-by-side. Vanessa did her best to smile at her friend.

"I kept thinking of the man who died."

"Of course you did. I'm surprised you could get out of bed after such a shock."

"I was glad to get out of bed, love. It was the only way I could escape my thoughts."

Martha smiled. She was now in her fifties, with a high forehead, a nose too long for beauty and a stern, straight mouth. When she smiled the lines in her face disappeared.

"We shall revisit the scene of your shock this morning. Daylight will bring it to the front of your mind where you may shine reason upon it, and expel it from your dreams."

"I'll do my best," said Vanessa. "But surely you do not need to walk all that way in order to comfort me."

"I am going to see your Captain Lonsdale play cricket, my dear."

"But we must see Mary before we leave."

"So we shall. And she is very well, expecting her husband home from Portsmouth today. Charles will be with him, and if it were not enough to have both Austen sea-captains and Henry the clergyman for dinner, we believe Edward will also join us from Kent."

Vanessa knew how unusual such an event would be. Charles, the youngest brother and like Francis a navy captain, had been without a ship since his frigate

Phoenix had run aground and broken in the Eastern Mediterranean in 1816. He was now in the Coast Guard, responsible for thirty miles either side of Plymouth, where he now lived with his wife and children. Mary's husband Francis, known to the family as Frank, was senior to Charles, but had been ashore on half pay for years. Edward, adopted by the rich Knight family as a boy, was now a country gentleman, having inherited both Godmersham House in Kent, and Chawton, where his brothers now lived. Edward made his family welcome in Kent as well, and also provided a cottage in Chawton village for his mother and sister.

Vanessa climbed the stairs to the first-floor drawing room, where the heavily-pregnant Mary was reclining on a long sofa. As Vanessa came closer she could see the pallor and perspiration on the woman's face. A cup of tea sat on a side-table, untouched.

"Are you drinking enough?" Vanessa asked.

"Hush," Mary said with a wan smile. "I've borne Frank ten children so far. I can manage one more, I believe."

Vanessa put a hand on Mary's distended belly, and felt an answering kick from the tiny body inside.

"Your hand is cold," Mary said. "Whoever is there does not care for the chill."

Vanessa smiled. "Poor little poppet, to be born in England. Cold is part of life here."

Mary shivered, and Vanessa took off her shawl. But Mary held up a hand to keep it away.

"As soon as you put it on me I shall become too hot. Talk to me instead. Tell me about this dreadful attack last night, and your Captain Lonsdale saving you. It sounds quite romantic."

"It wasn't. It was cold-blooded. Businesslike."

Mary nodded. "Frank would say that is how it must be. If you allow an instant to consider your enemy's humanity, you will die instead of him."

"I suppose so," Vanessa replied. She was eager to change the subject. "Tell me your news. Martha says we'll see both Frank and Charles this afternoon."

Mary's eyes brightened. "I pity them both. There was news of a frigate captain falling ill in Portsmouth harbor, and I expect there were a dozen half-pay officers circling like vultures, wondering how to get the posting if he died."

"Oh, dear," said Vanessa. "Do you suppose Charles could be set against Frank in this?"

Mary shrugged. "I believe Charles would *defer* to Frank, both as older brother and senior captain. But it cannot be easy for either of them."

"Charles must be unhappy in the Coast Guard."

"Nor is Frank much pleased at sitting idle in his brother's house."

Vanessa patted Mary's belly. "Not *altogether* idle."

Mary managed a faint blush. "No," she replied. "Not altogether." She turned her head away, towards the back of the settee. "Will you forgive me if I sleep?"

"I'll go to the cottage if you're certain that you will. May I bring you anything before I go?"

Mary shook her head, and Vanessa tiptoed out, worried.

Cassandra Austen and her mother had already arrived at Chawton House from their cottage in the village. The cart that carried them was about to leave for the mile-long drive to Alton. Cassandra insisted that Martha and Vanessa accompany it.

"We must not argue with Cassandra," Martha said softly to Vanessa. "She is by now so accustomed to dictating to her mother that she will brook no argument from anyone."

Vanessa knew this was true, and wasn't about to argue. But she wished Cassandra would speak to her. Cassandra's resemblance to Jane always brought a stab of recognition and sorrow. Both Austen sisters were tall and graceful, with dark hair, large eyes and small mouths. But where Jane's face had been animated, even in her last illness, by her lively interest and wit, Cassandra's seemed passive, whether from bitterness or stoicism Vanessa could not tell.

Cassandra was making a point of folding her mother's bonnet and straightening the border of her gown. Vanessa knew this was how she avoided conversation. Martha knew it too, and took Vanessa's arm to guide her outdoors.

The sunshine was back and after a few steps Vanessa turned back to look at Chawton House. In spite of her worries she smiled as the light played on the handsome Elizabethan manor. It was situated at the top of a gentle rise, with a short gravel drive leading down to the main road. She could see the old stone church of St. Nicholas on one side of the drive, the manor house stables on the other.

They walked to Alton accompanied by the same donkey-cart and deaf servant that had been with Vanessa the night before.

Martha spoke first. "I am under strict instructions from Mary to insist that Captain Lonsdale join us for dinner after the cricket."

Vanessa shuddered. "I don't know that I approve."

"By Henry's account the captain saved you from mortal danger. That is surely worthy of an invitation. Afterwards he may go back to his inn at Alton. *He* is in no danger walking alone at night."

Vanessa smiled. "What if he's promised elsewhere? Or the cricket runs too late?"

"So be it," Martha replied.

Vanessa had run short of ready money. She had a ten-pound banknote which she knew would be unwelcome at the cricket pavilion, where tea and strawberries cost no more than sixpence. There was a branch of Hoare's Bank in Alton, a branch she knew only too well. It had been the scene of her arrest for the supposedly-forged bank draft, six years ago.

Vanessa was certain the bank teller would remember her and give gold and silver for her note.

"My dear Miss Horwood," he cried as soon as she entered.

He was the epitome of a bank employee: small and of indeterminate age, with wisps of grey hair at the very top of his domelike head, neatly and formally dressed in a much-mended frock coat. But his cheeks were pink and his bespectacled eyes bright with enthusiasm.

He left his post behind the counter to come round into the foyer, bowing to Vanessa and Martha in one expansive gesture. Vanessa smiled at the grandeur of it, making sure her smile was gone before the teller straightened and could see her face.

"And Miss Lloyd," he added. "I am pleased to see you together once more. I recollect you both in this very place soon after the conclusion of, ah" – he nodded to Vanessa – "that most unpleasant incident. I still treasure the letter we received from our director acknowledging the error, and the validity of his signature on your draft."

Even after six years Vanessa's memories were painful, and she could tell that Martha sensed her discomfort. *Someone* could have changed her note at the cricket-ground, surely. What had compelled her to come to the bank? A return to the scene of the crime-that-had-never-been? And a reminder of what she'd survived, and the world of her own time she'd lost, seemingly forever?

Both Martha and the old teller were staring at her now. Vanessa forced a smile.

"I expected to be recognized, sir, but I am astonished you should recollect my name after all these years. And I have never been acquainted with yours."

The teller bowed once more. "Shuffleton, Miss. Aeneas Shuffleton."

Mr. Shuffleton was obliging about the banknote, and declared his intention to attend the last of the cricket as soon as the bank closed for the day.

"I shall watch for you, ladies."

Vanessa and Martha took their leave. When they reached the cricket pavilion they found Lonsdale at bat. As Vanessa pointed him out to Martha, another spectator turned his head.

"He's reached his half century. The married men are in despair."

Lonsdale had hit two balls for six and another three for four. The fielders were playing well back in hopes of containing him, and perhaps of a lucky catch.

The spectator went on. "He's hit enough over their heads that they've learnt their lesson."

Vanessa took Martha's arm, moving towards the far side of the pitch to get a better view. They passed into Lonsdale's line of sight just as the bowler was setting up to throw. Lonsdale was off-guard, missed the ball, and was out before he could get back behind the crease.

Vanessa could see Lonsdale's mouth move, and decided it was just as well she and Martha were out of earshot. But he smiled as he approached them, bowing.

"I suppose it's just as well. We were ahead last night, and with me out the married men have a chance to catch up. Will you come for tea?"

Martha knew cricket better than Vanessa. "How many overs have the marrieds bowled?"

"Just gone thirty-six when I was stumped. It'll be at least an hour before the bachelors take the field." He smiled. "Unless their bowling improves."

"How long will it all last?" asked Vanessa.

"We started last night in hopes of finishing by dinner-time today. Probably we should have let the married men bat first. Then we could have put them out, started ourselves about now, and we'd have passed their score by three o'clock or so. Now they're going to want all their overs to see if they can overtake us."

The pavilion had a coal fire warming a half-dozen kettles. Next to the fire a long table held containers of strawberries and clotted cream. Lonsdale filled a tray and showed them to a picnic table reserved for players. He wolfed down two dishes of strawberries and a platter of biscuits, insisting that the ladies do the same.

"Two dishes *between* us will be quite enough," said Martha, "and I suggest you not spoil your own appetite, as the Austen family is determined you should join them for dinner."

Lonsdale half bowed from his seat, spoiling the formality by the cream smeared on one cheek.

"I am honored, Miss Lloyd, but you must not allow me to delay your meal. Cricket matches have no precise schedule."

"We'll be waiting upon Henry in any event. At worst you two will get a cold collation after the rest of us have dined." Martha smiled. "But we shall certainly save you a bottle of wine."

Lonsdale shot a glance at Vanessa, who offered no encouragement. Finally he nodded.

"I look forward to it."

He turned to Vanessa, who finally met his gaze.

"Are you well?" he asked.

"Yes," she replied. "I'm not entirely helpless, you know."

"I never suggested you were. But you and Mr. Austen had nothing against his knife."

"Nor had you."

Lonsdale's smile had a hard edge. "I expect he did not see it that way."

After a moment's strained silence Martha touched Vanessa's arm.

"You speak to the captain as though he'd done you a disservice."

Vanessa took a deep breath. "I'm sorry. I *am* grateful. But I don't think the man deserved to die."

Lonsdale deliberately looked over her head. The sky was blue in all directions, not a cloud to be seen anywhere.

"It will rain tomorrow, I expect. Will you return with me to London?"

"Did you hear what I said?"

He nodded, still not meeting her eyes. "I have no answer for you."

Lonsdale turned back towards the pitch, and was astonished to learn that the married men had kept an expert bowler in reserve. While they'd been eating strawberries this man had stumped two of the bachelors, and retired a third on a weak fly caught by the wicket-keeper.

Another expert ball caught a fourth bachelor leg before wicket. Henry called him out and, just as his fellow had done yesterday, the batsman began loudly protesting he was nowhere near the stumps.

Lonsdale turned back to the ladies. "I'm just in time."

He strode forward to speak to the batsman, who gave a final glower at Henry and left quietly. Within fifteen minutes the bowler had retired the remaining bachelors, and both sides broke for tea.

"I believe we may expect the two of them in good time," said Martha. "Let's finish our shopping and get home."

As they were leaving they encountered Mr. Shuffleton, come to watch as he'd promised. He waved a small handbill.

"I give you joy, Miss Horwood. Such a venue, such a program."

"What is this?" cried Martha.

Vanessa blushed, eyes downcast.

"Is Miss Horwood so diffident, Miss Lloyd? It appears she is about to display gifts I did not know she possessed. Next week, in Winchester. Mozart and Beethoven, and our own English composer Mr. Pinto."

Martha turned to Vanessa. "Why didn't you say so?"

"There might be some at Chawton who would not approve."

Martha laughed. "So there might. We shall pay them no mind. And the rest of us will be there."

"As shall I," declared Mr. Shuffleton.

Vanessa and Martha took their leave and were back at Chawton by three o'clock. Frank and Charles had arrived and were in the upstairs drawing room with Mary. "And Mr. Edward Knight is here too," said the maidservant.

Vanessa and Martha left their packages and hurried upstairs to join the party.

Mary was still on the long sofa. She looked better than she had that morning, but her hand was under her belly, supporting her burden, and her face was still drawn.

Vanessa curtseyed to the gentlemen. Edward Knight was every inch the country squire, stocky and well-dressed, with a ruddy complexion. Frank, the senior of the two naval captains, was shorter than his brothers, strong and compact with a serious face – he was known in the navy as a praying captain – that lit up when he smiled.

The youngest brother Charles was nearly Frank's opposite, tall and rangy, with looks that had conquered many hearts and, according to some of the racier reports Vanessa had heard, more than a few bodies.

The three men were already on their feet, bowing.

"Mary is grateful for your presence, Miss Horwood," Frank said formally.

Charles grinned. "So is Frank," he said. "Anyone who can bring a little order to this household is welcome." He turned to Martha. "Now, my dear, we are told you have been to the cricket, where our brother dispenses the Lord's justice."

Frank frowned, but Charles raised a hand. "Even our reverend father described it so. And who better than Henry to succeed him?"

"Humph," said Frank. "I believe what my brothers want to know is how long the cricketers are likely to be."

"And how long," Edward put in, "we must wait for our dinner."

"I count upon two hours at least," said Mary. "It's too hot to eat sooner."

The cricketers returned just before six, bachelors triumphant but by a much smaller margin than Lonsdale had expected. Vanessa had to admire the way he greeted the Austen brothers, showing just the right touch of deference to his two superior officers, and a gentlemanly camaraderie to Edward Knight.

They sat for dinner at once. Lonsdale began to commiserate with Charles for the loss of his frigate in 1816, and with Frank for his long term ashore on half pay.

"These are bad times for getting on," said Lonsdale. "My regiment sails for India next month. Without another uprising there's no hope of promotion."

Frank and Charles nodded gravely.

"Just so," said Frank. "Peace is the grace of God and a blessing to most, but a sad lot for military men and their families."

Charles turned to Lonsdale, asking how he came to be in Hampshire. "Apart from the cricket, of course."

"I've orders to recruit a dozen men for my company before we sail, and I expect an advertisement in Portsmouth will find some unemployed marines."

"My brother and I can name a score, sir. We may spare you your advertisement."

Lonsdale smiled, half-bowing in his chair. "Thank you, Captain. I shall make note of any addresses you may have. I should add that I have relations near Selborne, which is how I came by the cricket. And of course Miss Horwood needed an escort."

"I did not," Vanessa replied, more sharply than she'd intended. "I have come to Chawton before on my own, and if I am invited I shall do so again."

"But we were grateful for his appearance last night," said Henry. "I trust you have finally expressed your gratitude to Captain Lonsdale."

Lonsdale grinned. "She has not, sir. Nor do I expect it. Miss Horwood goes her own way, and rarely listens to advice."

Martha spoke next. "And what advice do you offer, Captain?"

"A visit to India," he said promptly. "But in the meantime I suggest she decline her invitation to stay with the Marquess of Hastings when she returns to London."

All four Austen brothers froze. Charles was first to recover, setting his wine-glass carefully on the table. He glanced at Frank, who had returned a forkful of meat to his plate, then at Henry.

Finally Charles turned to Vanessa. "May I ask how you came by this acquaintance?"

"Captain Lonsdale is too modest," said Vanessa. "He introduced me."

All eyes returned to Lonsdale, who was discreet enough not to refer to the evening at White's Club. All he said was they'd been invited to Campden Hill for an evening of whist.

"The family was much taken with Vanessa."

Charles smiled. "As who would not be."

"And," Lonsdale continued, "the Marquess suggested he might be posted to Canada and would be pleased to discuss the place further. The next thing I knew she reported that the Marchioness had invited her to stay."

"You must not," said Henry, his voice cracking. "The man is untrustworthy, notorious."

Vanessa's head came up. "I had no such impression. I found him the perfect gentleman, and his wife and children charming." She smiled. "And when I partnered him at whist, we won."

"It is as well you did," said Henry. "If you had lost he'd never have paid, and even if he had his creditors would have been after you."

"I do not believe," said Frank, "we ought to dwell on creditors."

"Pah," said Henry. His voice was barely controlled, and increasingly bitter. "*You* might say so, but everyone in this room saving our guests knows that but for Hastings's treachery my bank would never have failed."

Edward's face had darkened. "Enough, Henry. It has been seven years since your bank failed, and you have said ever since how blessed you are to have become a clergyman. Yet whenever the Marquess of Hastings is spoke of, you insist upon his treachery. My warrant from the Exchequer Court says I may, as your surety, try to collect £6,500 from him. That is less than a third of my losses. Where did the rest of my money go?"

He turned to Vanessa. "I am grateful for this information and will write to him tonight. Perhaps you would be kind enough to deliver the letter."

"With pleasure, Mr. Knight."

Vanessa caught a glimpse of Lonsdale on her right. He was obviously fascinated by these exchanges, motionless as a beast of prey waiting to pounce. Now he saw his chance and leaned across towards Henry.

"Are you at liberty to say more about Lord Hastings?"

"There is no more to say, sir. When the Earl of Moira, as he then was, defaulted on his obligations to me, I was unable to remain current with my creditors. They became insistent."

"As creditors will," said Charles.

Edward spoke next. "Henry has been fortunate. I lost £20,000 by his bank's defalcation, our uncle another £10,000. My brothers lost their entire deposits."

He turned, fixing his eyes upon Henry. Mary, her pregnant belly touching the table, was seated between them. She leaned back in her chair, helplessly.

Edward's words sounded like an indictment. "You lived high for many years, brother. Your bank floated upon bills you were ill-advised to contract, and when it sank you became a public bankrupt. But for myself and our uncle you would, I believe, inhabit Marshalsea gaol. How much of our money did you spend on yourself, Henry?"

Henry's face was beet-red. He started to speak, but Edward raised a hand.

"You need not answer. Nor may you presume to tell me whether I should or should not write to the Marquess of Hastings."

Henry stood up, hands on the table, leaning across towards Vanessa.

"You should not see this man again, Miss Horwood. He is too dangerous."

"Sit down, Henry," said Frank. "Lord Hastings has greater concerns than our Canadian friend."

"And no more conscience about ruining her than he would have at swatting a fly."

With that Henry resumed his seat, but the dinner conversation never recovered. None of the other women had spoken a word, and Vanessa could see the relief on Martha's face when the men retired to the library for port.

Vanessa went up to the top floor nursery to put Mary's youngest to bed. She could hear the opening of doors and conversation below, and when the men joined the ladies in the drawing room someone – Cassandra or Martha – played a couple of popular songs on an out-of-tune pianoforte. When the music ended Vanessa went down, feeling obliged to say goodbye to Lonsdale.

He took her arm, walking her outside into the courtyard.

"Will you return to London with me when I am finished in Portsmouth?"

Vanessa shook her head. "I don't know. You seem determined on keeping me away from the Hastings family, and I don't understand why."

"Does what you heard tonight influence you at all?"

"I didn't hear enough. I intend to find out more."

"Don't," said Lonsdale. "There is more here than either of us can fathom."

"That's the point, Will. Within a year of Henry's bank's failure I was in gaol, on a false charge from the Alton bank that used to belong to him. If there's a connection I want to know about it."

Lonsdale shrugged. "That was six years ago. Why not let that wild goose go, and think about coming to India?"

She looked up at him, pleased and resentful at the same time.

"You've given me some wonderful adventures, but with each one you seem more determined to take what little virtue I have. I can't see any way I could go to India and not be in your keeping."

He smiled. "Would that be so terrible?"

She touched his cheek. "Not to some women. But I'm not the keeping kind."

He paused. "I'm afraid if I asked. . . ." His voice trailed off.

"Don't ask," she said softly. "If you won't fret about me staying with Lord Hastings, come for me day after tomorrow. But I shall go to his house directly from Charing Cross. And tomorrow I shall go to Portsmouth as well, with Martha and the two captains."

Lonsdale straightened, a military man once more. "We shall all go together. They say I'll have my recruits in half a day."

"Good," she replied.

She kissed him then. She could tell he wanted more, but the sound of the front door made her pull away.

"Vanessa?" It was Martha's voice.

She smiled at Lonsdale, raising a hand in farewell. He turned away, striding down the hill towards the road. There was no moon, but the stars were so bright she could see him until he disappeared behind a wall. Then she rejoined Martha, linking their arms together as they went back into the house.

CHAPTER IX
1823

The men had discussed the journey to Portsmouth over their port. Edward had apologized that he had no coach at Chawton large enough to lend, and Lonsdale and the two captains had decided to hire a private chaise.

The next morning Lonsdale arrived with the chaise from Alton. He was back in uniform, his lobster-red jacket making an agreeable contrast to the two Austen captains in their navy blues. Martha was soberly dressed as usual, and Henry had surprised them all by declaring he would come too. He looked every inch the clergyman in his black frock coat and white dog-collar.

Frank promised a night's lodging at Government House in Gosport, and Lonsdale would stay with friends. They arrived shortly after noon, leaving their portmanteaus at the House and taking the ferry across the narrow harbor inlet to Portsmouth proper.

The dockyard was bustling with activity, even in peacetime. Sailors and young officers bobbed their heads and saluted the two Austen captains. Vanessa smiled as she contemplated the two brothers. Frank's uniform was precisely arranged and he stood fully erect, his manner severe. Charles's uniform was just as perfect, but his bearing was more relaxed, even dashing. Their cocked hats gave a clue to the men underneath. Frank's was in the old-fashioned position, its points parallel to his shoulders. Athwartships, they called it in the navy, whereas Charles's hat pointed fore and aft.

As they approached the harbor-master's office Frank called to a man nearby. The man turned at once, coming to attention.

"One of your recruits, I'll warrant," Charles said to Lonsdale.

As the man approached he touched his cap to Frank, glowing with pleasure when told that Lonsdale was recruiting.

"Bachelors by preference," said Lonsdale. "India is not an easy place for a soldier's family. And the pay is not enough for a wife and child to live decently in England."

"More decent than they'll get from charity, sir," said the man. "I've some mates'll be glad to join, but not all bachelors."

"Their decision," said Lonsdale. "Shall we go find them?"

The man bobbed his head and led the way, with Lonsdale promising to return to Gosport in time for supper.

"Now," said Frank, rubbing his hands, "we shall make our useless call on the harbor-master, check on the health of our fellow-captain. . ."

"Wishing him a speedy recovery, of course," put in Charles.

"My brother," murmured Frank, "is sometimes in danger of hypocrisy."

Charles grinned, turning to Henry and raising both hands. "I rely on Henry for divine guidance."

Henry's good cheer, lost at last night's dinner, had not returned. He'd been silent on the journey from Alton and even now only nodded, refusing to comment. Frank turned to Charles, about to speak, but someone in the distance caught his eye.

"Isn't that one of Admiral Paget's lieutenants?"

Charles whirled. "And his pretty longboat crew. Our dinner is set, ladies."

He set off in pursuit. Vanessa could see him as he hailed the lieutenant, who turned and saluted.

When Charles returned his eyes sparkled like a boy's. "What luck! Admiral Paget gave us a standing invitation when last we met, and the King has once again postponed his cruise. We shall commandeer His Majesty's longboat to take us all to the *Royal George*."

He turned to Vanessa. "No serving captain will ever fail to feed his half-pay brethren, and I – stranded in the Coast Guard – am as much an object of pity as Frank. But we should never have dared impose on the royal yacht without the Admiral's express invitation."

Frank spoke next. "Charles served under him twenty years ago. For my own part I must say that Admiral Paget would not be my first choice as host" – he glanced sideways as Henry gave a pronounced cough – "but he will keep a very fine table."

"As indeed he must," added Charles. "He is the King's yachtsman."

He pivoted towards the harbor.

"Follow me closely, as the tide is starting to ebb. The longboat will cast off shortly."

"Oh dear," cried Martha. "I'm sure I won't be able to keep up. Perhaps I should take a cart back to Gosport."

Frank was at her side in an instant, slipping her arm into his.

"Of course you will not, my dear Martha. It is a short enough walk and Charles will see that the longboat does not leave without us."

The *Royal George* was at anchor half a mile offshore, accompanied by her companion yachts *Royal Sovereign* and *Prince Regent*. The sea was like glass and the longboat crew, turned out in matching white trousers and blue jackets, kept a precise stroke.

As the longboat pulled further out to sea Vanessa began to long for her own days as a sailor, far away in her own time. She'd hated sailing at first, when her Canadian uncles took her as a sullen fourteen year-old out in freezing weather, scarcely deigning to heat the tiny cabin and refusing to use the motor assist even in the midst of ice floes. But when they went again the next summer, sailing from Montreal out past Anticosti Island, Vanessa's heart lifted with the sea-birds and breezes and seemed never to return to earth. From then on she shared her passion for music with sailing.

But six years in England, struggling to adapt to a new, and at first terrifying world, had made her forget how it felt to be at sea. Now she felt like she never wanted to leave.

She knew she must have surprised Charles with the intensity of her smile as he pointed out to Vanessa the sandbar which gave Spithead its name. He grinned back, and pointed to Henry who, still silent, was beginning to turn green. All too soon the longboat was closing with the royal yacht, exchanging signals. No doubt, Vanessa thought, warning of impending visitors.

When they reached the yacht's side, both a rope-ladder and the boatswain's chair were ready at the longboat's port side. Charles scurried up the ladder and Vanessa could hear the stamp of feet and the sound of piping as the sideboys saluted his arrival on deck. The longboat lieutenant helped Martha into the boatswain's chair and as all eyes were upon her Vanessa reached for the rope-ladder and began to hoist herself up.

"Good lord," came a shout from Henry.

Charles looked over the yacht's side and began to laugh. The longboat lieutenant looked up, took in the situation and shouted "Eyes starboard!" to his crew.

Vanessa cast a look over her shoulder and stifled a giggle. All eyes were averted, but she was certain there was nothing indecent that could be seen from below. She had avoided the newly-fashionable flared skirts and was wearing the second of the two walking-dresses from her portmanteau. It came from an earlier time, square-cut and long, covering the ankles of her half-boots. If she was in any danger from voyeurs, it had to be from above, as her shawl hung loose and her square-cut bodice was quite low.

By now she was nearly at the deck, and Charles was there to help her aboard.

"You will give the crew the wrong impression, my dear Miss Horwood," he said softly.

She began to smile before she registered his expression and realized what he meant. Only one kind of woman climbed ropes to navy ships: women who were paid for their services. She blushed and looked away, straight into the eyes of the man who had to be their host. He was about forty-five, tall and good-looking in a round, fleshy way, with wavy brown hair and large eyes.

"Welcome to the *Royal George*, Austen," he said cordially.

Charles saluted. "Thank you, Admiral. I give you joy of your promotion, and present Miss Vanessa Horwood of Canada, a dear friend of our family. Miss Horwood, Admiral Sir Charles Paget."

"Lucky family," murmured Paget, bowing.

Vanessa made her curtsey, and as she rose she saw Martha being helped from the boatswain's chair, which was promptly lowered back over the side. Frank was already at the top of the ladder and was next aboard. He saluted the Admiral, who came forward to shake hands.

"Pleased to meet you, Captain," said Paget. "I'd hoped Charles would bring you along. Damned unlucky business about Trafalgar, what?"

"Thank you, sir," said Frank, as though the Battle of Trafalgar had been the week before instead of eighteen years ago. "I've not given up hope of another command."

"Nor should you," said Paget. "Nor should your brother, with all respect to the Coast Guard."

Henry was hoisted aboard as Paget was introduced to Martha. All went below for dinner.

They dined at once, at the Admiral's – and for that matter the King's – large and elegant table, with splendid views out the high stern windows. The captains from the other two yachts joined them, along with the *Royal George's* lieutenants.

They talked navy business for a time, again – inevitably – discussing the dearth of commands in the peacetime Navy.

The young captain of the *Prince Regent* was first to return the subject to Trafalgar.

"Shame about the *Canopus* and Trafalgar, Captain Austen."

Frank gave a wan smile, as the third yacht captain cut in.

"She distinguished herself at Santo Domingo, of course, but that wouldn't do, would it?"

Poor Frank, Vanessa thought. He'd been flag-captain of the *Canopus* under Admiral Louis, Nelson's second-in-command, sent to Gibraltar in October of 1805 for provisions. On the afternoon of their departure Frank and his Admiral had dined with Nelson. Admiral Louis had protested – Frank could quote him precisely – "The Enemy will come out, and we shall have no share in the battle."

Nelson had replied, "I send you first to insure your being here to help beat them."

But Louis had been right and Nelson wrong, and Frank had missed Trafalgar and all the glory that attended its captains. Those captains received promotions, treasure, and even new houses near the Greenwich shipyards. Only a few months later Frank and the *Canopus* had been part of another British fleet that inflicted an equally decisive defeat on the French near the Caribbean island of Santo Domingo.

But the Caribbean was far from England, and celebrations over the Trafalgar victory and lamentations over Nelson's death had exhausted the British public. After the Santo Domingo victory Frank languished ashore for more than a year. He was finally posted to the old 64-gun *St. Albans* and sent for convoy work in southern Africa and China.

Charles and Frank, seemingly unfazed by reminders of their misfortunes, continued their banter with the other officers. Martha engaged the youngest lieutenants with enquiries about their families, and soon they were revealing their innermost longings as though to their own mothers.

Vanessa received longing looks of an altogether different kind, including several from the Admiral himself as he worked his way through a second bottle of claret. But he recollected his manners, asking polite questions about Canada and showing considerable knowledge of music when Charles managed to turn the conversation in that direction.

Henry was the wet blanket, uncharacteristically replying to the few questions he received with monosyllables, and giving only the briefest of graces when invited to do so as the meal was set before them. By the time they rose, after a traditional spotted dick for pudding, a magnificently orange sun hovered above the horizon, angling bright beams through the stern windows.

The Austen captains insisted on a tour of the yacht, and as they climbed up and down companionways and ladders Vanessa reflected upon Henry's truculence. It dated, of course, from the introduction of the Marquess of Hastings into the dinner conversation.

'Treachery,' Henry had said. It was a strong word to use if the Marquess had simply failed to pay his debts as they came due. There had to be more to the story. Did any of the other Austens know what it was?

Vanessa was relieved when they came back to the main deck and the open air. She had a moment to herself by the stern rail, gazing first out to sea and then back at the graceful profile of Portsmouth. For an instant all she wanted was to go aloft, to haul on a line with the other sailors and feel the graceful yacht catch the wind in her sails. She longed to feel herself speeding close to that wind, away from the fog and cold of England to. . . well, Vanessa didn't know where. There *wasn't* anywhere else, or anyone else, for her.

She shrugged and turned away from the rail, well aware that any expression of interest in sailing might lead to an invitation from Admiral Paget which would be awkward to refuse.

Nevertheless she was sorry when the Austen captains said their farewells. Frank gently helped Martha into the boatswain's chair, as Charles launched himself down the rope-ladder to be sure he was in time to help her board the longboat.

Henry announced that he too would descend the ladder, waving aside Charles's cry from below that it was more difficult going down than coming up. After a few minutes another call brought Vanessa and the others to the taffrail. It was Henry, frozen halfway down.

By now Charles and the longboat crew had helped Martha aboard, and a grinning oarsman retrieved the boatswain's chair and climbed in. His mates hoisted him to Henry's level, where the brawny sailor scooped up Reverend Austen as though he weighed no more than a cat.

While Henry was deposited below Vanessa once again climbed onto the ladder.

"Eyes starboard," ordered the lieutenant.

She was past the halfway point, fifteen feet or so above the longboat, when one side of the ladder gave way. Reflexively she gripped the intact rope on her right, dangling for an instant as she heard part of the broken side splash into the water. She heard a shout from above and gasps from below, and then she had both hands on the good rope and let herself slide to the longboat, where a pair of strong hands gripped her from behind.

She felt herself lifted aboard and spun to face her helper. It was Charles, who had released his grip on her waist just enough to let her turn. He tightened it again.

"Are you all right?"

His voice was hoarse and his eyes bright. He'd never looked so intent or, Vanessa was startled to find, so attractive. For an instant she was overwhelmed by his masculine energy, wanting nothing more than to let her body melt against his.

But she managed to break their gaze. "Let me sit down," she whispered, hoping she would sound no more than faint.

He guided her to a seat astern, next to Martha who put her own arms around Vanessa and gathered her close.

"You poor child. What a fright you've taken."

But Vanessa hadn't been frightened, only surprised. She'd never doubted her ability to come down the rope, and now her mind was racing with two separate trains of thought. Why had a moment's contact with Charles Austen – a married man, after all – made her passionate in a way that months with Will Lonsdale had never done? And why had a rope-ladder broken on the King's own yacht, arguably the tautest ship in the Navy?

Charles had taken a seat next to Henry and was blushing, looking purposefully out to sea. He really was absurdly handsome, more so than any of his brothers, and far more than Admiral Paget, who clearly thought himself something of a Lothario.

Henry was staring in the opposite direction, frowning. Could he have sabotaged the ladder? And then called for the boatswain's chair knowing Vanessa would likely be the next person down?

Surely that was improbable. What reason could Henry have for trying to injure her, and how could he be certain that she instead of his brother would be next to descend the ladder?

No, she decided. He *could* be certain Vanessa would be next, because Frank would never allow her to be last. Could Henry be so determined to keep her from another visit to Lord Hastings that he would harm her to prevent it?

Vanessa pulled away from Martha and sat up straighter. Frank was sliding down the remaining rope, spry as any young sailor. He took a seat amidships and turned towards her, eyes gentle and concerned.

CHAPTER X
1823

Vanessa wanted to rest – and think – when they returned to Government House in Gosport, but there was still daylight and Frank asked if she was strong enough to walk.

"Of course I am."

She took a few minutes in the room she shared with Martha, as Martha remained downstairs with Frank. When Vanessa went down Charles had joined them. Henry was conspicuous by his absence.

They set off along a promenade that paralleled the inlet separating Gosport from Portsmouth. Frank pointed south.

"Ten minutes walk and we can look out to sea for the sunset."

After a hundred yards Frank turned to Martha.

"Tell me what you saw from the longboat."

"I saw Vanessa fall," she replied. "No more than that."

Charles nodded. "I was attending to Martha, and did not notice Henry on the ladder until he called for the chair." He smiled. "And I averted my eyes from Miss Horwood until I heard the rope hit the water."

Frank turned to Vanessa, his eyes bright. "You handled yourself like a sailor."

"Indeed you did," added Charles. "We shall rate you 'able' here and now."

Vanessa didn't smile. "Are you are all wondering the same thing I am?"

Frank nodded. "Has Henry any reason to wish you ill?"

"Not that I know."

"And yet," said Martha, "he has been glum, well, glum as a parson since you mentioned the Marquess of Hastings yesterday."

"Just so," said Frank.

"Were you in England when Henry's bank failed?" asked Vanessa.

"I was," said Frank. "Charles was in the Mediterranean. It was the more damnable luck for him. We both lost our savings, but for Charles the news came hard upon the loss of his frigate at Smyrna."

"Never say *more* damnable," Charles retorted. "You had a wife and six children to feed. Henry's failure left you with nothing but your half-pay."

Frank nodded, and for a few minutes they strolled in silence, Vanessa and Martha arm in arm.

Martha gave a reminiscent smile. "In some ways Henry was the least affected of the family by the disaster he caused."

"It's true," said Charles grimly. "Henry never had savings. He said he lived off the fat of the land."

"Yes," Martha added. "And that after his bankruptcy his dreams of affluence ended. It was time for him to return to the Church, he said, the best of all professions. And thank God it took him."

"Then why," asked Vanessa, "if he was so untroubled by his bankruptcy, might he try to hurt me? To prevent me visiting the Marquess?"

"If he *did* try," said Frank.

"Of course," said Vanessa.

She held onto Martha's arm. She could give Henry the benefit of the doubt about the rope. It could have been frayed already. But *something* was bothering Henry.

She turned to Frank. "Do we confront him?"

"Perhaps not directly," he replied. "We'll gather for supper in an hour or so, and Charles and I shall take the measure of him."

Lonsdale was waiting when they returned to Government House.

"We had not expected to see you so soon, sir," said Frank. "But I believe Miss Horwood will be pleased to take an early supper. Have you been successful?"

Lonsdale bowed. "Entirely through your good offices, Captain. I've had to turn away recruits, and those I have taken are capital prospects."

"Better than you deserve?" asked Vanessa, forcing a smile.

"Never," said Lonsdale. He looked at her more closely, and then at the others. "What's happened?"

Frank turned to Charles, who answered. "We dined on the royal yacht this afternoon. Miss Horwood had an accident."

Lonsdale's face went hard. "But you are not certain it *was* an accident."

"I am uninjured," said Vanessa. "Except for a little burn on my hand."

She held it up for Lonsdale's inspection.

Charles laughed. "We rated her honorary able seaman on the strength of her skill, but she'll have to develop the calluses."

Lonsdale refused to share the joke. "What *happened?*"

"A rope gave way as she came down the ladder," said Frank.

"And you suspect. . ." said Lonsdale.

"I suspect no-one," said Vanessa.

"But," continued Frank, "our brother Henry descended the same rope immediately before."

"And could have cut it," said Lonsdale. "Did you search him for the knife?"

Frank stiffened. "No, sir. He is our brother."

A few minutes later they convened in a small dining-room on the ground floor, where Henry remained glum and evasive. There was a cold shoulder of mutton and pickled onions on the sideboard.

"It's July," complained Vanessa. "Surely there could have been *something* fresh for our plates."

"Naval fare," said Martha cheerfully. "Remember where we are, love."

Charles smiled. "At least you may enjoy some bread and butter, Miss Horwood. At sea we'd have hard biscuit."

"And hammer it on the table to knock the weevils loose," Frank added.

The meal continued in silence. Finally Charles burst out. "Something is troubling you, Henry. If you cannot speak of it to us, to whom *shall* you speak?"

Henry glared at him, his face reddening. "You have offended me, sir."

"*Offended* you!" cried Charles.

"Indeed," replied Henry. "You assured me we should have a respectable dinner on board the royal yacht. I was concerned enough at any association with our disreputable monarch, but to put me at the table of one of the adulterous *Pagets*! It is more than any decent person could countenance, and I am astonished you would so impose upon the ladies, and upon me."

"Oh, lord," sighed Charles.

"You will recall," Henry continued, "that even our sister Jane, most liberal of spirits, deprecated, even abhorred that family."

"Enough, Henry," said Frank.

"It is not enough. . ." began Henry.

"By God it is, sir," roared Frank. "Admiral Paget may have got preferment because of his family's connection with the King, but he's been a fighting captain from his first command."

"Oh, yes," said Henry sarcastically. "They are all fighters as well as adulterers. The worse they are, the more honors the King bestows. And the worst of all become marquesses."

"Henry," called Martha from across the table. She was the oldest of their party, and there was a maternal imperiousness in her tone that Henry, though full of his own indignation, could not ignore. He half-bowed to her from his chair.

"It is discourteous in the extreme," Martha continued, "to cast such aspersions upon men who have devoted their lives to serving our country. And upon one who has shown such kindness to Vanessa."

"And besides," Vanessa put in, "I have no idea what Henry is talking about."

Charles laughed. "Henry is comparing one of the Pagets - the Marquess of Anglesey – to the Marquess of Hastings. Anglesey eloped with the Duke of Wellington's sister-in-law. Wellington refused to serve with Anglesey until after Bonaparte escaped from Elba, and then Anglesey led the great charge at Waterloo that ended the war once and for all."

Vanessa took no pleasure in the story. All she could think of were the battle-field dead and broken families. Mothers separated from their children. In her heart she knew Henry was responsible for her so-called accident. But why? And how far back did the mystery of his connections with Lord Hastings go?

She caught Charles's eyes upon her and looked away quickly, only to see Lonsdale staring at them, one after the other. She remembered the surge of desire she'd felt when Charles had held her after her near-fall. Life was more complicated than she wanted to allow.

CHAPTER XI
1801

Moira was surprised when the package containing Jane's novel arrived at Moira House within an hour of her departure. He smiled at the cover sheet. It was standard form, although some female novelists preferred anonymity even so far as their sex: "Susan. A Novel, in Two Volumes. By a Lady."

He read the manuscript straight through that evening, sometimes laughing out loud. At others he imagined Jane herself as the young heroine, obsessed with her 'horrid novels' and suspecting villainy and mayhem behind every door. When, he wondered, had she written this? And upon what families had she based her characters?

"I have one criticism and one question," he told her the next day, after collecting her at Henry Austen's house in the phaeton. Its hood was up, his coat-of-arms on the sides obscured, and the coachman rode postillion on the lead horse, safely out of earshot. They were on their way to Hampton Court to see Henry VIII's palace.

"Criticism first," replied Jane. "Let's get it over with."

"Your General Tilney is not sinister enough."

Jane smiled. "And the question?"

"Did you write him after you met me?"

Her laugh was gentle, musical. "Would I were so facile. I have scarce known you a month. Do you think me capable of both carrying on a romance and writing a novel in so short a time?"

"It is very accomplished," he said.

"It is not," she said shortly. "It is a girl's ramblings. I shall finish revising *First Impressions* and indulge myself in no more unless there are a few crowns to be had."

"A practical woman."

"A necessitous one, like Susan. And like hers my family is numerous, and by no means respected in its own neighborhood."

"That is false. Your family is eminently respectable, your father esteemed in the Church, your brother Edward highly regarded in his county – I know this from my own Kentish connections – and your two Navy captains likely to rise on account of merit rather than accident of birth."

"Just as you did," she said softly.

She touched his arm. It was gratitude for his kind words, he supposed, but it gave him a pulse of excitement. He damned himself for spending too much time with the Prince and his hangers-on, surrounded by demi-reps who would fall into bed or onto a sofa – or the floor for that matter – at a moment's notice. It gave a man's body certain expectations, presumptions, which the rational mind could not entirely control.

But he could control his *behavior,* by God, if not his emotions. He pulled away just enough to break contact, smiling at her in the hope she would not take offence. She held her shapely body proudly, head high as she met his gaze.

But she must have felt his excitement. After a moment she dropped her eyes, blushing as she picked up the thread of the conversation.

"How should I make the General more sinister?"

"From your own experience. Now you know a real general you may make Tilney more like me."

Jane reached across to touch his cheek. She had to be teasing him, aware of his longing for her. But she gave nothing away.

"Taller?" she asked. "Darker? Narrowed eyes and lowering eyebrows?"

"All of those," he said.

Jane smiled. "But I believe he already *is* you: 'a very handsome man, of a commanding aspect, past the bloom, but not past the vigor of life.'"

"I never bloomed," said Moira.

"Hush," she replied, her own brows furrowed. After a moment she spoke again.

"I decline to change him. When Susan suspects General Tilney of either murdering or shutting up his wife, she is not *entirely* unjust to his character. The only reason he encouraged his son's courtship was in the mistaken belief it would be an advantageous connection. *You* would not behave so."

"No," said Moira softly. "Though there are those who would say I should."

Half an hour more saw them to Hampton Court and its stately old palace. One corner of the building had partly collapsed, and was much admired on that account.

"Very picturesque," Jane remarked.

"I believe they intend rebuilding it now they have restored the Great Hall," said Moira. "But let us wait to go inside. I can smell rain coming."

There was mist in the air as they began to tour the gardens, but the rain held off at first, coming in earnest only when they reached the middle of the famous hedgerow maze.

They ran in what they thought was the direction they'd come, only to reach a cul-de-sac. They tried again, and again, with Jane doubled over laughing after their third failure. She cried for them to try yet again, but her muslin dress was in light summer style and her shawl did little to keep the rainwater off.

When he caught her arm she was shivering. Moira bellowed for the gardener, concerned she might catch cold.

Once inside the house she professed herself perfectly well.

"I must see the Great Hall at least."

Moira called for tea and a fire. Jane hung her shawl and bonnet on a chair close to the heat, and they ate stale cake and drank weak tea. They completed the house tour, but it seemed dull after their race through the garden maze.

Back in the chaise Jane returned to the unwelcome subject of Moira's finances.

"You say your advisors counsel you to marry wealth. Have you confessed your attachment to me?"

"No," he said. "No-one knows but Charlotte."

"Even the man who receives my letters?"

"Even he," said Moira. After a moment he sighed. "I have been the most consummate fool over money, and never truly regretted it till now."

He looked at Jane. Her face was attentive, loving, with no hint of disapproval. She was inviting him to explain, and he did.

"It started with my Irish volunteers during the American rebellion. I paid and equipped them at my own expense, and when I came to the Lords I thought I must make another grand impression. I could have paid my debts when I inherited from my uncle. Instead I became more profligate."

"Is that when you took in the French princes?"

"Yes, but that was only part of it. I borrowed to rebuild Donington Hall, and borrowed again to have Repton do the park. Only then did I invite in the French

— and leave cheques on their bureaus so they would not need to beg for money." He smiled sadly. "That was 1793."

"And now it is 1801 and they still expect the cheques."

"Yes. And so does the Prince of Wales."

"How bad is that, dear Moira?"

He shrugged. "The Prince first took my money in 1787 and has done so ever since. It wasn't long before I couldn't get full value for my promissory notes. My man Captain James does his best, but sometimes the discount is upwards of ten percent."

"But how much do you owe, entirely?"

"I can only guess. I have properties for sale in Yorkshire and Ireland, and my managers are doing what they can to increase the income of others. But I shall not play *Castle Rackrent* with my estates."

"How I laughed at that book!"

"And I too, but there is too much truth in it for comfort."

"Very well," said Jane. "And what is *your* truth?"

Moira shrugged. "If my projects go well I might bring my debts below fifty thousand by the end of next year."

Jane recoiled. "Fifty thousand pounds? It is a king's ransom."

Moira took her hand. "Oh no, dear Jane. It is less than the Prince spends in a year."

"There can scarcely be a woman in the kingdom who could bring you so much money."

"Exactly so," said Moira. "That is why I shall marry for love."

CHAPTER XII
1801

Lady Charlotte had told Moira that two wagons full of clothing and bric-a-brac recently arrived from Ireland must be sorted and everything they could part with – and there would be much – should go to charity. Thus it was that when Jane arrived at eleven o'clock next morning she found Moira and Charlotte covered in dust and laughing like children.

"And it is children we became," he said, "with all there was in those boxes."

"It's odd," said Charlotte. "Our mother was such a generous spirit, yet she saved all our childhood clothes instead of giving them to the poor."

"Which," declared Moira, "we are about to correct, although the children who get them will be monstrously unfashionable."

Then he grinned. "But I saved this to show you." He held up a small embroidered waistcoat. "Mine, at school. Listen." He shook it, and there was a slight jingle. He unbuttoned a pocket and tipped some coins into one hand.

"Treasure," he said, handing them to Jane.

"Treasure indeed," Jane replied, turning them over in the palm of her hand. "Six ha'pennies, by my reckoning."

"But Irish," cried Moira, taking one from her hand and tossing it in the air. "And matter for sport."

Jane grinned back. "Pitch ha'penny! I could best my brothers by the time I was seven, and keep myself in pin money."

"Could you now?" said Moira. "Our dear St. Patrick's harp is on the tail of the Irish ha'penny. So for us the game was head and harp."

He looked at her, half-smiling, half-serious. "Are you thinking you could best *me?*"

Jane replied solemnly. "I have not remained in constant practice, but if you have not weighted one side of the coins or otherwise come it the flimflam, I believe I might relieve you of your fortune."

"Flimflam indeed," said Moira. "To show I am no cheat you may play with one of my own sacred halfpennies."

"And then there's no sport to it!" cried Jane. "What joy shall I take in winning if I have nothing to lose myself?"

Moira beamed at her. "A woman in a thousand, is she not, Charlotte?"

Charlotte smiled. "I'll not complicate your game, children. You may toss your coins and cry your heads and tails in peace. And yourself in your own dirty clothes, my lord Moira."

Moira felt himself blush. "You're leaving us alone, sister?"

Moira saw Charlotte's gaze turn to Jane, and his heart leaped as he saw the affection in it. "I do not believe," Charlotte replied, "that either of you will abuse my trust."

Jane's head came up. "Is that a dare, Lady Charlotte?"

But Charlotte only laughed, raising an arm in farewell as she left the room.

Moira turned back to Jane, taking her hands. She looked up at him, eyes mischievous.

"If you squeeze my hands so hard, dear Moira, I shall never manage to give my ha'penny the touch it needs to win."

"You aim to flesh it?"

"How not?"

He knew she was joking, but he had to ask. "Are there other ways you would cozen me?"

She met his gaze, instantly serious. "There are not, my lord. Although it has been my fate seldom to treat people as well as they deserve."

He laughed then, releasing her hands. "We must send our coppers to the ceiling, and trust in fate and nimble thumbs. Are your English rules the same as ours?"

"We must cry the outcome in the same instant. And should we both cry 'heads' or 'tails' there is no winner and we throw again."

Moira nodded. "Just so. And both ha'pennies must show the called side for one of us to win, must they not?"

"Oh, yes," said Jane.

"One of each is a nil, just as if we both cried 'skull' or 'music.'"

"You've lost me, my lord."

Moira grinned. "A boy's way of calling. Skull for the head, and 'music' for the tail – which on Irish coins is the harp."

"So be it," she answered. "Now enough bother and on to the game. And then you must promise to walk with me, as the sun is shining. I am a desperate walker."

Moira nodded. "Swap your English Britannias for three of my harps so we can cry alike."

Jane duly handed over three English halfpennies, and Moira watched as she reminiscently fingered the edge of one of the Irish coins.

"On my mark," he said. She flashed him a grin and he cried "Up!"

The coins flew into the air. "Harp!" cried Jane. "Music!" shouted Moira. Moira's halfpenny struck the ceiling and was the first to hit the floor, landing on the boards and rolling towards the fireplace. Jane's coin hit the carpet, heads up. She peered at it and then rushed to the fireplace as Moira's coin slowly settled, showing the harp.

"A tie either way," she declared.

"Again," said Moira. "One, two, three. . . Up!"

"Skull," he cried, as Jane in the same instant shouted "Music!"

He watched her coin sail smoothly into the air, neither spinning nor rotating. It landed once again on the carpet, flat and almost without sound. "Tails," she announced.

Moira's halfpenny struck the floorboards again, bounced once, and came to rest, also harp-side up.

He began to laugh. "You *did* flesh it, by God! Duels have been fought for less."

This time her look was coy, even flirtatious. "And shall we duel, my lord?"

Moira looked towards the drawing room door, firmly shut. Then he seized – gently – her shoulders and kissed her full on the lips. For an instant he felt her tense, and then her body responded, relaxing into his own. They held the kiss in silence, but a clatter of footsteps made them both leap back. Jane's face was scarlet.

Moira was bowing to Jane as Charlotte entered the room.

"I must change my clothes," he said. "Shall we walk to Bond Street afterwards?" He struggled to keep a straight face as he looked at his sister. "I rely on you to join us, Charlotte."

"Of course," she replied, looking intently from his face to Jane's, unable to repress a smile of her own. "You'll visit poor Lieutenant Dermody, will you not?"

"Yes."

Charlotte turned to Jane. "I never understand how he makes time for his sick and crippled soldiers."

Moira flushed. "It's the government should care for them, but casts them aside once they're used up. And then presses the next ones."

He caught his breath, embarrassed. "Forgive me. And while I see Dermody, you and Miss Austen may inspect the latest at Mr. Tabart's."

Jane looked blank, and Moira explained. "A children's bookshop. Dermody lives upstairs."

"Have you planned so far ahead?" murmured Charlotte, eyes on Jane.

Jane's blush had started to fade, but now it returned in full force. Once more she dropped her eyes.

"Oh, my dear child," cried Charlotte, waving her brother towards the door as she rushed to Jane's side. As Moira climbed the stairs to his bedroom he could hear his sister's voice. "I beg you will forgive my teasing. It is because I have never in life seen him so happy."

CHAPTER XIII
1801

Jane seemed fully recovered by the time Moira returned to the drawing room. "You are dining with us tonight. . . ." It was half statement, half question. "If you may not, will you take something before we walk out?"

"Indeed she is," said Charlotte, smiling. "She gave us her undertaking yesterday. And" – this to Jane – "we shall dine early, at four o'clock as my brother must go to the Lords afterwards. I shall be very glad of your company, and our carriage will return you to Upper Berkeley Street whenever you wish."

"There is no need," Jane replied. "I'll walk to my brother's office in St. James's Street. He will be there until seven o'clock at least, and will see me home."

Moira nodded, unable to take his eyes off her. She was composed, almost grave, he hoped for Charlotte's benefit rather than his own.

He adopted a similar reserve. "Captain James and Mr. Clifton will join us. James is already acquainted with your brother and will see you safely to his office."

It was a short enough walk to Bond Street from Moira House. They went without servants, dodging carriages until they could walk three abreast on the Piccadilly pavement.

"I never know how Dermody will manifest," said Moira. "Even when he's not drunk he can be either purest charm or deepest gloom. Or so full of poetry that he declaims as soon as he opens the door."

"Is it not so with all Irishmen?" asked Jane.

"Oh, ho," cried Charlotte. "Answer that, dear brother."

Moira smiled, feeling the stab of an old sorrow. Then he shook his head.

"I could wish it so, but the muse who visited me when I was young declined to stay when I became a soldier."

Jane caught his sadness. "Well, sir," she said gently. "Perhaps as compensation you are spared those black moods said to be peculiarly Irish."

Moira smiled. "I shall never indulge one in present company."

"That may not be enough," said Jane with a smile.

"Oh," said Charlotte quickly. "I think it may." She glanced at her brother, who stepped back to allow the ladies to precede him onto the narrower pavement of Bond Street. Moira walked behind as Jane asked her next question.

"And is he kind, Lady Charlotte?"

"Absurdly so," she replied. "Where shall I begin?"

"It was said in Bath that Mr. Evelyn planted groundsel for the songbirds wherever he lived."

Charlotte laughed. "Mr. Evelyn, was it? It is true of the Earl of Moira as well, so much that the gardeners complain that the groundsel overruns the roses. There is enough for all the birds in the park."

"So there should be," murmured Moira.

"And," Charlotte continued, "the servants have a menagerie of stray dogs and cats he's rescued, and any soldier he's ever commanded knows where to call if he's down on his luck."

"Ah," said Jane. "This explains Lieutenant Dermody."

"Thomas Dermody," said Moira, "was our mother's legacy. He could write Greek and Latin verse by the age of nine, and she took him up after his father drank himself to death. But drink was in his blood, and he began insulting our mother when she didn't send as much money as he asked."

"Truly?"

"Oh, yes. I have a letter somewhere where he complains of 'receiving half-a-crown from that hand which has bestowed many guineas.'"

"But he was a good soldier, was he not?" said Charlotte.

"He was that," said Moira. "Our sister got him a place in her husband's regiment. No preferment, just a private. But by the year ninety-four he'd made sergeant and when he came to me I promoted him lieutenant under Captain James in the wagon-corps. One poet to another."

Moira stopped, not wanting to pursue the recollection any further. But Charlotte took up the story.

"The ministry betrayed my brother. He should have had men and supplies to attack the coast of France, but they never arrived. Instead he was forced to Flanders to rescue the Duke of York and his army. And all he has to show for it. . ."

"You need not repeat it, Charlotte."

"But I shall," she insisted. "All he has to show for it is a bill for fifteen thousand rations which he ordered to deceive the French into thinking his corps had twice as many soldiers as it actually did."

Jane stopped short. "You cannot mean, my lord, that the government has sent you a personal bill to requite your success?"

Moira smiled, stepping up to take her arm. "You are standing directly in Stafford Street, Miss Austen. The carriages will show you no mercy."

And at that moment a male voice from above cried "Hold hard!" and with a cacophony of neighing and jangling a coach-and-four labored to a stop. A dark, coarse-looking man with an out-thrust jaw leaned down from the driver's box.

"Why, what a sight is this? Moira – Moira the picture of manly rectitude, sauntering along Bond Street in the company of women?"

"Drive on, sir," said Moira calmly.

"Drive on?" cried the man. He looked behind, beginning to shout at a groom uneasily perched on the platform behind the empty passenger seats. "God damn and blast you! Do you not see I need you to hold the horses?"

Although dressed as a coachman, the driver's manner had nothing of the servant about it. He was fully equipped, as the saying went, *en cocher*, from his cape downwards, his livery rich and elegant. His large mouth drew down in a sneer as he pointed his whip at Charlotte.

"I know your sister well enough, Moira, but who" – he angled the knot towards Jane – "is *she*?"

He struck the thong against his boot for emphasis. As his groom approached he raised the whip once more, preparing to strike his servant.

Moira jumped up to the box, wrestling the whip from the driver's hand.

"Go along, Sefton," he said quietly. "You may speak to me in the House, should you choose to make an appearance."

Moira sprang down, flicking the whip at the horses. Sefton briefly struggled with the reins as the coach started to move, but was soon back in control. The thunderstruck groom was just in time to leap up to the rear platform. Moira tossed him the whip, and he recovered his balance just in time to catch it.

"I shall discover her, Moira," Sefton shouted, as the coach reached the far side of Bond Street. Then he was lost in the traffic.

"Who was that?" asked Jane softly, as Moira resumed his place between the two women, taking an arm of each.

"Lord Dash-along," said Charlotte. "And a loathsome lord he is." She turned to her brother. "But it was surely unkind to tell him to speak to you in the House, when you must know he has only an Irish peerage and may not appear."

"Never mind," said Moira, glancing around and taking a deep breath. A few passers-by had stopped to stare, but it appeared that no-one of importance had remarked the scene. He resumed his place behind the ladies as they mounted the curb.

"I perceive," said Charlotte, "that my brother does not presently care to discuss Lord Sefton and his like."

"The Prince of Wales," said Moira quietly, "does not always discriminate in his choice of friends."

Charlotte smiled. "What he means is that the Prince's friends are an embarrassment. Sefton is actually one of the. . . perhaps we should say one of the less indecent, unpleasant as he is. His greatest affectation is to dress himself as a coachman, as you saw, and show off his skills around town."

"But," said Jane, "he must want more than that, or he would not have asked who I was."

"They all crave gossip," replied Charlotte. "And because Moira is above reproach and yet better-loved by the Prince than any of them, they are jealous. The Prince will hear of Moira's mysterious companion by the end of the day."

"Sooner," said Moira, surveying the pavement once more. He came up closer and dropped his voice.

"The Prince has a lively and intelligent mind. If he'd been given responsibilities at the time of the King's first illness, I believe he would have risen to them. But he remains idle. His hangers-on provide amusement."

"You are too kind," said Jane indignantly. "Even clergymen's daughters know of the Prince's depravities. He has abandoned his wife and child for all manner of women. He. . . ."

"Say no more, my dear," interrupted Charlotte. "Moira knows it all, only too well."

"And apart from that," said Moira, managing a smile of his own at last. "We've arrived."

Mr. Tabart's Juvenile and School Library stood at the corner of New Bond and Grafton Streets. The shop door was set between two large windows. In the one on the left were educational maps and toys, a colored and dissected pictorial alphabet within a wooden frame, and sheets of colored engravings of birds, beasts, and insects. Below these last was a decorative title-label, "The Infant's Path Strewed with Flowers. By Mrs. Lovechild." In the right-hand window were rows and rows of books, some plainly bound in leather, others in bright floral-patterned pasteboards.

Moira's face lit up at the sight of someone inside the shop.

"James, by God! Just the man I wished to see."

As they entered Captain James turned and bowed, taking in the ladies with a sweeping gesture. But Moira could see the man's eyes on Jane, full of curiosity.

"My lord, ladies," said James with a broad smile. "May I anticipate that you come on a similar errand to my own?"

"Dermody," said Moira. "And some books for the ladies. My sister you know, but may I present Miss Jane Austen of Bath, who evidently has a great many nephews and nieces entirely dependent upon her for their education and amusement. Miss Austen, I give you Captain Charles James, my confidential man of business and, I am pleased to add, my friend."

"Lord Moira overstates the plight of my nieces and nephews, Captain James."

The sound of a clearing throat made all turn. It was the proprietor of the shop, now bowing.

"Pray forgive the intrusion, my lord, ladies, sir. If your lordship and the captain intend a visit to Mr. Dermody, I suggest you go upstairs without delay. He is lately inclined to go out at about this hour, and is seldom conversable upon his return."

Moira cast a regretful look at Captain James, and turned to Jane.

"Dermody has gone back to the bottle, perhaps as solace for the wound he took in my service."

Captain James shook his head. "No solace, my lord. Alcohol is in his blood. Shall we go up? We need not stay long."

Moira nodded, turning to the shopkeeper. "A word with you, Mr. Tabart."

The two went to the far corner of the shop where Moira spoke in a low voice.

"I believe Lieutenant Dermody's rent is current, and he does not overly inconvenience you?"

Tabart nodded. 'He is fortunate in your patronage, my lord."

"Thank you. And now, sir, kindly take this five-pound note and put it to my credit here in the shop. Do not speak of this, but if my sister or Miss Austen chooses to buy you are to decline their money. Make whatever excuse you must, but do not take their money."

Tabart bowed, and Moira returned to the ladies.

"Where may I find you if Dermody keeps us longer than the books keep you?"

Jane smiled. "I could happily spend a fortnight here, my lord."

"But not I," declared Charlotte. "You have twenty minutes, sir, and then Jane and I are off to the milliner's."

"Cooper's?" asked Moira.

"Where else?"

Moira bowed, gestured to Captain James, and the two men went out a side door and up the two flights of stairs to Dermody's garret.

Moira could hear singing as they approached the top floor. He knew this boded ill for their visit. He gestured to James, who smiled and entered first.

"General's inspection, Lieutenant," he snapped. "On your feet."

"T'devil take the General, sure," came the reply, and then Moira was inside.

The room reeked of alcohol and urine. Dermody had managed to stand and, though scarcely twenty-six, was stooped and haggard. Behind him was a filthy pallet, surrounded by books, and a table covered with papers and guttered candles.

"What am I to do, Dermody?" said Moira. "The Captain and I got you these quarters so you could write. Am I to put you in a hospital, where you will find pen and ink hard to come by, and privacy impossible?"

Dermody raised bloodshot eyes. "I've written, General, I have indeed. Listen.

Behold the haughty soul, o'er heav'n that flew,
Submissive for a paltry pittance sue!
Behold those lines that feed the general ear,
Despis'd, discarded, by the listless peer!

James stepped forward. "You are impertinent, sir."

Moira only laughed. "There is nothing new in that. But pay attention, Dermody. I have reason to believe you are disturbing Mr. Tabart and his family. If he chooses to evict you I shall not interfere, and you will have no further rent from me. I know you have received some money from the booksellers this year. . ."

Dermody gave a sharp laugh. "Aye, two guineas here, a guinea there. Never twice from the same man."

"If you spent the money honestly and did not invade their shops, drunk, to importune for more, your fortunes might improve."

"So they might, my lord." Dermody waved at the table behind him. "I am writing elegies and epitaphs. Dozens of 'em, and most upon myself."

He waved again, but the gesture was too much for him. He lost his balance and toppled backwards.

James was quicker than Moira, catching Dermody in mid-fall.

"Damn you, man," said James. "You are the finest poet of us all, better than I, better than Tom Moore. . . ."

Dermody's eyes slowly focused. "Moore spends his days at his lordship's houses, I am told."

"And so would you," said James. "If you were fit for human company."

Dermody clutched his old leg wound. It was a theatrical gesture, and he winked at Moira as he made it.

"Help me sit, Captain, I beg you."

James had missed the wink, and eased Dermody down to his pallet, where the poet covered his face with both hands. Finally he looked up, and now his expression was tragic. Moira wondered if this was another theatrical ploy, but Dermody sounded, for the moment at least, sincere.

"There is no saving me, your lordship. But I thank you both."

Slowly he pulled himself back to his feet.

"You've resolved me to stay out of my cups, at least for today. But when Tabart finally sends me packing, I suggest you do not search for me."

He came to something like military attention, touching his right hand to his forehead in salute.

"General, Captain, I thank you both, and I bid you farewell."

Moira led the way out, shutting the door behind him. As they descended the stairs he spoke softly to Captain James.

"How long do you think he'll live?"

James shrugged. "A year, at the outside."

CHAPTER XIV
1801

C harlotte and Jane were still in the bookshop. Jane was at the counter, arguing with Mr. Tabart.

"It is none of your concern, sir," she said firmly, "that Lord Moira is in credit with you. My transaction is entirely distinct, and you are a fool to decline my offer of ready money."

The counter was at the far end of the shop, and all Moira could see of Jane was her back, ramrod-straight with indignation. Tabart cast a supplicating look over her shoulder.

Moira glanced sidelong at Captain James, who managed to remain expressionless.

"Not a single book, Charlotte?" Moira said to his sister as he and James drew close to the counter.

"*Our* nephews and nieces are old enough to choose their own. Or so they tell me. But Miss Austen has accomplished all."

Jane shook her head. "I have not, my lord. Mr. Tabart is unwilling to accept my money, and I am at a loss how else to pay for these books."

"I have credit with Mr. Tabart," said Moira. "You would honor me by letting me pay for your books."

"And I hope, Miss Austen," added Charlotte, "that Lord Moira and I shall have the opportunity of meeting all these relations before too long."

Moira could see the astonishment on Captain James's face. He should never have seen these exchanges.

"Pray, Mr. Tabart," declared Moira. "State the total amount owing. I perceive I shall have to accept it from Miss Austen before she will let you deduct it from my credit."

"Just so," said Jane firmly. Then she turned to Moira, her face bright with pleasure.

"I cannot tell you how pleased I am with this shop. I had no notion that *Anecdotes of a Boarding School* had been reprinted. Having given my own copy to my niece in Hampshire, I have found, of course, that my niece the same age in Kent feels herself slighted."

She smiled. "Tranquility will soon be restored."

Jane insisted on taking the books with her, so Moira carried the package as they strolled back to Moira House. The ladies went ahead, allowing him some private conversation with Captain James.

"Will you see us home, Captain? I'm sure we have much to discuss before our other guests arrive."

"Thank you, my lord. Will Colonel McMahon join us?"

"Yes. And young Clifton, and my ward Harriet. McMahon is certain to bring the latest bills from the Prince."

"There seems no end to them," replied James. "Has his Royal Highness made any offer to pay down the principal?"

"No," said Moira. "And each time a note comes due I believe I must suffer a greater discount to have it compounded."

James nodded. "That's true, my lord. I am still attempting to reconcile the Prince's accounts and I confess that after a year I am no closer to doing so. And if that isn't enough, I yesterday had a cheque drawn by one of your French expatriates. Surely there cannot be many more of those outstanding?"

Moira winced. "I kept no memoranda. I relied upon their honor."

"The story does *you* honor, my lord. But it is still in general currency. I am concerned that these newer cheques may be forgeries."

"Guard against them, Captain. My honest debts are large enough."

Moira looked ahead, where Jane and his sister were absorbed in conversation. He felt a burst of longing, then helplessness.

"What would you have me do, Captain?"

"If there is no hope of the Prince paying his debts, I suggest a large bond or loan. This would create an efficient fund to absorb the mass of floating paper, and secure us both from the regular importunings of Colonel McMahon."

"'Importunings' sounds harsh, Captain. You must remember that the colonel acts on behalf of his Royal Highness."

"Who has trespassed to the uttermost upon your lordship's loyalty and generosity."

Moira thought of his conversation with Jane, the day before he left Bath. 'Va t'en,' the echo returned. Get away. His tone softened.

"Can you calculate the amounts we owe on the Prince's account?"

"I have not given up, my lord."

"Do your best. We must tell McMahon that it is time to end this – well, what shall we call it?"

"Association, my lord?"

Moira nodded. "Association will do."

CHAPTER XV
1801

Captain James used an office in the basement of Moira House, where all the accounts were kept. He retired there immediately.

"You will meet Lord Moira's ward this evening, my dear Jane," said Charlotte, taking her leave. "She is all charm and youthful energy, and I must rest before I face her."

Jane and Moira were left alone in the drawing room.

"You must continue your discussion with Captain James, dear Moira."

"James can wait."

Jane shook her head. "It is scarce two hundred yards to my brother's office. Surely I may be trusted to find my way."

"Of course you may. But will you find your way back for dinner?"

Jane smiled. "You perceive my difficulty. I have no gown suitable for dining in this house, and when I accepted your invitation I did not imagine you would have other guests. I am not inclined to face a young woman of style in my brown cambric, with my hair uncurled."

"Harriet will see beyond that, and we dine early enough that you will not need an evening dress." He smiled. "I shall ask Charlotte not to change either. And nor will I. Will that give you comfort?"

Jane hesitated. "Yes," she finally replied. She passed him a small handbill. "I wonder if this might amuse you. Did you see it on the wall as we came out of St. James's Street? The bill-poster used so little paste that it practically fell into my hand."

As he surveyed it she added, "It even seems to be Irish."

"Ach," said Moira. "The Dublin lottery." He read it aloud:

ARE YOU IN LOVE?

If you are, and the want of Money be a ban to your Union with
the object of your Affections, the Sum of Six Thousand Pounds
may be obtained by a Sixteenth Share of a Ticket, All in One Day.
Time is precious, purchases are numerous, and delay may
prevent your obtaining that which the Possession of might
make you Happy for Life.

When he looked up her eyes were upon him, sympathetic and sad.

"I could not help overhearing some of your conversation with Captain James. You are pressed even now, this moment, are you not?"

Moira began to shrug, and then straightened his shoulders. He would not dissemble to Jane.

"I am. Even if I won this lottery the six thousand pounds would do little to forestall my creditors. The interest alone on my debt is enough to devour a fine estate. I told you I have property for sale here and in Ireland, but I can find no relief."

"People are horridly poor and economical in Hampshire, my lord. Perhaps I might offer you lessons."

Moira laughed. "Life with you would never be horrid."

"It might. I cannot live like my improvident brother Henry, who declares that bankers must keep up appearances. I wish to have money first, before I spend it."

"I had supposed you were above caring about money."

"No indeed. I am greedy and want a very great deal of it."

To Moira's relief she began to laugh. He sighed, and by unspoken agreement both fell back onto a settee. He took her hand for comfort and gazed out the window overlooking Green Park.

"Since I met you I have thought of giving up politics. My agent believes a buyer might be found for Donington Park, and my houses in Essex and Monmouthshire are so far unencumbered. . . ."

"Monmouthshire, dear Moira. Essex is too close. Your friends would never let you rest until you came to town and saved the country."

He turned to her. Her eyes had been merry before, but not now. Her small mouth pursed.

"I was not in earnest, my lord. Politics is your very self. You must not give it up. I believe you must marry an heiress after all."

"No!" he cried. "I'd rather starve."

"Oh, no," she cried, pulling her hand away and standing. The sparkle was back in her eyes.

"You must never starve. Heiresses come with legacies, and legacies are the most wholesome diet of all."

Moira had risen with her, and she put her arm in his. He walked her downstairs to the front door, which the footman opened with a bow.

Moira raised an arm in farewell. "I shall send Captain James in an hour."

Then he went down to the basement.

James was hard at work at an oversized mahogany desk, copying numbers from what seemed an inexhaustible stack of bills.

"Four of the Prince's for every one of yours, my lord."

"It doesn't matter. I have accepted them all."

"But surely the Prince must be sensible of his obligations."

Moira shook his head. "He might have paid if he'd become Regent years ago. Now he has forgotten them, and looks for lenders elsewhere."

"McMahon does not forget."

"Colonel McMahon has no means to repay principal. He borrows for the Prince's account, and the Prince spends. Then McMahon moves on."

Moira reached down for a sheaf of the bills, riffling through them. All were denominated in hundreds of pounds, some in thousands.

"Have you a total?"

"Close to a hundred thousand, my lord."

"And your opinion?"

"With your present income you cannot retire them. The accumulated debt will only increase as the interest is compounded."

Moira nodded. "Young Clifton, who will be with us this evening, may be useful. He is presently employed at Hoare's bank, but wishes employment with me. This would bring him closer to my ward, but she favors him so much already that it hardly signifies."

"I confess I do not much care for him. But if he has a strategy for these" – he held up another stack of bills – "I cannot object to working with him."

Moira flung his handful back on the desk. "Thank you, my friend. Let us leave these for another day, and go up. We shall be seven at table, once you've fetched

Miss Austen from her brother's office. May I count on you to divert McMahon, and entertain the ladies?"

"I may divert McMahon and your sister, my lord, but never Miss Austen. Surely you've noticed she's in love with you."

CHAPTER XVI
1801

J ane returned with Captain James before the other men arrived. Moira's young ward was already upstairs, and Charlotte had left a message that Jane should join them. Charlotte's maid took Jane in tow, and as they retired upstairs James entreated one more private word. For the moment Moira and he had the drawing room to themselves.

"Mr. Henry Austen has embarrassed his sister, my lord."

"How?"

"He greeted me as a friend because of an old connection we had through the Oxfordshire militia. He's insisted on visiting tomorrow."

Moira was already on edge: about money, about hiring Clifton, and – perhaps most of all – about Jane's foray into his intimate circle at dinner.

"Stop him," he snapped. "Why should he do this?"

"He was not circumspect, my lord. He is an army agent and more recently a banker. He wishes to serve you."

Moira shook his head decisively. "I don't want to owe *her* brother money."

A long pause followed, during which Moira looked at everything in the room except the Captain. Finally there was nowhere else to look.

James's face was expressionless. "Les affaires du coeur sont toujours les plus difficiles."

"God *damn* you and your affairs of the heart, sir. Next you'll be reciting one of your poems."

"I dare not, my lord. Only yesterday I looked at them, and saw I'd written one about the 'native radiance of the Prince's generous heart.' I can ask no man's indulgence after that."

Moira gave a snort, and clapped James on the shoulder. "Very well. And this business of Miss Austen remains among ourselves?"

"Ourselves and Lady Charlotte, my lord. And I expect anyone who ever sees the two of you in the same room."

Moira flushed, he wasn't sure whether with anger or embarrassment. A noise at the front door distracted him, and he surprised himself by starting to laugh. He knew James was right.

"I shall endeavor to improve, Captain. Immediately."

William Clifton and Colonel McMahon had met on their way to Moira House and, recognizing each other, discovered they were bound for the same engagement.

Moira gestured them to chairs as the footman showed them into the drawing room.

"What?" cried McMahon. "No ladies?"

Colonel McMahon was a small, bustling Irishman with an oval face, prominent nose, and mottled pink complexion. Moira knew him well. McMahon had been a common foot-soldier when they'd first met in America. Moira transferred him to his own command, promoted him, and later introduced him to the Prince, who was struck by McMahon's charm and impeccable manners. To Moira's dismay the Prince now employed McMahon for all his confidential errands, including the most unsavory.

"Patience, Colonel," said Moira. "There will be time for your gallantries later. In the meantime, Clifton, what do you think of being trapped in a room with the men of business for two such famous debtors?"

"I protest, my lord!" cried McMahon.

"Save your protests, Colonel," said Captain James. "It's no more than the truth."

"But what will our young friend think?"

Clifton smiled. He was only a little taller than McMahon, but by comparison almost classically handsome, with regular features and a shock of brown hair. His only shortcoming, if he had any, was that each of his features was so individually perfect that the overall effect was bland. Moira himself had passed him on Piccadilly earlier in the week without recognizing him, and that was after Clifton had called at Moira House at least a dozen times.

"Great men must have great debts," said Clifton. "Otherwise discharging them would be unremarkable."

"Well spoken, sir" declared McMahon. "Whoever said that gentlemen may not be bankers?"

"No-one in this room, surely," said Moira. "May I take it, Clifton, that you have been of service to Colonel McMahon and his Royal Highness?"

"As far as I was able, my lord. My principals at Hoare's are meticulous about endorsements."

McMahon's face, perpetually pink, reddened. "Let us not air our dirty linens in such distinguished company, young man."

"No indeed," said Charlotte, making a somewhat theatrical entrance. "Especially not in *mixed* company."

At first Moira tried to spread his gaze evenly as Jane and his ward followed Charlotte into the room. The effort didn't last long. Jane entered last, uneasy in one of Charlotte's dresses. How fast had the ladies worked to take it in so much at the waist? And who'd given Jane's auburn ringlets such perfect shape? He couldn't take his eyes off her.

Charlotte cleared her throat, and Moira recollected his duty.

"Gentlemen, you know my sister and my ward. May I give you Miss Jane Austen, of Bath?

The men bowed in turn as Moira gave their names. McMahon immediately cast an inquisitive look at Captain James, whose expression revealed nothing. Clifton, having performed his bow, was all eyes for Moira's ward, Harriet. She was slightly taller than Clifton, in full evening dress at the height of current fashion, its train bordered with a key pattern from a Grecian urn and the bodice with a low, rounded décolletage.

Lord, thought Moira, watching Clifton. Do I seem as besotted around Jane as that puppy does now?

The footman entered. "Dinner is served."

Clifton jumped up, followed by Captain James who offered his arm to Jane. McMahon did the same for Charlotte. Moira was last, entering the dining room alone.

CHAPTER XVII
1801

Charlotte had been careful with the seating. As always, she sat at the foot of the table, opposite Moira. But instead of putting Jane at Moira's right, she placed his ward there instead, with Clifton opposite and Jane between him and Captain James, who was on Charlotte's right. Colonel McMahon took the place on Charlotte's left, and no sooner were they seated than he launched his first question.

"Nobody truly comes from Bath, Miss Austen. Where, exactly, are your people seated?"

"Steventon, Colonel, in Hampshire."

Moira saw danger in this line of questioning, but James was faster.

"Miss Austen is a considerable reader, Colonel. She bought no fewer than seven books this afternoon."

"And she writes as well," put in Charlotte. "Like you, Captain, and indeed like my brother, though he would blush to allow it."

All eyes turned to Moira who, feeling himself under fire, managed to hold steady. Jane was quick to take pity on him.

"A writer, Captain James. Pray, of what manner?"

Charlotte laughed. "Of what manner is he not? Apart from screeds of political pamphlets, not least that bothersome vindication of the French revolutionaries, he has just published a compendium for soldiers – what did you call it, Captain?"

James's face was pink. "*The Regimental Companion*, my lady."

"Just so," continued Charlotte. "And his poems have seen, I believe, three editions."

Charlotte had the attention of the entire table, and was clearly enjoying herself.

"James wrote that he would never – how did you put it, sir? – 'never visit the paths of flowery panegyric to flatter rank.' But listen to this:

> All is not lost; Britannia still shall find
> Its guardian genius in a Rawdon's mind."

"Better, my lady," cried McMahon. "I believe I can go one better in quizzing our friend Captain James. Here's another of his effusions:

> Though Milo's paper floats about the town,
> And in loose ways by looser hands be shown,
> The breath of Slander cannot reach his name;
> His worth is spotless and untouch'd his fame. . . ."

"Enough," said Moira. He hadn't raised his voice, but it was a command nevertheless. The table fell silent.

"Your soup will get cold," he added mildly.

"Indeed I have forgot myself," cried Charlotte, gesturing to the servants. As the dishes came and the wine was poured Captain James turned back to Jane.

"Now they've had their fill of me, I believe I may ask you to speak quietly of your own writing. Are you a poet as well?"

Clifton had begun talking across the table, and it was all Moira could do to eavesdrop on Jane's answer.

"My poems are, as Mrs. Piozzi says, flight and fancy and nonsense, but I confess an aspiration to novel-writing."

Jane was studying James's face. "I perceive, sir, that I meet with no approbation. I am not surprised. Novels you imagine as desultory things, full of circumstances of apparent consequence which lead to nothing."

"I have no such conception of novels, Miss Austen."

"Then you do not read them, sir, for I describe no more than what is. But my family are great novel-readers and not ashamed of being so."

Colonel McMahon saw his opportunity, and interrupted.

"Bath is a fine place for novel-reading, Miss Austen. But I am myself acquainted with Hampshire and cannot place your father's seat there."

Jane's head came up and her gaze was firm as she looked directly across the table.

"He has no seat, sir. My father is a clergyman."

"A poor clergyman, I infer. Are you another of his lordship's objects of charity?"

Moira rose from his chair. "You are insufferable, Colonel."

McMahon, unabashed, raised his eyes to his host.

"I withdraw the question, my lord. Will you forgive me, Miss Austen?"

"I shall answer you, sir. I am no person's object of charity. My father is a gentleman; I am a gentleman's daughter. I honor his lordship's rank, but it is not outside my own sphere. One of my brothers has his seat in Kent; two others are officers in the Navy. I am told that Mr. Clifton is heir to a baronetcy, yet he aspires to the same profession as still another of my brothers."

Moira sat down, feeling a surge of pride. Jane had stood her ground like a soldier.

"Brava," said James softly.

"Brava indeed," repeated Charlotte. "It little becomes you, Colonel, to en-quire after Miss Austen's family, when my brother's generosity has spared you enquiries into your own. Let us turn to happier subjects."

Young Clifton intervened. "Surely it is not improper for Colonel McMahon to make such inquiries?"

Charlotte turned to face him. "Perhaps not altogether improper, sir. But cer-tainly less than genteel. But we are changing the subject, Mr. Clifton. I under-stand you have secured tickets to the theatre this evening?"

Moira's ward replied first. "Oh, yes," said Harriet breathlessly. "They have revived *Lovers' Vows.*"

Moira laughed. "Immorality and Jacobinical sedition. Did you not see it when it first appeared, two years ago?"

She blushed. "My father would not allow it."

Charlotte came to the girl's rescue. "He'd have considered you too young, my dear." Moira felt her reproving glare as she continued. "There would have been no other cause, surely."

Moira waved a hand. "Did you fear I should forbid her to go, even if the play *were* seditious? I, who am called seditious for no more than defending the rights of my fellow-Irishmen?"

James raised his glass. "On behalf of all Catholics I offer our heartfelt thanks, my lord."

"You are Catholic, Captain James?" asked Jane, clearly surprised.

"But not Irish, Miss Austen," put in McMahon. "Doubtless you are aware that Irish Catholics may not serve as officers in the regular army."

"The Irish are to be cannon fodder merely," said Moira. "They may groan under the most absurd and disgusting tyranny that any nation has ever known, and then be expected to fight and die in the service of those same tyrants."

"I perceive this is one of your convictions, my lord," said Jane mildly.

Moira nodded, embarrassed. Jane's eyes were upon him again, wide-open in an expression that conveyed amusement, puzzlement, and affection all at once. He was coming to recognize that it was the turn of her mouth which gave the clue to what was uppermost. Pursed was puzzled, or with eyes narrowed could mean disagreement or annoyance.

But when her lips parted, just slightly, as they did now, Moira knew affection was in the ascendant. He took heart from this, as he had never sounded Jane on her true opinion of the Irish. Many Englishwomen dismissed them as incorrigible paupers, unworthy of notice. All at once he longed to be alone again with her.

The servants saved him by entering with the roast. Conversation ceased for a time, and Moira took a moment to consult his pocket-watch. There would be further debate on the Debtors' Relief Act that evening, and he had lobbied so many of the peers about his proposed amendments that he knew he had to be in the House before the bill was once again read.

As they finished the main course Moira prepared to depart. But Charlotte held up a hand.

"Tomorrow, dear brother. . ."

"Yes?"

". . . will be Miss Austen's last day before she leaves for Kent. It's Wednesday, and surely we may get tickets for Almack's if you can be spared from the Lords."

Jane's eyes were bright. "Almack's? I have no gown suitable for Almack's. It is the most elegant venue in London – in the entire country, surely?"

Charlotte smiled. "I shall see to your gown, Miss Austen. We are not so very different in size, after all."

Moira hated the stuffiness of Almack's, the pretensions of its lady patronesses in their determination to be final arbiters of all taste. But Jane's ardor was infectious.

"I shall try to keep my concerns from the Lords for a few hours. And appoint a proxy if I fail. Almack's it is."

He rose. "And now I must go."

CHAPTER XVIII
1801

The usher wore the long-suffering look often seen on those responsible for the day-to-day workings of the House. But it did not occur to Moira that the man was coming for him until he heard his name whispered.

An old Scottish earl had the floor. He was ranting that if the Pope came to terms with Bonaparte, the restoration of Catholicism in France could lead to a holy war against Britain. Moira had heard it all before, in public and private. He didn't hesitate to follow the usher out of the chamber.

Moira's stable-boy was hopping with excitement. "Two men in yer house m'lord. I'm to tell you one of 'em's Lord Sefton an' you're needed at once."

Moira's horse was outside. He leaped astride, leaving the boy to find his way home on foot. He passed St. James's Palace at a gallop, loudly damned for his hard riding by a half-dozen pedestrians and a couple of coachmen. Two minutes later he was inside Moira House.

The butler pointed towards the drawing room, but Moira could already hear the voices. Something garbled and male, and then a cry from Charlotte.

Taking the stairs two at a time he heard Jane speak calmly. "Come no closer, sir."

Then he was inside.

If Moira hadn't been so angry he might have laughed. Jane stood by the fireplace, holding a poker like a quarterstaff. Lord Sefton was close too, much too close, but keeping a safe distance from the poker.

Charlotte was behind the piano, tears of rage on her cheeks. Sefton's particular friend Sir John Lade was on a settee, foppishly dressed as usual, wringing his hands.

Jane was as angry as Moira, eyes bright and color high in her cheeks, ready to use the poker to good effect. A glimpse told Moira she was unharmed. Then he was upon Sefton, knocking him to the floor with a single blow.

"Out."

"My lord!" cried Sir John, his voice slurred. "There 'sh no harm intended."

Sefton came to his hands and knees, dazed. "'Twas you the bitch was quizzing, Lade."

"Enough," roared Moira. He turned to Jane, who managed a smile.

"There's justice in that, my lord. I asked Sir John if he was truly the subject of verses by the immortal Doctor Johnson."

Moira grinned. "Ever the literary one." He turned to Lade, who shrugged.

"I am mortally sick of those lines." Nevertheless he giggled and began to recite:

> Call the Bettys, Kates, and Jennys,
> Every name that laughs at care,
> Lavish of your grandsire's guineas,
> Show the spirit of an heir.

As Lade declaimed, Sefton reached up to the arm of a chair and hauled himself to his feet. His outthrust jaw was swelling where Moira had hit it. He weaved on his feet, glaring as hard as his unfocussed eyes allowed.

"God damn your eyes, sir. 's cause for a mortal challenge."

Moira turned to face him, matter-of-fact. "It is that," he replied. "Send Lade tomorrow if you choose. Captain James will be my second."

"By God, I shall," bellowed Sefton. "You will come out."

Moira straightened, eyes flashing. His voice became deeper, ice-cold and with a hint of Irish.

"Never doubt it," he said. "You have challenged. I shall choose weapons." He paused. "They will be sabers. I shall cut you down like a dog."

Sefton wasn't too drunk to be alarmed. He recoiled, almost falling again as Jane came to Moira's side.

"No," she said firmly. She was still holding the poker. "Lord Sefton has suffered enough, my lord. Let him apologize for his insults and go."

"I never apologize," said Sefton, voice still slurred. "'s a matter of honor."

"Of which he has none," said Moira. "Do not trouble yourself over him."

Sir John Lade approached, gripping Sefton's arm.

"Don't be a fool, Sefton. The lady will accept your apology, and if she does, so must Moira."

For a moment the room was silent. The front door opened, and was followed by footsteps in the hallway. The butler, shamefaced and clearly hoping to recover some of his dignity, announced Mr. William Clifton, who entered, bowing.

"Clifton!" exclaimed Sefton, his red face turning pale. "The young one a greater villain than the old, I'll warrant."

Clifton cut his bow short to stare. "My lord Sefton," he said finally.

"Hah," said Sefton. "Look at the boy's face. He's got his talons into Moira now." Sefton turned to Moira, bowing low.

"You have my most profound apologies, my lord, and" – he turned to Jane – "you as well, my lady, whoever you may be."

Moira looked from Sefton to Clifton and back. Clifton appeared shocked and angry. Sefton's coarse features had, suddenly, an unexpected dignity.

"Come along, Lade," said Sefton. Then he bowed to Lady Charlotte. "My most humble apologies, ma'am. Your brother has enough trouble now. I shall not compound it."

The two men brushed by the butler, still at the drawing-room door, stumbled downstairs, and let themselves out into St. James's Place.

Moira looked around the room. Jane's face was grim, and Charlotte suddenly lost her balance. Clifton was closest and rushed to her side, helping her to the sofa.

"Get her maidservant," he said to the butler.

"No, no," protested Charlotte, waving an arm. "I am perfectly all right. Miss Austen must sit too."

Jane took an adjacent armchair as Moira turned to Clifton.

"What business have you had with Sefton?"

"None, my lord. I believe he had some dealings with my father on a matter of gambling debts. I have never seen him before this evening."

"And yet you called him by name," said Jane.

Clifton smiled. "There's no mistaking Lord Sefton. Every printseller in town has his image."

"Quite true," said Charlotte. "'Lord Dash-along, bent on driving.'"

"You called him that in Bond Street," said Jane.

"Yes," said Charlotte. "Mr. Gillray's caricatures are always telling."

"I shall seek them out when I return to Bath."

Once again Moira wanted Jane to himself, to apologize and to tell her how well she'd acquitted herself with Sefton. But Charlotte was in no state to walk out of the room, and he dared not let Clifton see him leaving with Jane alone. Nor, for that matter, could they ever be seen alone by the town. Damn Gillray and the rest for making Moira's face as well known as Sefton's. And no prettier, come to think of it.

Jane's hazel eyes were upon him, wide and uncertain. Was she starting to regret ever knowing him? He'd told both Captain James and Clifton she was Charlotte's friend. James had seen through the ploy at once. He dared not give himself away to Clifton, at least not yet.

"Captain James will return at any moment, Miss Austen."

"I confess," Jane replied, "that until this evening I should not have hesitated to walk to my brother's office on my own. Now I am not so certain."

"May I assist?" asked Clifton.

"Have you time to accompany Miss Austen to her brother's office in St. James's Street?"

"Of course, my lord. Our play doesn't begin for another hour."

Moira thought for a moment. "Will you join my sister tomorrow, Miss Austen? I expect she would approve a quiet day with you."

"I must work on my gown if we are to attend Almack's, my lord."

Charlotte, fully recovered, began to laugh. "Almack's indeed. I am afraid we must forego Almack's, my dear Miss Austen."

"Why?" asked Moira.

Charlotte was almost coquettish as she replied. "Lady Sefton is one of the patronesses."

Jane joined in the laughter, as did Moira. Clifton smiled, not entirely sharing the joke.

After a moment Jane spoke. "Perhaps, Lady Charlotte." She hesitated, uncertain. "Perhaps you might allow me to offer morning coffee in Bond Street? I have already imposed upon your hospitality here, far more than I ought."

"Indeed you have not. But yes, let us meet in Bond Street. Or, better, at Brunswick House, in Prince's Street off Hanover Square. And then we shall go to the dressmaker's."

"Thank you, my lady. Shall we say eleven o'clock?"

Charlotte nodded her assent.

Jane rose, offering her arm to Clifton. Moira wanted to push him out of the way but forced himself to remain still. He saw them to the front door, surprised at his own jealousy. When he returned to the drawing-room Charlotte gave him a knowing, sisterly appraisal.

"You are truly smitten with this young woman, are you not, brother?"

"I imagined myself too old to be smitten."

"Oh, no. The blow falls harder as one gets older. Be glad you are not sixty, or you would have no control at all."

CHAPTER XIX
1823

After supper at Government House Lonsdale and Vanessa walked outside into a soft sea-breeze. Vanessa was still puzzling about the accident at the *Royal George*. She wanted comfort from Lonsdale, but his first words made it clear she wasn't going to get it.

"Your sea-captains let their brother off too easily," said Lonsdale.

"What more could they do?"

"Get the truth! If they'd left him to me I'd have had it."

Vanessa was angry, and showed it. "If they'd left him to you he might be dead."

Lonsdale looked down at her in the twilight. "That is unfair, but I won't argue. There's a hostler here who has an arrangement in Alton. I shall ride to Selborne tonight and take the London coach tomorrow morning. Will you join me?"

"You know I won't," said Vanessa. "I'm staying here tonight, and return to Chawton tomorrow. I must see Mary before I go to London. Her baby may come soon."

"Will you go to London tomorrow?"

"Yes. Lord Hastings is expecting me to supper."

"The two o'clock coach then," said Lonsdale.

Vanessa wasn't sure why he was so insistent, but she knew she would rather travel with than without him.

"Agreed."

The Austens' chaise reached Chawton before noon the next day. Mary's condition was unchanged. Vanessa didn't like her pallor, and she still seemed feverish. But Martha didn't seem overly concerned. Nor, she reported, was the midwife.

"Return in time for your music in Winchester, love, and come sooner only if it suits you." She smiled. "Henry is the only one of us who wishes to deprive you of your visit with the Marquess of Hastings."

"Thank you." Vanessa put her arms around her friend. "I know you and I are the childless women in the house, and we should defer to Mary. But I still believe I should come back soon."

Edward Knight was not at home, but his servant had the letter for Vanessa to deliver to the Marquess. The donkey-cart carried her case to the coaching inn at Alton where Lonsdale was waiting. This time the ride was uneventful.

CHAPTER XX
1823

During the coach journey Lonsdale made Vanessa promise she would hire a carriage to take her to the Marquess's house at Campden Hill. As it drove from Charing Cross to Kensington, she changed her mind, deciding it would be a nice touch if she could arrive with a gift for the house, perhaps some tea or spices. She wasn't sure why she was so happy at the thought of returning to Lord Hastings and his family, but she was. She didn't want to arrive empty-handed. She called to the driver to drop her by a small parade of shops in Kensington's high street.

The driver offered to wait, or to return for her after her shopping. But Vanessa knew there would be daylight for at least another hour. She wanted to stretch her legs after the long coach ride from Alton, so she demurred, paying the driver to deliver her portmanteau to Campden Hill and to tell the servants she would arrive shortly.

One of the shops had ready-packed tea canisters from Messrs. Twining. Vanessa bought a large, hand-painted one. She knew the turn that led north up to Campden Hill was no more than a hundred yards from the shop. The lane was tree-lined and scented, peaceful in the waning light of a summer evening. She prepared to enjoy the walk.

As she progressed up the hill, the houses at the lower end, closest to Kensington, gave way to more open space. The cluster of four houses at Vanessa's destination was in sight when the sound of someone alighting from a nearby carriage made her look back. A bearded man approached her, waving urgently.

"Miss," he cried. "Wait."

It was too much like the scene in Alton after the cricket, where Lonsdale had killed a man. But there was no Lonsdale to protect her now.

What if this were another rescuer from her own time? No ordinary outsider could have any idea where she might be. But as the man drew closer instinct told Vanessa something was wrong. It was too late for her to run away, and she doubted she could outrun him anyway. He was holding something in his fist, and the closer he got the worse he looked.

Would he tackle her? She readied herself for a leap sideways, but as he came within ten yards he slowed, panting. It was then Vanessa realized that his beard was false, as false as the moustache and side-whiskers in her own portmanteau. That does it, she decided.

Vanessa had practiced martial arts in her own time, and they remained part of her exercise ritual. She took two quick steps forward, pulling up her skirt. Then she kicked with all her might, directly at the man's groin.

He went down, wind and strength knocked out of him. A set of brass knuckles fell from a nerveless hand as he writhed by the roadside, gasping for air.

Vanessa reached down and snatched the knuckles, keeping her distance from the fallen man. As she did so his carriage rattled past, giving her a single glimpse of its dark-skinned driver. Her blood was up, and she wondered if she needed to kick her assailant again to keep him from coming after her.

"Who are you?" she demanded.

Both the man's hands were covering himself. He shook his head, moaning.

Vanessa took a step backwards. "I'm going to leave now, but if I see you get up before I reach the top of the hill, I'll do worse than I did just now. Do you hear me?"

The man's head jerked in a nod. Vanessa kept backing, and when she could no longer bear it she turned and ran. She was breathless when she reached Lord Hastings's courtyard at the top of the hill.

The clatter of her feet on the gravel must have roused the servants. The front door of the house was open before she got there.

A footman bowed. "Lord Hastings is upstairs in the drawing room."

But Vanessa could hear measured steps on the main staircase, and when she looked up it was the Marquess himself.

"We are pleased you are so anxious for our company as to run, Miss Horwood, but could you not simply have remained with your carriage?"

Vanessa started to laugh, but she recognized the same hysteria she had felt in Alton. She cut it short.

"I've been attacked, my lord. Close to this house."

Hastings was on the alert at once, seeming to grow taller as he barked commands. He had the assailant's description from Vanessa as four dark-skinned and formidable young men arrived from different directions. Hastings ordered them out.

"Find the site and fan out. I do not expect he would come this way, but make certain before you disperse.

"Watch for dirt on his trousers. He may easily lose the beard and the jacket. If you get him, bring him here whatever he may say. We'll fetch the constables after."

When they were gone he took Vanessa upstairs, where a worried Marchioness was standing in the open doorway to the drawing-room.

"Brandy, my love," ordered Hastings, his voice softening. "Miss Horwood is distinctly pale."

Vanessa fell into a chair, reassured by the room where she and young Lady Flora had played and sung only a few days earlier. She set down her reticule to take the brandy, and then snatched it up again.

"Oh," she cried. "I have something for you."

She pulled out Edward Knight's letter, exchanging it for the brandy. The liquid burned its way down her throat, and she took a deep breath.

"Much better," said Hastings. He glanced at the letter's address panel. "This will wait, my dear, while you tell us what exactly has happened."

Vanessa managed to smile. "I'd been in a coach all day and wanted to walk."

"So your driver said when he left your case."

"And I wanted to bring you this," she added, once again rummaging in her reticule, bulging with the tea-canister. She had crushed the bow where the shopkeeper had tied the wrapping with a bright ribbon, and she tried to straighten it as she rose from her chair to hand the package to Lady Hastings.

"How kind of you," said the latter, untying the ribbon and pulling aside the paper. "Ah," she added. "What a lovely tin."

"Tea," said Vanessa.

"Tea," repeated the Marchioness faintly.

"Oh lord," cried Vanessa. "You've just returned from India. You must have a houseful of tea already."

"Never too much," said Hastings. "Even in Newcastle they must have coal for their fires."

The Marchioness smiled. "My husband is gallant, is he not?"

"Miss Horwood is no stranger to gallantry," said Hastings. "Your Captain Lonsdale is a fine young officer. He'd have received promotion had his regiment stayed with me after the Nepalese wars."

"But now," he continued. "I hear my men returning. By their footsteps I surmise they have not succeeded."

"He could have gone anywhere, couldn't he?" asked Vanessa.

"Yes. There is open country in all directions. If he was intent upon mischief he could not have chosen better ground."

Vanessa shuddered. "But why *would* he?"

"A moment, Miss Horwood."

Hastings strode to the door and descended, much lighter on his feet than he'd been when Vanessa arrived. She could hear part of the exchange, as the men explained where they had looked, and that they had found the place where Vanessa had taken her assailant to the ground.

"Have you sent someone to the constables?" asked Hastings. "And reported to Clifton?"

"Sir William has returned home," someone said.

"Surely not," said Hastings. "The Marchioness invited him and Lady Clifton to join us for supper."

"No, sir," came the butler's voice. "He said he had pressing business, and I saw him leave just after Miss Horwood's case arrived."

"Very well," said Hastings. "As the children have retired, please let the cook know it will be just the three of us. In half an hour."

"Yes, my lord," replied the butler.

By the time Hastings returned upstairs Vanessa had remembered something else. She held up the brass knuckles for inspection.

Lady Hastings gasped, but the Marquess took the knuckles with a smile.

"You are more of a fighter than you admitted. These are appurtenances of professional criminals."

"I didn't know he had them till he went down," said Vanessa. "Although I knew he was holding *something* in his fist."

"How did you know he meant you harm?" asked Hastings.

"I can't say that I knew. I felt it as he approached. And then I saw the false beard."

Hastings nodded. "That was enough. No soldier could ask for more."

Lady Hastings gave a faint smile. "He has paid you his highest compliment, Miss Horwood." She rose. "I must see to the children before we dine." She smiled again. "Do not fear I shall change before we dine. And nor must you."

Hastings stood as his wife left the room, and proceeded to the sideboard to pour himself a glass of the brandy he had offered Vanessa.

"To your very good health, young lady."

Something about the way he spoke, the sympathy in his voice, the sheer *kindness* in a man so nearly overwhelmed by his own troubles, brought tears to Vanessa's eyes. She remembered her happiness in the carriage, little more than an hour ago, as she anticipated this visit. What *was* it about this man – and his family too, she quickly told herself.

She raised her glass and took another swallow of the powerful brandy. No, she thought. It was Lord Hastings himself. He made her feel looked after, safe, even in the midst of danger. She hadn't felt this way in a long, long time.

"My lord," she began.

Hastings bowed, and was about to sit opposite when Lady Hastings returned.

"I am not needed," she declared. "Let us begin a cold collation at once, while Miss Horwood still has strength to eat."

Supper was everything Vanessa had been denied the night before in Gosport. No meat at all, but lettuce from the Marchioness's kitchen garden, hothouse tomatoes, and fresh bread. And the second course consisted of root vegetables cooked with rice in a spicy sauce.

"Curry," said Lady Hastings. "His lordship became very fond of it in Calcutta, and this" – she handed Vanessa a condiment dish – "is called chutney. It will lessen the effect."

Lady Hastings chose to retire immediately after dinner.

"We do not stand on ceremony when we are alone, my dear," she told Vanessa. "Please forgive us if we treat you as one of our family."

Vanessa made her curtsey, and at the Marquess's invitation she joined him for a glass of madeira back in the upstairs drawing-room.

He sprawled on a settee, stretching his long legs. Vanessa took a chair opposite, sipping at the sweet, slightly syrupy wine. After a moment she spoke.

"Will you forgive an impertinent question, my lord?"

He smiled. "Any young woman beset on her way to my door is entitled to at least one."

"Thank you. The question is not my own, and I am concerned you may think it an insult."

Hastings cupped his hands behind his head. "Captain Lonsdale, then."

"Yes. But before I ask I must tell you that this evening is not the first time I've been accosted. Three days ago on the coach to Hampshire a young man had words with Captain Lonsdale. He alighted at Alton, as we did, and that night he approached me on my way back to Chawton."

Hastings's arms came down. He was fully alert now.

"You were alone?"

Vanessa shook her head. "I was accompanied by Mr. Henry Austen, one of my hosts."

"Austen! But I mistake – you told me of this visit, did you not?"

"Yes. Captain Francis Austen's wife is expecting another child, and I promised to help in the house. The captain and his family are living at Chawton House. I must return day after tomorrow."

Hastings nodded. "You were walking to Chawton House from Alton when the man accosted you. Could it have been the same man as this evening?"

The horrors of that night blended with the shock of today's attack, and Vanessa shivered.

"No. This evening's man is still alive. The one at Alton is dead."

"I am sorry to distress you," said Hastings. "Take your time."

"The young man produced a knife, and Captain Lonsdale killed him."

"Shot him?"

"No, my lord. With a blow to the neck."

Hastings replaced his hands behind his head, once again leaning back against the settee.

"I believe I may infer your question. Lonsdale wonders if I am somehow implicated."

Vanessa nodded and Hastings smiled. "It is damnably impertinent. And entirely reasonable. You change your plans – you notice I do not enquire what sort of plans you made beyond dressing yourself up as a man and playing cards at White's."

She met his gaze, blushing.

"Just so," said Hastings. "As I said, you change your plans in order to visit my house. The next day someone attacks you. Lonsdale's question is made more telling by the fact that you returned to my house today and once again someone attacked you, almost on my doorstep."

"And I should say that both men, as well as today's accomplice in the carriage, were dark-skinned like your servants."

Hastings dropped his hands to his sides, intent, almost brooding.

"I may tell you I had business with Henry Austen for a number of years, until I left for India. I owed his bank money when I departed, and it took me some years to repay it."

"He blames you for his bank's failure. But surely that's not enough of a connection."

Hastings's head came up sharply. "What do you mean?"

"Not enough for someone to wish me harm."

"I agree."

"Is everyone in your household accounted for?" asked Vanessa.

"Twenty lascars from India accompanied us on the voyage home. Some of them had relations already in England."

"Lascars!" blurted Vanessa. "Lonsdale said the man he killed had a lascar knife."

Hastings shook his head. "That means no more than the dead man was likely from army or navy service himself, and thereby known as a lascar. There are thousands of such men in England, including the four I dispatched in pursuit of your attacker. Eight more of mine live down amongst the potteries by Ladbroke's estate. I cannot speak for their exact whereabouts, but Clifton will know."

"But these lascars are all Indian, are they not?"

"Some intermarry. What did your man in Alton look like?"

"Very like your four men. Handsome, in fact. With an accent I could not place."

Hastings looked thoughtful. Then he shrugged, smiling.

"Let us speak of other things, or you will have nightmares."

"Wait," cried Vanessa. There was too much trouble in her life to allow Hastings to return them to small talk. She wanted him to know the rest of her story. As soon as she'd seen her assailant's brass knuckles she knew he could not possibly have been coming from the future to rescue her. And if this man was an enemy, surely the man Lonsdale had killed on the path from Alton was another.

She was certain Hastings would have told her the truth if he'd seen a link between himself and her attackers. What advice might he give if he knew the rest of her story?

He was sitting calmly opposite, like a general expecting a report from a junior officer. Not long after her release from gaol she had tried to tell a new friend the truth of who she was and where she'd come from. Some force — a quirk of time itself? — had frozen her tongue. It was time to try again.

"My lord, I must tell you. . . ." There it was again, the same force.

Hastings was leaning forward, expectantly.

Vanessa tried again, and again. Finally she burst into tears, all her fears converging in a series of sobs she felt would never stop.

After a few moments she felt Hastings's hand on her shoulder. She managed to raise her face so she could look into his eyes.

He smiled. "I have not seen such sorrow since we sent Flora off to boarding-school."

Vanessa managed a weak smile and Hastings returned to his sofa. He seemed about to ask a question, then shrugged and returned her smile.

"If I may serve you in any manner, at any time, Miss Horwood, you have only to ask. But I shall say this before I send you to bed. If you must return to Hampshire so soon we shall keep you busy tomorrow. My daughters wish you to play music with them, and to have your opinion of their drawings. By noon we must go to town. We shall leave Flora and my wife in Bond Street whilst we dine with Murray."

"You remembered!" cried Vanessa.

"Of course I did, my dear. Murray says your friend Miss Austen's letters are not so entertaining as Byron's, and that he has only a few. But he will produce them for our inspection."

He paused. Vanessa could see his uncertainty as he spoke again.

"Have you letters of your own from Miss Austen?"

"Only one, three lines confirming she intended a visit to Winchester gaol."

Hastings smiled. "Did she make regular visits of that kind?"

"I don't believe so, my lord. But by the time I knew her she was ill, and the last time I saw her was a month before her death."

Now it was Lord Hastings's turn to show grief, the same expression Vanessa had seen at his whist table on her previous visit. Both times the conversation had been about Jane Austen. Was he hiding some secret as powerful as Vanessa's own?

Once again he soon mastered whatever feelings he had. His face impassive, Hastings put a hand in his jacket pocket.

"You handed me a letter earlier. Let us see what it has to say."

He put the letter in his lap, and leaned forward to set a fresh candle in a lamp. He lit it, and tore the letter open.

"Edward Knight. Ah . . . brother to Mr. H.T. Austen." Hastings looked up. "And to Miss Jane Austen of whom we just spoke." He returned to the letter. "In possession of bills of your Lordship's to the amount of £6,500 actually paid by myself. . . your Lordship's honorable and unequivocal expressions of your sacred obligation to discharge the Bills. . . ."

"If you repaid Henry Austen's bank, how can Mr. Knight have a court warrant to collect more?"

"He told you as much?"

"Yes."

Hastings shook his head, making her think of an old and weary lion. "My finances have reached a point, Miss Horwood, where I owe so much to so many that I can no longer keep track."

He replaced the letter in his pocket, lifted the lamp, and stood up.

"Come, child." He led the way, pausing before he opened the drawing-room door. "I should warn you that your room is next to Selina and Flora's. If you wake them they will certainly keep you up all night."

Vanessa had risen along with her host. She curtseyed.

"I shall tread lightly, my lord."

He smiled. "Angelically, I do not doubt." He walked her up the stairs to the top floor, handing over the candle as they reached her bedroom door. Then he bowed.

"Good night, Miss Horwood."

"Good night, my lord Hastings."

CHAPTER XXI
1823

Vanessa woke early next morning in the unfamiliar bed, but even so Flora and Selina were waiting for her. Both were anxious to prove themselves competent pianists, and soon woke the rest of the house as they demanded points of technique from Vanessa and insisted on practicing them at once.

Soon they declared her much better than any teacher they'd had either in London or Calcutta. Then they were ready to display their watercolors.

Vanessa was surprised how good they were. There were scenes from India, portraits of their family, and sketches of friends.

"This is Sir William Clifton," said Selina. "He embarrassed Papa in India, but he has always been kind to us. And this is his wife, with their two children."

"And this notebook is all sketches of Papa," said Flora, handing it proudly to Vanessa.

There were dozens of them, all accomplished in loving detail. At his work-table, on his horse, reading to a child in bed, dozing with a cat in his lap.

"You admire your father, don't you?"

Selina interrupted. "She writes verses about him too."

Flora blushed, but when Vanessa asked again she began to recite:

My dear Papa in vain I strive
In vain I strive t'express the flow
Of love for you which while I live
Will never, never cease to glow. . . .

"Oh, well done, Lady Flora," said Vanessa. "Is there more?"

Flora shook her head modestly. "That's enough, I'm sure."

After a few more minutes the Marchioness arrived.

"You must allow Miss Horwood to dress, children. As must you, Flora. We shall leave for town in half-an-hour."

"May I not come, mother? Please?" asked Selina.

Lady Hastings smiled. "You already know the answer, my love. But your father says we may bring something back for you from Cooper's. Ribbon, perhaps?"

"Oh yes," cried Selina. "Let Flora pick the color."

When Vanessa went downstairs she found Lord Hastings in his study. There were stacks of papers on his desk, and she recognized Edward Knight's letter at the top of one of them. When Hastings turned to greet her his face was lined with worry. But he smiled nevertheless, complimenting her gown as though it had not been the same one she'd worn on her first visit, less than a week earlier.

They climbed into his old phaeton carriage sharply at noon, Vanessa and Flora perching on the rear platform while Hastings drove with the Marchioness at his side. He stabled the carriage off New Bond Street, and before they walked out Hastings handed his wife some banknotes.

"There is a small amount owing at Cooper's," he said. "This will cover the debt, and allow you and Flora both new dresses, I believe."

Lady Hastings winced as she took the money, but Flora went up on tiptoe to kiss her father.

"And may I buy a ribbon for Selina as well?"

"You may buy something more grand than ribbon, my dear," he replied. "Your mother will advise."

Cooper's millinery shop was towards the north end of New Bond Street. When Hastings and Vanessa left the two shoppers he directed her further north to Oxford Street instead of south, which was where she knew John Murray's house in Albemarle Street lay.

"It is some time since I was seen in town with a young woman, Miss Horwood. Allow an old man the indulgence of your arm, whilst we attend to one more errand before Murray's."

Vanessa had no idea what the errand could be, but she found out soon enough. It was a gunmaker's premises.

"Joe Manton," said Hastings. "I sent him one of Collier's revolving pistols from India and he produced a pair of much better design. This is another bill I must settle."

Manton came immediately from his workshop when his callers were announced.

"I never doubted you would honor your debt, Lord Hastings, although I confess there were others who did."

Hastings smiled. "Pay attention to those doubters next time you seek their advice, Manton. But you should know I admired those pistols enough to bring them home with me. And now I have another commission for you, which I shall pay with ready money."

Manton waved an arm. "You need not, my lord."

"But I shall, sir," replied Hastings. "I want your smallest, most accurate pistol for my companion here. She must have it now, this instant, and we shall instruct her in its use before we leave."

"No, Lord Hastings," cried Vanessa. "This is unnecessary, and much too generous."

"Absolutely necessary, given yesterday's circumstances. You've shown you can fight, but you might not be so lucky next time."

"Then let me pay for my own pistol."

Hastings winked at the gunmaker. "Manton would overcharge you."

"Indeed I should, Miss. You must never argue with such a great man."

And so Vanessa was conducted through a sequence of work-spaces, with all manner and sizes of guns in various states of manufacture. Manton knew exactly where he was going, and paused at a long table to speak with one of his men. A moment later he had what he sought, and guided Vanessa and Lord Hastings into a warehouse. At the far end were stacks of baled hay, to which were affixed small paper targets.

"Should your lordship care to try it first?" asked Manton.

"I should indeed," said Hastings, taking the little gun from Manton's hand and looking closely at it. "Forsyth's percussive cap, I perceive. Have you ready-made cartridges for it?"

"I've brought a dozen. If you tell me how many you'd like to take away, my man will make them up while you practice."

Hastings cast an inquiring eye at Vanessa. She was thoroughly taken aback by the entire proceeding, but a voice inside said 'this is a good idea.'

"How long do they keep?" she asked.

"Excellent question," declared Manton. "We have them in multiples of ten. An unopened package should last your lifetime, young lady. Opened and kept dry, perhaps a year in this climate."

"Make up four packages of ten," said Hastings. "And now show us the mechanism."

Manton pulled back the hammer and slipped in a small paper-covered cone.

"The main charge is at the front, powder and ball, so make sure this copper nipple – begging your pardon, Miss – is at the rear. The hammer will strike the copper and the spark will ignite the fulminate of mercury within, which in turn will fire the gunpowder."

"What range?" asked Hastings.

"It will surprise you, my lord. The cartridge burns more even than a flintlock, and with the rifled barrel, short as it is, you may rely on thirty, perhaps even forty yards in the hands of a marksman."

Hastings smiled. "Or woman."

Manton next showed them a small metal flange next to the pistol's hammer.

"This will prevent accidental discharge while the pistol is loaded. You may safely carry it for a day or two without fear of losing the charge. But you must disengage the flange as you cock the hammer, or your business will remain unfinished."

Hastings took the pistol, feeling its heft in his hand. "Just the size for a young woman's reticule, I believe."

He held it up, sighting along the short barrel. In what seemed to Vanessa like a single movement, he cocked the hammer with his thumb, flicked the safety-flange aside with his forefinger, and fired.

"Damnation," he said softly. "Missed altogether."

"Indeed not, my lord," said Manton. "You nicked the edge of the target, six inches off the bulls-eye. An admirable first shot."

"It will do, I suppose," said Hastings, his eyes on Vanessa. "The next shots are yours."

"Will you show me the trick of sliding the flange out of the way at the same time you cock the pistol?"

Hastings smiled. "With pleasure, my dear, although I expect Manton could do it better."

Manton waved an arm in self-deprecation, and Vanessa approached Lord Hastings. He'd bathed with something unusual, and smelled, she thought, of India. She placed the scent: sandalwood.

He showed her how to shake hands with the wooden pistol grip, lifting her finger and thumb into the appropriate positions. But Vanessa remained distracted. She already knew how distinguished Hastings was, and she'd seen his kindness the night before. But now she felt something of the magnetism he must have had when younger. Old he might be, but this is *not* the ugliest man in England, as the satirists once had it. Far from it.

Her pianist's fingers soon had the knack of the safety flange, but her first two shots went wild. Lord Hastings drew close once more, showing her how to hold the pistol steady.

"Use both hands if you must," he said. "And squeeze the trigger slowly. Most important of all, do not anticipate the recoil. Hold steady."

Vanessa took a deep breath, relaxing as though preparing to play a piano recital. When she raised the pistol again she slowly let out her breath as she fired. Her next six charges all struck the target, the last from the back wall of the warehouse forty feet away.

"She'll do," said Manton. "Would you care for some cartridges for your revolving pistols as well, my lord?"

Hastings nodded. "Let Miss Horwood fire a few more rounds whilst we settle."

Ten minutes later they were on their way to John Murray's house.
They arrived sharply upon their three o'clock hour, with Murray himself greeting them at the door. He was a compact, good-looking man in his early fifties, his face marred only by a clouded, obviously blind right eye.

"My lord Hastings," he crowed, arms wide in welcome. "I am delighted you should find time to return to my humble house so soon."

He turned to Vanessa, bowing. "And this is your guest, I perceive. Had I known her age and demeanor I should have summoned a dozen young poets to join us for tea later."

Murray offered Vanessa his arm. "Are you any relation of Horwood the map-maker?"

"No, sir," replied Vanessa. "At least not that I know of. My family has been in Canada since General Wolfe's time."

"Ah," said Murray. He guided her up the stairs, looking back at Hastings, who followed.

"We shall dine as soon as the others arrive, my lord. But in the meantime I have retrieved some letters for your perusal."

He walked them into a small antechamber, where a half dozen letters from Jane Austen lay on a table. Hastings looked intently at them, leafing through each before sliding it along towards Vanessa. Then he looked up at Murray, who shrugged.

"I believe I told you they gave no great impression of their writer, who showed great charm in person. Byron's letters, on the other hand, are often better company than the man himself."

Hastings nodded. "Nevertheless, I believe Miss Horwood and I are satisfied. By the way, Murray, I do not believe I mentioned when I saw you last, that I dined with Byron in Genoa not two months ago."

"How could you have failed to tell me so, my lord? I have not heard from Byron for months, not since I declined the rest of his *Don Juan*. Does he persist in this Greek adventure?"

Hastings nodded. "He does more than persist. He solicits money, men, and arms, already imagining himself a conquering hero."

Murray smiled. "It is always the way of men with satirical minds. When they become serious, they become serious indeed."

A bell from below caught Murray's attention.

"Our other guests have arrived, my lord. I must ask your indulgence, as Judge Richards had a standing invitation for today, upon which I could not renege. I proposed another time, but he maintained that he would not miss your lordship's presence for the world."

A footman entered. "Mrs. Murray advises that the other guests are at table, sir."

"Very well," said Murray. He extended an arm to allow Vanessa and Lord Hastings to precede him, following them downstairs to the dining room.

"I was about to say, my lord," he added softly, "that although we are only eight I believe the last two guests will please you."

A moment later Murray held a dining chair for Vanessa. He turned to the footman.

"Any of my writers who turn up for tea at four o'clock may be served." Then he addressed the table. "We may join them when we choose."

"Thank you, Murray," replied Hastings, standing behind his own chair. "I appreciate your indulgence to an old man."

Before Vanessa could sit, a stooped, elderly, and obviously infirm gentleman slowly pushed to his feet from his place opposite.

"You are not the only old man present, my lord."

"Lord Hastings," said Murray. "I give you Chief Baron Sir Richard Richards and his lady."

Hastings bowed. "Pray resume your place, Sir Richard. In my turn I give you Miss Vanessa Horwood."

Vanessa curtseyed. "Sir Richard. Lady Richards."

Another couple were likewise on their feet, a well-dressed and attractive but rather careworn woman, and her elegant husband, both in their forties. The man's patrician, slightly fleshy, features were alight with anticipation and pleasure.

"Tom Moore," cried Hastings. "My dear sir!"

"My lord Hastings," replied Moore fervently. "It has been a *very* long time."

"I was certain your fellow-Irishman would please you, my lord," said Murray mildly, "but I did not appreciate you were already acquainted."

Moore smiled broadly. "You have not read the dedications of my books, Mr. Murray."

"It was near twenty years ago, Tom," said Hastings.

"It was," replied Moore. "I proposed comparing your lordship to Hercules and you replied, if I remember rightly, that you were no better than an out-of-fashion piece of furniture, not fit to figure outside the steward's room."

"If it was true then," said Hastings, "How much more true now?"

Moore beamed at Hastings, his eyes full of sympathy. "True neither then nor now, my lord. But sit, I beg you. We may reminisce at leisure."

"Indeed you must sit, my lord. And Miss Horwood," said Murray. "And you too, Moore. Pray, sir, how did you and his lordship meet?"

Vanessa could tell that Hastings was feeling his age. He leaned back against the chair until its joints creaked. Moore, by contrast, seemed all energy.

"A mutual friend in Dublin secured my invitation to Donington Park. I shall never forget my first night there, when your lordship lighted me to my bedroom."

Moore turned to the table at large, enjoying his moment in the limelight.

"Imagine this tall and stately personage stalking on before you through the long gallery, bearing in his hand your bed-candle, which he delivers to you at the door of your apartment. It is all exceedingly fine and grand, but at the same time rather discomfiting, is it not?"

Vanessa smiled. Lord Hastings had done the same thing for her last night.

Murray gestured for serving to commence, and then spoke.

"Let us do more than reminisce. I have already shown his lordship's friend a glimpse of my meager correspondence with Miss Austen the novelist, dead these past six years."

Moore grinned. "I know what you are about to say, Murray. You propose to show her your Byron letters after dinner."

"That I will not," said Murray, his accent nearly broad Scotch for an instant. "They are sometimes as indecent as that memoir you cherish, and which we must destroy."

"Don't do that, Mr. Murray!" cried Vanessa.

"Forgive me, Miss Horwood," said Murray. "I have upset you."

"Great writers should be allowed their own monuments," declared Vanessa, surprised by her own temerity. "What seems to you indecent might not be so to another generation. How will *they* know Byron's true feelings if you have destroyed his autobiography?"

"Pah," said Judge Richards. "The young lady espouses the licentiousness of today's young. Licentiousness which the likes of you, Mr. Moore, and your friend Byron have encouraged. My lady and I commend Mr. Murray for declining to publish any more of that blasphemous *Don Juan*."

Vanessa saw the alarm on Murray's face, but it was Mrs. Murray, at the foot of the table, who intervened.

"Attend, your lordship, ladies and gentlemen. Our soup arrives. Let us eat, and resume the debate afterwards."

It was halfway through the main course, after Vanessa had replied to some questions posed by Mrs. Murray, that Judge Richards re-entered the conversation.

"I fancy myself a scholar of accents, Miss Horwood. You attend Lord Hastings, but your accent is not of the Indian continent, nor of these islands. Surely you are North American."

"Canadian, sir," replied Vanessa.

"Canadian," he repeated. "And who are your people."

Vanessa's head came up defiantly. "Transported felons, sir. The dregs of society."

"Nonsense," interposed Hastings. "You are ungracious, Sir Richard. We might just as well inquire by what name you are known around the law-courts."

"Stumpy Dick!" cried Moore. "It was even so in my Middle Temple days."

"Humph," snorted Judge Richards. "And you, my lord Hastings. Are you unaware that I was forced to pronounce upon that scandal involving the Austen banking house in the year seventeen? Your solicitor cried 'usury' over bills you had surely contracted knowing you could not repay them."

"That is a falsehood, sir."

Judge Richards had worked himself into a dudgeon. He was straining himself upright in his dining chair, his small eyes squinting with malice.

"How many score of creditors are dunning you, my lord? Will you put another bank into the gazette of failures, now you have returned home?"

Hastings rose to his feet, his dark skin flushed with anger.

"In another time, sir, I should have declared those fighting words."

"So have bullies ever replied to the truth," said Richards.

Hastings turned to his host and bowed. "Mr. Murray, I thank you for the meal, which I regret I shall not stay to finish. I rely upon your continuing courtesy to Miss Horwood."

Both Murray and Moore were on their feet, speechless with embarrassment. The ladies, including Lady Richards, were likewise silent, eyes downcast. The judge's face was bright with triumph.

Vanessa didn't hesitate. She stood as well, crossing to Lord Hastings and taking his arm.

"I thank you too, Mr. Murray. Perhaps we may look at more correspondence another day."

She watched as Lord Hastings's eyes met Moore's, both like soldiers hearing the trumpeter sound retreat. Hastings raised a hand in farewell.

"Goodbye, Tom. I doubt we shall meet again."

Murray himself accompanied Vanessa and Hastings to the door, murmuring apologies. As they walked up Albemarle Street her indignation grew. Judge Richards had been more than ill-mannered. He'd been vicious, baiting Lord Hastings beyond reason. Was the judge speaking the truth, as he insisted? It was hard to imagine he was not, and Vanessa knew from this morning's outing that Hastings had been obliged to settle previous debts at every shop he visited. How many more shops was he avoiding? How many other creditors?

His deep voice intruded on her speculations.

"I am put in mind of the first evening our dear Jane Austen dined with us."

Vanessa froze, and a pedestrian behind nearly ran her down. After apologies and curtseys she and Hastings resumed walking. Hastings seemed – it was hard to be certain – both amused and appalled. A man who'd let a cat out of a bag.

"You knew Jane Austen?"

"She and my sister Charlotte were friends. I grew fond of her."

No, Vanessa thought. He's holding back. He's put on his stoical mask to hide something. But what?

Hastings continued. "As I was about to say, the Prince's, now the King's, man of business, my sometime friend Colonel McMahon, quizzed Miss Austen as unkindly as the judge did you today. The spirit of your defense was the very echo of hers."

Vanessa was longing for more, but she could see in Hastings's face that she wasn't going to get it. She took his arm.

"Thank you, my lord. But the judge saved the worst of his bile for you."

Hastings drew her arm closer. "I have heard it all before."

They reached the end of Albemarle Street. A right turn and another fifty yards saw them into Bond Street, where Hastings surprised her by mentioning Jane once more.

"On the corner here" – Hastings pointed – "used to be a fine children's book-seller, Mr. Tabart. Ahead of his time, I believe. Miss Austen bought an armful of books one afternoon and adamantly refused to let me to pay for them."

They walked north, turning right, and then left into St. George Street. Another few minutes brought them to Hanover Square.

"Flora was certain you would wish to see Schrader's Piano-Forte Manufactory, Miss Horwood. She and her mother are taking tea in Brunswick House oppo-site. If you would be good enough to collect them, you may have half-an-hour at Schrader's whilst I fetch the carriage."

Hastings bowed with his usual courtesy, but Vanessa was certain there was more grief behind his elegant manners. Grief at the insults he'd borne at dinner and a quieter, permeating grief that he, who'd been used to coachmen and other servants constantly at hand, was now reduced to going to the stables for his own hopelessly out-of-date carriage.

The image of his face stayed with her as she entered Brunswick House. Was there any way for a man so compromised to retrieve himself?

CHAPTER XXII
1823 AND 1801

Hastings lengthened his stride as he left Brunswick House, needing exercise to settle his nerves. He was still seething from the encounter at Murray's, and he'd broken a decades-old resolution never to speak of Jane Austen. He hoped mentioning his sister and the bookshop had put Miss Horwood off the track. For a moment he'd been tempted to tell her the entire story.

He crossed Oxford Street, barely avoiding a post-coach, and then lost track of himself, consumed by memories. He must have walked a mile before he stopped. All at once he knew where he was, outside Henry Austen's former house in Upper Berkeley Street.

He thought again of McMahon's abominable behavior towards Jane that first evening she'd stayed to dinner. But of course McMahon's rudeness had been completely overshadowed by Lord Sefton's intrusion later the same evening.

At least McMahon had been taken in by the pretence that Jane was Charlotte's friend. As far as Hastings knew, McMahon had never mentioned Jane to anyone, let alone the Prince. But how had Sefton intuited her place in Moira's heart?

Or had McMahon seen Moira's heart too? If so he'd remained silent, as discreet about Moira's affairs as he'd always been about the Prince's.

Hastings shrugged as he turned towards Bond Street and the stables, smiling as he remembered how Charlotte had explained to Jane that they would not be going to the Wednesday ball at Almack's, all those years ago.

**

If Moira regretted losing Jane's company at Almack's, as he certainly did, it was the only thing about Almack's he was sorry to lose. At least he could console himself with the knowledge she would have a quiet evening with Mr. and Mrs. Henry Austen.

She was leaving the next morning for her brother Edward's house in Kent. Moira longed to drive her there himself, but his parliamentary obligations gave him no choice but to remain in London.

Jane wrote from Kent to say her brother Edward intended to visit their parents in Bath and that they would travel roundabout, with a stop in Hampshire to visit still another brother. Sometime in July the family – at the very least Jane, her parents and her sister – would spend some weeks in Devonshire.

In the meantime, Jane enclosed a souvenir.

It was another manuscript, titled *First Impressions*. This one contained more of the Jane he knew than *Susan*. The new story was less determinedly satirical, gentler, more affectionate.

'Do not mind my proud hero,' Jane had written in her accompanying letter. 'Had I met you sooner I expect his manners would have improved. And I should add, dear Moira, that the ms. has the distinction of being already refused, unread, by no less esteemed a bookseller than Mr. T. Cadell in the Strand. . . .'

The more he read *First Impressions*, the more he determined to join Jane in Devonshire. Parliament would be in recess by August and he could take an entire month if he chose.

He'd travel incognito once again, and adopt the 'Mr. Evelyn' persona he'd used in Bath. He could never arrive as the Earl of Moira in a small Devonshire town without everyone, including Jane's family, hearing of it. He'd be a rumpled country squire, arriving by post-coach.

He enlisted Captain James's advice. But James was indignant.

"You must never believe you won't be recognized. Do you think Mr. Gillray's caricatures, if nothing else, have not penetrated as far as the western sea?"

"No one will make the connection," insisted Moira. "Nor will anyone's gaze linger on a face as ugly as my own."

James smiled. "Except, I surmise, Miss Austen's."

"You are presumptuous, Captain."

"No, my lord. Perceptive. I should be no use to you otherwise."

Moira's manservant was equally outraged, this time at Moira's suggestion that he travel alone.

"Even a country gent's entitled to a manservant, m'lord. How will you shave yourself? How dress?"

"I am perfectly capable of dressing. And there are barbers, even in Devonshire."

But on this point, if no other, Moira finally gave in. His man was the colossus of Moira House for the three days before their departure, and on the last he declared it was no use his *master* buying a country wardrobe if his servant wasn't similarly attired.

"Second-hand for you, my man," said Captain James. The servant claimed a sister in the East End who would provide, and Moira gave him two guineas for shopping.

"Much too much, my lord," said James, when the man was gone. "You are generous to a fault, as always. Now your man will come home drunk, and you'll have the devil's own time getting him on the coach tomorrow."

Next morning proved James right: Moira's man wasn't fit for service until the end of the day, and they had scarcely packed in time for the one coach James had determined worth taking. It was the Exeter Mercury out of Cheapside, and left at either three o'clock in the morning, driving full tilt to arrive late the same evening, or two in the afternoon, with the passengers spending a night on the road and arriving the following day.

Moira, having prepared his disguise, was on fire to get to Jane. He took the early coach and regretted it. It was crowded and uncomfortable, the fleas in the upholstered seats ravenous, and by mid-day the summer heat was stifling His man, riding atop, complained at every change of horses. Soon enough Moira realized he could not possibly call upon the Austens the same evening he arrived. He'd be lucky if he could walk at all.

Jane had written that the family had taken lodgings in Sidmouth, a newly-fashionable watering place eight miles from Exeter. But, she'd added, they might also be with her father's former pupil in the village of Colyton. She would have no control over when and how long they might be at either place.

Colyton was another eight miles from Sidmouth, inland and further to the east. If he knew the Austens were in Colyton, Moira would prefer to stay in Lyme Regis, an altogether more genteel town. But Jane had said the family's lodgings would be in Sidmouth, and so to Sidmouth he must wend his way.

When the Mercury finally arrived in Exeter, Moira discovered he had to wait for a private chaise. A baronet had taken precedence by rank, followed by an army colonel. Moira, who would otherwise have been first, had by virtue of travelling incognito relegated himself to third place. Two hours passed before the baronet's carriage returned.

But it all proved worthwhile. The next morning brought bright sun and a gentle sea breeze. He called at a small terraced house as early as he dared, and Jane's face became radiant. Her father was cordial, greeting him as 'Mr. Evelyn' and treating him with the same affability he had shown in Bath. Jane's mother took her cue from her husband, declaring that such a fine day surely called for a walk along the seashore.

But Moira hadn't reckoned with Jane's older sister. Cassandra Austen resembled Jane, but her nose was longer, her cheek paler, and her mouth firmer. Where Jane was warm and welcoming, Cassandra appeared cold and forbidding. She looked at Moira as if to say 'I know you are a humbug and will break my sister's heart.'

And so, of course, Cassandra declared herself their chaperone.

Jane was perfectly content. "You must walk between us, my – Mr. Evelyn, and you must declare to my father that you will provide the proper amount of exercise, a modest amount of wine, and perhaps a slight excess of food. Most of all you must tell him when we shall return."

"I should prefer we all dine together," said Moira. "Will you suggest an inn, Mr. Austen, and allow us to meet you there?"

"You are uncommonly generous, sir," replied Mr. Austen. "Let it be the London Inn, at two o'clock. This may well be our only opportunity, as I have a letter this morning that summons us to Colyton for the next fortnight."

Moira had given this possibility some more thought on the long coach journey.

"You must allow me to convey you there tomorrow. I shall continue to Lyme Regis, and I believe the detour will be slight."

Mr. Austen bowed. "You are too kind, Mr. Evelyn. It is indeed scarcely out of your way. On behalf of my family I am pleased to accept."

"In the meantime," said Moira. "I beg you, Mr. Austen, to point a direction for our walk, and to tell me how far to go before we turn back."

"Walk by the sea," said Mr. Austen. "My daughters will show you the way."

Mrs. Austen smiled. "You should walk half the distance you intend entire, and then commence your return."

Moira bowed. "Such good sense might transform the world, ma'am."

The three walkers remained silent for most of the first mile. Moira considered the lie of the land, placing imaginary troops at the tops of cliffs and behind hillocks as though the French were about to invade the place. He was so content to be arm in arm with Jane and so intent on his strategies that he nearly jumped when Cassandra spoke.

"My sister tells me you met in Bath."

Moira smiled. He had reviewed his past subterfuges and was ready for questioning.

"Indeed, Miss Austen. Through the kindness of our mutual friend Mrs. Chamberlayne."

"Did you lodge with the Chamberlaynes at the Charitable Repository?"

Jane colored and nearly spoke, but Moira laughed.

"I regret I did not, though I count myself sympathetic to the poor."

"Perhaps," Jane interposed, "*you* might have persuaded her to sell her black beaver bonnet on their behalf."

"I do not recollect such a bonnet," said Moira.

"Men would not," said Jane. "And by the time Cassandra arrived, who would have shared my horror equally, the Chamberlaynes had left Bath."

"I forgive Mrs. Chamberlayne's beaver bonnet," declared Moira. "Indeed I forgive Mrs. Chamberlayne anything. Without her introduction I should never have had the pleasure of meeting you, or reading your two novels."

"*Two* novels," cried Cassandra. "I understood Jane had lent you the second copy of *Susan*, but the other can only have been *First Impressions*. Did you make a second copy of it as well, Jane?"

"I did," replied Jane firmly. "I began it for Martha, and finished it for Mr. Evelyn. And now, sir, I have discovered I must change its title."

"Why?" asked Moira.

"Another lady novelist has appropriated it. Mr. Lane's Minerva-Press has" – she smiled at him – "shall I say stolen a march?"

"*First Impressions* suited your story well. What will it be now?"

"My sister suggests I borrow from the last chapter of Miss Burney's *Cecilia*, which is called 'Pride and Prejudice.'"

"Yes," said Moira. "*Pride and Prejudice* has the proper gravity. Your *Susan* has an ironical charm. But this other turns wit to better purpose. It gave me tears of happiness. Had I not promised to keep the manuscript strictly to myself, I'd have given it to my sister at once."

"Indeed," replied Cassandra. "You admired it so much. And you have a sister."

"I have three sisters," replied Moira. "But only one remains unmarried. It is my joy that she often chooses to stay with me in London."

"She is entirely amiable," said Jane. "I have told you as much, dear Cassandra."

Cassandra lapsed into silence. By now they were out of town and could look back along the esplanade. In the distance were the famous red cliffs of Devonshire, and directly ahead of them a fairly sharp ascent.

"Do we go up?" asked Moira.

Jane nodded. "The path becomes level there, and we may follow the coastline."

Moira was pleased to have such exercise after so long a time in yesterday's coach, and he was pleased to see that neither Jane nor Cassandra seemed in the least fatigued by the climb. He watched Jane as closely as he dared, not wanting to reveal too much to her sister.

Cassandra seemed to have taken against him. Had she sensed he was in love with Jane? Or was she naturally jealous, as he could easily imagine in an older sister likely destined for spinsterhood.

"Cassandra is my deepest critic," said Jane. "She does not care for desultory novels, and is fearful on that score for *Susan*. Now you have spoke your mind I may declare myself as well. *First Impressions* is my own darling child."

She stopped, blushing. Moira halted as well, wondering if something was wrong. Cassandra went a little further before realizing she was alone. She did not seem happy to retrace her steps.

Jane held up a hand, drawing her sister's attention and at the same time keeping her at a distance. Moira could tell that Cassandra was intent upon her sister's face as Jane continued.

"And you, dear Moira, are the darling of my heart, and the hero of my novel as he discovers himself at its end. I shall conceal these facts from my sister no longer." She took Moira's hands. "You may rely upon her discretion as much as my own."

Cassandra's features were set and grim. But as she looked upon Jane's face, shining with happiness, her own began to soften. When her smile finally came it was like the sun coming from behind a cloud.

She began to speak, so softly that Moira had to lean closer.

"Have you declared yourself to my sister?"

"I have," he replied. "I should speak to your father this afternoon were Jane to allow it."

"No," cried Jane.

She sounded alarmed, almost frightened. Cassandra and Moira turned to her in surprise.

"Dear Cassie, do you know who this is?"

"Mr. Moira, Mr. Evelyn, what am I to think?"

Then her eyes grew wide. "No," she breathed.

"Yes," cried Jane. "My own dear Lord Moira, Lord Longbow the Alarmist in the Gillray caricature. Do you not recall that I retrieved it for you at the Literary Institution?"

She took Moira's arm. "I do not consider you bound by your promise while you settle your affairs. You have the Prince pulling you in one direction, politics another, and Bonaparte expected on our shores at any moment. You must not pretend you were not devising the town's defenses as we walked through, not an hour since."

"You know me too well, dear Jane. But let us consult your sister, now she has learned our secret. Miss Austen, would you not counsel an early wedding, for richer, for poorer?"

To Moira's astonishment Cassandra burst into tears. They lasted only a moment, but when she raised her eyes her expression was bleak.

"Forgive me, my lord. I once had a confidential engagement of my own, and only after my betrothed perished in the West Indies did I learn that his employer would never have allowed the risk of such travel had he known our intentions."

Cassandra turned, beginning to walk along the cliffside path.

"Come, both of you," she said. "I wish to leave these memories behind. There is room here for the three of us to walk abreast. And if any come from the opposite direction I shall rely upon Lord Moira to heave them into the sea before they may interrupt our discourse."

Once again Moira took his place between the women. This time Cassandra gave him an arm as well as Jane.

After a few moments' silence Cassandra spoke again.

"Jane has been very sly, very reserved with me, my lord. It is conduct unbecoming a sister, and for the past few minutes I have been gravely displeased."

Jane released Moira's arm, leaping ahead to confront her sister. Moira stopped short.

"Dear Cassandra," Jane began.

"Hush," replied her sister. "I have recovered. I have questions for his lordship, and I intend to address him as though he were not one of the first men in the nation."

"I should wish you would address me as a brother," said Moira.

"No, my lord," replied Cassandra as they resumed their walk. "Much as I might wish it, you are not yet a brother. Jane alludes to your settling affairs. What do you fear about these?"

"You come directly to the point, Miss Austen, do you not?"

"That is my intent, sir."

"Well," said Moira. "I am severely compromised. So much that were my creditors to decline compounding my notes as they come due I believe I might be bankrupt within a year."

"But this is not his fault," declared Jane.

Cassandra nodded. "You are reputed to have borne the Prince's debts these last ten years."

"Not all of them, but far too many," said Moira. "I need not have endorsed his notes, but he has been my friend."

"Does he require more of you?"

Moira shrugged. "His requirements are inexhaustible. But I have no more to give."

"Dare I invoke Shakespeare, my lord?"

"I deny you nothing, Miss Austen."

"'Neither a borrower nor a lender be. For loan oft loses both itself and friend.'"

"*Hamlet*," said Moira. But there is another line from Shakespeare that troubles me more."

"May we guess?" asked Jane. "Anything to relieve this inquisition."

"No," said Cassandra. "This is too important. Speak your speech, my lord."

Moira smiled. "Mine is from *Antony and Cleopatra*: 'The band that seems to tie their friendship together will be the very strangler of their amity.'"

"Oh!" cried Jane. "And how like Antony you are. I dare not think on it, lest I be devoured by snakes like Cleopatra."

"*Hush*," said Cassandra again, more sharply. She turned to Moira once more.

"Should you marry my sister will you lend the Prince more of this money you do not have?"

"No," said Moira flatly. "I should rely upon my wife to restrain my extravagances, as I should rely upon her to conceal my failings and promote my respectability."

"And your own career, sir?"

"Enough!" cried Jane. "Lord Moira is a great man, destined for still greater things."

Cassandra smiled. "And now I may invoke my sister's own *Susan*, although in the form of another line of Shakespeare contained in it. There stands Jane, a young woman in love, 'like Patience on a monument, smiling at Grief.'"

Moira was now entirely won over by Jane's sister. He smiled back.

"What am I to do with this Patience on a monument?"

"Speak to our father, sir. Marry her at once. I have learned too well that happiness forestalled may be lost forever."

Moira looked at Jane. There were tears in her eyes as she shook her head.

"No, dear Moira. I am normally the most compliant person in the world, especially to my sister. But if you are not entirely ready, I shall wait."

There was a long pause before Cassandra spoke again.

"I have done what I could," she said. "Now I shall show that I may be compliant too."

She withdrew her arm from Moira's. "Let us turn back, my lord. We should not wish to keep our parents waiting."

CHAPTER XXIII
1801

Both sisters agreed that for Moira to reveal himself to the Austen parents would only cause distress. As a result the family dinner was uneventful, with the conversation ranging from politics – Moira, knowing Mr. Austen as a staunch Tory, was careful on this topic – to literature to the state of the Church. The elder Austens were clearly pleased with "Mr. Evelyn," and Jane and Cassandra played their parts as demure daughters.

The next morning Moira remained the rumpled country squire, his manservant atop a hired chaise as he and the Austens drove to Colyton. Once on his own Moira became himself again, and was so announced at the entrance to the largest of Lyme Regis's inns.

He was relieved that Jane's parents had agreed to allow Cassandra and Jane to join him at Lyme within the next two or three days. This would, Moira knew, be all he could expect of Jane's company during the fortnight.

Should he have taken Cassandra's advice and made himself and his intentions known? Then he'd have had all he could wish of Jane's company. But he considered her reticence a sign of her love, and was grateful for it.

Now it was up to him to secure his finances, to sell whatever he must to pay down his loans, and to deny the Prince both the money and the extravagant parties – always at Moira's expense – he craved.

As if to emphasize the point, the next morning a letter arrived from Captain James, forwarded from the inn at Sidmouth. Some of the bills Moira had endorsed for the Prince, and which McMahon had failed to list, had been dishonored upon presentation at Messrs. Coutts, Moira's principal bankers. James's letter enclosed a note from Thomas Coutts himself, regretting his action but declaring he had no choice in the absence both of funds in Moira's account, and of any direction from Moira himself.

Coutts wrote:

> . . . I am always afraid of these money dealers being possessed
> of your Name to Bonds & Papers which, without your having
> had any value for, may give you much trouble to get rid of.

Moira flung the letter down. He'd take the sea air before breakfast, as a way to get this latest indignity out of his system. Then he would give James some conclusive direction about managing this sea of floating debt.

But what direction? Where would he begin? He walked down the steep pavement to the sandy beach, where the incoming tide advanced along the shore with the help of a fine south-easterly breeze. He basked in the morning sunlight as it rose above the eastern hills, and in the lively smell of the sea. All things seemed possible in this weather.

He finished his promenade with a circuit of the famous Lyme Regis Cobb, and returned to his inn with a healthy appetite. A note from Jane was waiting, dispatched soon after her arrival at Colyton. Rev. Buller was required the next day by his parishioners. Her mother was once again indisposed but her father had given his blessing for Jane and Cassandra to spend a day in Lyme Regis. Rev. Austen considered Mr. Evelyn a man of "sound principles" and hoped his daughters would learn from him. A farmer's cart was leaving for Lyme early the next morning – *this* morning, thought Moira – and the two sisters would be on it.

He had not ordered his breakfast, and could easily enough wait till Jane and Cassandra arrived to share it. He wondered what they might like most. Everything, he decided. From Spanish oranges to pork sausages, eggs and all manner of pastries, and both coffee and tea.

He sat in high anticipation for another hour, and then they were so dusty from the road that Moira insisted the innkeeper's wife take them in hand while their breakfast was prepared. After they ate Cassandra pleaded fatigue, retiring to the room Moira had reserved for them while Jane and he window-shopped along the steep streets of the handsome town. Afterwards the two made their way to the comparative privacy of the paths above the seashore.

"Cassandra and I were up half the night," Jane began.

He'd been distracted by her closeness and her pressure on his arm. He made himself pay attention.

"Not unhappily, I hope?"

"Hope is what she gave me, and her blessing for our happiness."

Jane dropped her eyes. "As she spoke to me I came to understand that I had spent the last three months as though in a dream. You have been my handsome prince —"

"Far from handsome. . ."

"My detestable ogre," Jane continued without hesitation, eyes still on the pathway. "And all along I'd been waiting to wake up, for you and the entire dream to disappear. Cassandra has made you real."

"Dearest Jane," Moira cried. "There is nothing to keep us from announcing ourselves to the world."

Jane raised her eyes at last, slowly shaking her head.

"If you married me now your friends would turn against you, thinking me unworthy." She smiled. "And they would believe you a greater fool than even you are, for wanting me in the first place."

"But. . ." he began.

"Hush." She stopped on the deserted path, putting a finger to his lips. "And your enemies would rejoice, declaring you so far reduced that you could marry no-one but the daughter of a poor clergyman."

"What would you have me do?"

"If you love me you will discharge your debts and detach yourself from the Prince. Cultivate those in your circle you wish to keep. As you spend time with them you will discover whether they would accept someone like me as Lady Moira, and then you may come for me if you choose."

"If I choose!" he cried.

"You may recall I released you from your promise, dear Moira. But I beg you" — there were tears in her eyes now — "I beg you will let me know your intentions as soon as you may."

Moira folded her in his arms. "Oh my sweet love. My intentions will never change. And I have never received more sound advice."

Cassandra joined them for an early dinner at Moira's inn and then they shopped for gifts to the elder Austens. For Jane, Cassandra, and himself Moira bought sheaves of writing paper, pens, and ink.

"I may not write to you under my own crest," he said. "And this way we are linked." He smiled. "And when the two of you write to each other I trust you will have a kind thought for me."

Then he turned to Jane in the high street, in full view of all the passers-by, and pulled a tiny box from his waistcoat.

"I want you to have this."

He opened the box and removed a gold ring. The outside was incised with a foliate pattern, and inside was a short rhyme:

"In thee my choyce I do rejoice."

He took her hand. "The ring has been in my family for two hundred years, I believe. Shall our fates be decided by whether it fits your finger?"

"No!" cried Cassandra.

"Indeed not," said Jane firmly. She held out her right hand, and pointed to her forefinger. "We shall keep it well away from the wedding finger."

Moira took her hand as she continued. "But if it fits that finger, so it will the other. And then it may serve us twice, as it is the most beautiful ring I have ever seen."

Moira slipped it on, and Jane raised her eyes to his. "Perfect," she declared. Then she slipped it off and handed it back. "But not yet, dear Moira. You must keep it until we declare ourselves."

Moira sent his manservant with the chaise that took the sisters back to Colyton.

"You are to return directly." Then Moira smiled. The man had been with him for years and they had always got on well, in spite of his affection for the bottle. "I promise a drink with your supper, and we shall pack in the morning."

His man bristled. "Not for the bloody – begging your lordship's pardon – not for the Mercury again, my lord, I beg you."

Moira looked out the window of his room. There was a fine view of the sea and the bed had been comfortable. He need not hurry to return to London.

"No," he replied. "We shall go as far as Salisbury tomorrow. I've a mind to see the Cathedral. And then we shall ride post to London. But I must tell you one more thing."

His servant looked surprised. Moira had surprised himself with the harshness of his voice. "My lord?" the man asked.

"No-one but Captain James knows where we have been, or whom we've seen. If any news of it spreads, it will be your doing. Do you understand?"

The man nodded, and Moira smiled. "I shall not say you would be a dead man. You know me too well for that."

CHAPTER XXIV
1801

A stack of letters was waiting for Moira in London. At the top was one from the Prince.

"It can wait," Moira said. He called for bath water and a change of clothes.

As he soaked he considered once again how to change his life. And now he had what was bound to be a summons from the Prince, reminding him how hard it would be. Would the Prince importune for another loan? Invite him to a rout in some hanger's-on house, emptied of furniture the better to fill it with the *haut monde*?

Instead the letter was all kindness, declaring Moira to be the Prince's "dearest Friend (to whom I ever have through a long series of Years unveil'd the most secret thoughts of my Heart & Soul)." It included an invitation to a small dinner with the Duchess of Devonshire, and enclosed a manuscript by the Prince's long-abandoned mistress, the actress Mary Robinson. She'd died both young and poor, and the poem had been among her papers:

> In these degenerate times the Muses blend
> For thee a wreath, their guardian and their friend;
> Thee, lib'ral Moira, in whose glowing mind
> Exulting Nature ev'ry grace combin'd!
> Honour's nice sense, by judgment wisely taught;
> And hardy Valour, with soft Pity fraught. . .

Moira smiled, but there was more, four stanzas more, all in the same vein. The last few lines made him pause and think of Jane:

> Haply, when Contemplation sighs to scan
> The weedy pathway mark'd for wretched man,
> This humble Flow'r may fragrance still impart;
> If not to charm, to harmonize thy heart. . . .

Jane would no doubt blush at the poem's author. He'd scarcely met her, but he knew the story of her scandalous life, her libertine novels, her public literary battles. She'd fallen from grace and fortune and died surrounded by creditors. A fate, he knew, that could be waiting for him.

Moira's return was bound to be known, and he could scarcely refuse an invitation from both Prince and Duchess.

"You must wear a black tie, brother," his sister Charlotte counseled. "Your hair is already in best Brummell style, *à la Brutus*, and your cutaway jacket and white breeches will make you the most handsome man at table."

Moira laughed, but his vanity was touched. Charlotte was also invited, of course, and declared she'd reserved her newest gown for just such an occasion.

The Duchess of Devonshire, scarred as she was by recent attempts to save her eyesight, remained a model of discreet charm. She had returned to London and politics only a few months earlier and greeted Moira as a long-lost friend. Then she took a step back

"The Prince wishes a *tête-à-tête* with you. Charlotte may share the other gentlemen with me until you return."

A footman conducted Moira upstairs to an elegant withdrawing room, where the Prince, sprawled on a sofa, surprised Moira by being entirely sober. As usual he was extravagantly dressed, with silk jacket and breeches and one of his signature waistcoats, embroidered and studded with precious stones.

"Dear Moira," he gushed. He pulled his feet from the table in front of him, straining the buttons of his ample waistcoat, but he did not stand.

"Where have you been?" he continued. His small eyes were upon Moira's, lashes a-flutter, all but simpering. "As if I didn't know. Sefton's story has spread like wildfire. Lover's rage becomes you, he says."

Moira tensed. He knew what was coming next.

"Who is this paragon you defend so valiantly?"

"A clergyman's daughter," said Moira.

"Oh, excellent," replied the Prince. "Will you share her?"

Moira knew he was flushing, knew he would be unable to conceal his anger. He turned away, looking out the window across Piccadilly.

"I have offended you, my friend," said the Prince. "Surely you do not intend marriage."

Moira faced him once more. "You are kind in speaking to me as a friend, Your Highness. If I take offence it is only on account of someone who is not here to speak for herself."

"Hah!" replied the Prince. "Dare I quote our much-lamented Mrs. Robinson? You manifest your 'inborn Dignity, which springs elate.' You may rely upon my discretion, dear friend. And I shall insist that her father stand aside, to allow me to give the bride away at your wedding."

"You honor me, Your Highness. And may I hope for some relief from Colonel McMahon, to allow us to remain in London?"

The Prince's face darkened. "Do not speak of money, sir. Surely the Colonel has spoke to you of my father's latest parsimonies. I am myself *in extremis*."

Moira bowed. "Let us return to this another day. Shall we rejoin the Duchess?"

The Prince extended an arm. "Help us up, Moira. There was not a drop to be found in this room, and that damned footman never said a word. I am fairly parched."

As they descended the stairs Moira wondered how long the Prince's promised discretion would survive his customary intake of champagne.

But to Moira's surprise the Prince said not a word of their conversation, and indeed was overheard to whisper to the Duchess that he wished Moira placed well away at the dinner-table. But if Moira was banished, Charlotte was not. She sat next to the Prince, and the two were in close conversation several times during the meal.

Charlotte leaned on her brother's arm during the short walk home from Devonshire House.

"I am drunk, dear brother," she declared. "The price of companionship with the Prince. Every time he cried a refill for himself he insisted upon one for me."

"Will you tell me what he said?"

She tilted her face up to his. Her eyes were a little bloodshot, but her smile was pure affection.

"Can you doubt it?" she asked, laughing. "We spoke of you and your Miss Austen, the entire time."

"And?"

"He complained you had asked him for money. Declared himself quite taken aback."

"And yet it was he, all those years, who insisted they were loans, and would be repaid according to the strictest schedule."

Charlotte laughed again, but with a harsher edge. "Has the schedule not been strict? He has unvaryingly scheduled no return at all."

They crossed Piccadilly into St. James's Street, their footmen stepping out ahead with their torches.

"I shall find a way out for *you*, sister, even if not for myself."

"Oh, stop," she cried. "Do you not see what the Prince sees, what I and everyone *must* see? That your only hope of retiring your debt lies in marrying an heiress. And no ordinary heiress at that."

"As God is my witness I shall not give her up."

"Then you and Captain James must become magicians."

CHAPTER XXV
1801

James arrived at Moira House first thing the next morning. At once he and Moira closeted themselves in the downstairs office.

"As you know, my lord, I had two more bills from Colonel McMahon in your absence, along with one of yours. I punctually discharged your own, of course, but after Mr. Coutts declined the others I had no choice but to call on Mr. Austen."

"Austen!" cried Moira. "I gave you the clearest possible direction we were not to encumber him."

"He was insistent, my lord. He even called at my lodgings to press the case for his usefulness. Said he had months where his revenue as army agent lay fallow for want of creditworthy borrowers, and that working with your lordship's floating paper would suit him ideally."

Moira sighed. "How much?"

"Two thousand for eighty days."

"And the discount?"

"Twenty pounds. We could not do better, my lord."

"See to it that we do not embarrass him."

James straightened with indignation. "I have embarrassed no-one, except perhaps Colonel McMahon, who embarrasses us all."

Moira clapped James on the shoulder. "Forgive me, my friend. You are a model of discretion and honor, but this matter of Austen touches me closely."

James smiled. "I understand, my lord. And in my turn I honor those sentiments. Dare I ask. . . ?"

James's voice trailed off. The two men had been hovering over a large desk, but now Moira stepped back, flinging himself into a leather armchair. He waved James to another.

"Sit, Captain. I unburdened myself to the Prince last night, and was foolish enough to trust to his discretion. Why should I not trust yours, upon which I know I may rely?"

James was all attention, his broad face half-smiling in sympathy.

"Miss Austen and I have declared ourselves, but so far only to each other. The Prince does not know her name, and I must trust those who do to keep the secret. So far these are yourself, her sister, and Lady Charlotte."

"And your servants, my lord."

"Have you reason to doubt them?"

"No," James replied at once. "But I suggest you speak to them, so they will recognize the importance of the matter."

"Thank you, Captain. I spoke to my man in Dorset, but you are right about the others. Now, you should know that last night I asked the Prince to repay some of my loans."

"God's blood," cried James. "Did you have any more luck than I've had with McMahon?"

"I did not."

James nodded. "This must affect your plans to marry."

"It must not, sir. Although the Prince dared tell my sister I must marry an heiress."

James said nothing, and after a moment Moira gave a wan smile.

"You have enough of my accounts to make the calculation, my friend. I told Miss Austen I believed that if my creditors declined to compound my bills I could be bankrupt within a year. Am I right?"

"Not yet, my lord. I have kept current with that possibility as best I may. At present land values you could come clear, but only if you sold your remaining estates in Ireland, as well as Donington Park, Essex, Yorkshire. . ."

"Stop," cried Moira. "Would I be left anything at all?"

"Last year you might have kept Moira House and Monmouthshire, my lord. This year you could keep Monmouthshire, and I believe you would have a few thousands, a very few, remaining."

James was almost unbearably matter-of-fact. Moira tasted bile as he asked the next question.

"In other words I should require lodgings to attend Parliament."

"Others do, my lord."

"Damn it, man. I am *not* others."

James rose at once, practically coming to attention.

"Forgive me, my lord. I have spoke out of turn."

Moira slumped in his chair. "Sit down, sir. You precisely answered what I asked. It is no fault of yours if I do not care for the truth."

A knock on the door brought a footman with a letter.

"From the House of Commons, my lord. I am to say it is a matter of the gravest urgency."

Moira gave James a wry look.

James smiled back as Moira tore open the letter. "They bind you with adamantine fetters, my lord."

Moira looked up. "The Prime Minister has terms for peace with France. Fox says I am best placed of our party to advise on them. If I approve he believes these preliminaries may pass without division in the Commons."

"Your finances will keep for a time," said James.

Moira stood. "Will they?" replied Moira. "I am a man caught in a bog, believing if I go just a little deeper I may yet come out the other side."

James was on his feet too, bowing. "I do not deny it, my lord."

CHAPTER XXVI
1801–1802

Final agreement was reached on the Peace of Amiens in October of 1801. Jane visited London that month, staying with her brother.

"Henry boasts of his business with you," declared Jane. "He believes it places him in the first rank of London bankers."

"If only he knew," replied Moira, shaking his head. "But Captain James tells me there is hope. Our people are digging for coal on my estates in the north. Elsewhere we have begun smelting iron. We may have twenty thousand a year if we are successful."

"Twenty thousand a year," said Jane, smiling. "Lord, sir, you make a young woman swoon."

Much as he longed to take Jane into society, Moira knew he could not. So they took country walks and gentle rides when the autumn weather was fine, and Jane attended galleries and the theatre with Charlotte when it rained. As winter turned to spring in 1802 Moira was enlisted to advise on the reorganization of the army and the conversion of the volunteer forces into militias.

This last was something Jane knew about. Her brother Edward had worked with the volunteers, and was pleased at the prospect of a force where the contributions of the local gentry would be more formally recognized. She told Moira that Edward was ready to fund a company in the new militia, once the rules were set.

Meanwhile James kept Moira apprised of his ever-increasing debt. Spring turned to summer, and summer to autumn, as it was rumored that the new ministry was determined to bring the nation's finances under control, and was looking for ways to repay the debts of both the King and the Prince of Wales.

Moira was too much a natural optimist not to be elated at the prospect. Any timetable for repayment of the Prince's obligations would allow Moira to set up his own schedule with the bankers and so resolve the worst of his personal indebtedness. In the meantime he was constantly engaged at the highest level of Whig party strategizing, indispensible both for his military expertise and as an intermediary between the parliamentarians and the Prince.

But negotiations for discharging royal debts dragged on, and in September of 1802, as Parliament was about to begin, Moira returned from a visit to Bath to find his own affairs interrupted in the worst possible way.

William Clifton had asked for a confidential meeting. The young man's experience at Hoare's Bank had proved highly useful as he worked with Captain James in negotiating terms for extending Moira's payments. Clifton had managed to consolidate many of Moira's bills of exchange, meaning that fewer and fewer unpleasant surprises arrived at the door of Moira House.

They met in Moira's downstairs office, the desk as usual covered with Captain James's papers and ledgers. Both men remained standing. Finally Clifton spoke.

"I know how long and how closely you have worked with Captain James, my lord."

"Indeed," said Moira, purposefully at his most formal.

"I trust you will credit me when I say I should not have raised the subject had I not several incontrovertible instances of the Captain's impropriety."

"Get to the point, sir."

Clifton flushed.

"It has recently come to my attention that Captain James has presented himself as the sole endorser on paper that should have had a banker's signature, paper that has compounded large amounts at critical periods."

"So he has," said Moira coldly.

"He has further stated he has taken no commission and requested your lordship's remuneration in whatever amounts your lordship thought proper to allow."

"I do not believe this is any of your business."

"Forgive me, my lord, but it becomes my business when I approach your various bankers to negotiate terms and they ask if they are required to give me the same allowance as Captain James."

"That is enough, sir. I trust you will supply a list of these bankers and the specific commissions discussed."

Clifton's flush had long since faded. "I shall do so, my lord. I must first consult my notes of these conversations. Obviously Captain James never allowed these irregular commissions to appear on the bankers' books, let alone your own."

"Obviously," said Moira. He was furious at these charges against an agent he also considered a personal friend. But he had to give Clifton credit for speaking up.

"Thank you, Mr. Clifton. I appreciate your intervention."

Clifton bowed his way out, and Moira fell into his armchair. Usually he was a man of quick emotions and high temper. Now his anger was slow in coming. But come it did. He felt utterly betrayed, and an unexpected rage began to fill his heart.

CHAPTER XXVII
1802

September turned to October and Clifton still had not provided his list. Moira returned from the Lords after a particularly miserable week.

It had been unseasonably hot, and with endless debate about the King's and the Prince of Wales's debts. A Tory peer had advanced a bill under debate in the Commons, proposing relief for all documented debts other than those endorsed by middlemen.

Moira's direct loans to the Prince were largely undocumented. What the bill meant was that banks which had lent to the Prince directly would recover, but banks which had insisted upon additional security in the form of an endorsement, such as Moira's, would continue, unless the Prince made voluntary repayments, to collect from the endorsers.

It was a neat parliamentary trick, however mean-spirited. Moira and other Whig lenders – the Prince's private lenders were always Whigs – would lose out entirely. Angry as he felt, the strategist in Moira had to applaud the Tories' effort.

From the entry hall of Moira House he could hear voices from the upstairs drawing room. He felt a rush of pleasure as he realized one of the voices was Jane's, and started up the stairs.

"Dear Captain James," Jane was saying. "Will you be my confidential man of business, as far as you may without giving away my lord's secrets."

James gave a strained laugh. Moira was ashamed of himself for eavesdropping. But he wanted more, and remained where he was as James replied.

"I cannot imagine, Miss Austen, there is anything his lordship would not wish you to know, but I may divulge very little without his permission."

"Tell me only this, if you may," Jane asked. "Are his lordship's financial affairs better or worse than a year ago?"

"Worse. More than that I cannot say."

"I may infer the rest," Jane replied. "If he is unable to pay all the interest, let alone the principal, the two must be added together. Thereby his burdens increase."

"You must know, Miss Austen, that I would do anything in my power to relieve his lordship, but this past month I have found that my influence over him, and my knowledge of the real state of his affairs, have diminished.

"But I shall say this. I have known his lordship a dozen years and more, under his command or in his service for most of them. I believe him to be blessed with the happiest temper, and possessing the warmest and most generous heart, of any man living. If his fortunes sink, they do so for no reason other than his benevolence."

By now Moira was more than ashamed. How could he have doubted James's loyalty and honesty? Had the state of Moira's finances left James in distress as well, driven to desperation? Were confidential bankers' commissions keeping James solvent, or had Clifton invented the entire story?

Moira trod more heavily as he mounted the remaining stairs. James smiled as he entered the drawing-room.

"My lord, here is Miss Austen, come to visit Lady Charlotte who is not at home. She has had to make do with me."

"The time is upon us, Captain. Speak privately to land-agents and calculate with Clifton how we may achieve our goal most discreetly. I must be free of debt by next year, come what may."

James frowned. "I cannot promise that, your lordship. Nor, if I may speak freely, may I countenance such a decisive step. What of the Prince's debts, and Parliament?"

"The ministry has managed a trick which will deny me anything."

James came to attention like the soldier he was. "Very well," he said. "I shall speak to Mr. Clifton."

He bowed to Moira, and again to Jane. Moira saw the look James gave her as he straightened. Something was amiss, but Moira could not tell what. Before he could ask James was gone.

CHAPTER XXVIII
1802

No sooner had the front door closed than Jane drew close to him.

"Is this wise, dear Moira? The captain seems unhappy."

"His happiness is not my concern at present." He kept her arm in his as they walked to a sofa.

"We shall open a bottle of champagne. Let us drink to our happiness, my love."

"Our *poor* happiness?" asked Jane.

"Poor indeed. But I have three dozen in the cellar. We should have them even if I may buy no more, and we should drink them soon in case James's calculations are amiss and the bailiffs come to sequester them."

"Don't say it."

"I know I shouldn't tempt fate. But we shall dine well tonight before I return to the House. Charlotte will be with us momentarily, and James will return with Clifton and McMahon. It will be like the first evening you were here."

"Happier, I trust," said Jane. "Colonel McMahon has all but given up trying to speak to me."

The party drank three bottles of champagne before dinner. Charlotte and Colonel McMahon began to tell each other jokes about the Irish.

"Ah," cried Charlotte. "Do you know the one about the Irishman and his house?"

McMahon shook his head.

"Paddy hired the best land-agent in Dublin to write up the particulars. Then when he read them over he cried to the agent to cancel the sale. 'Why?' said the agent. Paddy replied, ''Tis a house too good to part with.'"

She and McMahon began to laugh, but when they noticed how glum the other faces at table were, they stopped.

"You look as though you've lost your best friends in the world," declared Charlotte. "Off to the Lords with you, dear brother. Perhaps the rest of us may retrieve our humor once you are gone."

Moira rose and bowed. "I accept, dear sister, though you might have put it more kindly. I shall take the phaeton to the House, and the coachman may deliver Miss Austen to her brother's house thereafter. I expect I may be all night."

"Thank you, my lord," said Jane. Moira knew her eyes were following him as he left the dining room, her mouth pursed in that combination of concern and puzzlement he'd come to know so well.

Moira's expectation of an all-night session proved accurate. It became clear by early morning that if the bill for the relief of the King's and the Prince's debts were to pass at all, the exclusion of debts like those owed to Moira would be part of it.

There had been a crowd outside the Palace of Westminster as Moira's carriage approached the night before, and it had grown larger by morning. A few held placards objecting to another rise in food prices; others protested the manner in which returning soldiers and sailors had been turned onto the streets without pay after last year's peace with France.

Disbanded soldiers were a familiar sight to Moira. He'd done his best for them, both in Parliament and during his time in the army. Some of the peers tried to avoid the crowd by leaving through a side entrance. Others left the House in disguise.

Moira walked directly from the main entrance into the crowd, determined to clear his head with some fresh air, and to make his way home on foot, snatch a few hours sleep, and take his first steps towards financial freedom with James and Clifton.

"It's Lord Moira," someone in the crowd shouted.

"Top of the morning to you, General," came another voice. "Did you manage to get anything for the common people out of their lordships, last night?"

"Not a thing," Moira called back. "But not for want of trying."

"Huzzah for Moira," came a ragged shout.

"Let's see him home," cried the first voice.

Moira had nearly come through the crowd by now. He turned back to face them, raising both arms, invigorated by their support.

"You need not walk with me, lads."

But there was no helping it. The crowd – Moira refused to think of it as a mob – fell in behind him and began to sing. He led them into St. James's Park, hoping some would begin to fall by the wayside as he set a fast pace towards the Mall. Some did, but he had to admit he was proud that most stayed with him as he took the long way around, leaving the Park at New Street, into Spring Garden and around the west side of Charing Cross.

They blocked carriage traffic the entire length of Pall Mall, all the way to St. James's Street. They passed the royal residence at Carlton House and Moira wondered whether the noise might rouse the Prince, who invariably slept, or tried to sleep, well past noon.

As Moira made the right turn into St. James's Street the crowd surged around him and he found himself once again caught in the middle. He knew the crowd could easily run rampant, that it was his own authority keeping it under control. And he knew such leadership was his natural talent. Could he give it up? Would Jane understand if he could not?

Someone threw a bottle at a hackney-chaise as it emerged from King Street. As the coachman pulled up to look for damage a familiar figure ran into the street. Even at a distance Moira could see Jane was weeping. She held a handkerchief in front of her face and her shoulders were shaking as she called up to the driver.

Moira tried to break through, to reach her before the carriage could drive on. But a sudden surge of placard holders to the front of the crowd blocked both his path and his view. By the time he pushed past them Jane had disappeared. . . .

CHAPTER XXIX
1823

For the second morning in a row Vanessa woke early in Lord Hastings's house on Campden Hill. The sun was very low in the east – it might not yet be six o'clock. But she could hear footsteps along the back stairs and murmurs from the children's bedrooms down the hall.

She'd played music with Hastings's daughter Flora the night before, part of the program Vanessa would soon perform in Winchester.

She sat bolt upright. Not soon, she thought. Tomorrow.

She climbed out of bed and put on her clothes. She was surprised she'd slept so well, after the dramatic afternoon at John Murray's house. She'd also been anxious about her upcoming travel on this morning's coach from Charing Cross. Her plan was to reach Chawton in time for dinner and some more practice on the Austens' old, out-of-tune pianoforte.

But she hadn't yet considered how to get across London. . . . No, she corrected herself. She *had* considered, several times, without coming to any conclusion. Even another private chaise seemed risky. Dared she ask if one of Lord Hastings's servants could fetch it for her? And even then could she feel safe? If one assailant had found her in Hampshire and another in Kensington, why could there not be a third? Or a fourth?

Having Lord Hastings's pistol was a comfort, but the greater comfort was his companionship. And his family's too, she added quickly. Then she smiled. No, it was Lord Hastings himself who mattered. What *was* it about him that was so compelling?

She brushed her hair and put her nightgown in her portmanteau. If there's another early riser in the house he or she is about to have company. Downstairs she found what she'd hoped: Lord Hastings in his study, seated at his overflowing desk. He too was fully dressed, his face dark with melancholy.

"Please don't let me interrupt," said Vanessa.

Hastings smiled, waving at the stacks of papers.

"Any reason to avoid correspondence is a good one, as far as I'm concerned. I must now rely on people I scarcely know to manage my affairs. They tell me all will come right, but I do not believe them."

He led the way to the small dining room. "I breakfast at half-past six, almost always alone. Your presence will please the cook, I believe."

A serving maid entered, bobbing a curtsey. "Cook asks his lordship whether he and his guest would care for kedgeree."

Hastings nodded at Vanessa. "You need not, my dear, but it will set you up nicely for travelling. I trust you know the dish?"

Vanessa smiled. "It is a favorite of the Austen captains. I tasted it this year for the first time. I can think of nothing I should like more."

Soon the sideboard was covered with a large toast rack, a basket of pastries, a large pot of coffee, and a steaming dish of buttered, saffron- and curry-scented rice and smoked fish, mixed with chopped hard-boiled eggs, parsley, and sultanas.

"I hope you like it buttery," said Hastings, as the maid began to serve.

"I like it any way it comes."

"Unlike my children, who *complain* however it comes."

"Unfair, papa," came an amused voice from the hallway. It was Flora, who curtseyed to Vanessa. "I wished to say goodbye, Miss Horwood, and to thank you again for the wonderful music last night." She glanced at her father. "And I am pleased to correct my father's mistake. I *do* like kedgeree."

"Children have no respect for their elders nowadays," declared Hastings, smiling affectionately at his daughter. "Was it so in Canada?"

"Never say it, Miss Horwood," cried Flora.

Vanessa couldn't resist. "We seldom saw our elders in Canada. They were manning stockades against Indian attacks, while we children skinned the buffalo."

"No!" said Flora, starting to laugh. "Even I know Montreal is not like that. And besides, you would never have learned to play the pianoforte if all you did was skin buffalo."

"Touché," said Hastings.

They set to their breakfasts then, and Vanessa reveled in the flavors of the Anglo-Indian dish, and the equally rich coffee. Fully ten minutes went by before another word was spoken.

"And now," said Flora, as businesslike as a seventeen year-old could possibly be, "I should like to know more about your insistence that I sing the violin part of that Beethoven trio last night. You said you were going to perform it. When, if I may ask. And where?"

"Tomorrow," replied Vanessa. "In Winchester."

"Oh, Papa," said Flora, her face bright with enthusiasm. "We must go, surely. You said we were due for an outing."

Hastings shook his head.

"No, child, we may not. I fear that the outing I have in mind is further than Winchester, and not of my own choosing. And for now I must remain in London. I expect a message from the King this afternoon, and tomorrow morning I meet once more with my friends at the East India Company. All depends on the outcome of these discussions."

He turned to Vanessa. "I have said too much, Miss Horwood. We have known you scarce a fortnight, and I speak in your presence as easily as if you were my own family."

Vanessa regarded him carefully. Yesterday he'd revealed a connection with Jane Austen, and today he'd given her a glimpse of his current troubles. In his eyes she saw something close to heartbreak.

"You honor me, my lord. Whatever you or anyone in this house says in my presence goes no further."

Hastings smiled at her, seemingly determined to shake off his cares. He finished the last of his coffee and stood.

"Flora recognizes that I have changed my routine this morning. I usually ride to Park Lane at daybreak and then return for breakfast. But today I have ordered the phaeton so I may drive you to Charing Cross."

Vanessa had risen along with her host. She began to protest, but Hastings cut her short.

"It is my pleasure as well as my exercise."

"May I come too, Papa?" asked Flora.

"You will be on the back bench, my dear."

At that moment George sidled into the dining-room, dressed but sleepy-eyed.

"Is Flora going to do something I am not allowed?"

165

"Indeed she will not, if you so choose," said Hastings. "But you too will be on the back bench, holding tight to Miss Horwood's portmanteau, and without your breakfast."

"And," said Flora, tossing her head. "You will stay on the back bench for the return, as I shall take the front seat next to Papa."

"Just so," declared Hastings. "We leave at once, before anyone else awakens. Does this suit you, Miss Horwood?"

"I can be at the doorway before the carriage appears."

"You are gainsaid," replied Hastings. "The phaeton is already at the door."

Vanessa ran upstairs as quietly as she could. Her case was packed, but her new pistol, along with a small box containing four rounds of ammunition, was on a side-table next to her reticule. She clenched her teeth as she loaded a cartridge. The pistol embarrassed her, but she wanted it ready.

A footman was outside her bedroom awaiting her portmanteau. She followed him to the carriage, where he handed the case up to George.

"Guard it as though it were your own, young sir," said the footman.

"No, indeed," said Hastings, pulling at the reins as the four horses began to paw the gravel. "Guard it much more carefully than that."

The footman helped Vanessa to the seat next to Lord Hastings, and the old phaeton began its journey. Hastings was an attentive driver, alert to the pedestrians and tradesmen's carts in Kensington High Street. Once into the park he picked up the pace, clearly enjoying himself as the phaeton overtook a few solitary riders next to the Serpentine. Hastings circled the park before turning south and east to pass the construction works at Buckingham House, but even so they arrived at Charing Cross well ahead of time. Hastings sent a loiterer into the inn, who returned with the message that it would be another quarter hour before the Alton coach would take on passengers.

"We shall stay till you are safely aboard," said Hastings, guiding the phaeton into the courtyard behind the public hackney-carriages. "There is time enough."

Hastings climbed down, directing George to hand over Vanessa's case and then climb to the driver's seat.

"Father," said George, looking down at the carriage doors as he changed position. "Why are there panels covering our crest?"

"I prefer to choose when to be recognized," replied Hastings. "I shall say more in due course. You have a very important task just now, which is to look after your sister and the horses as I speak to Miss Horwood."

Hastings gave George the reins, and then came round the carriage to hand Vanessa down. He held her case with one hand, and she linked her arm with his as they took a few steps away, where the jangling of the hackney-carriage harnesses offered something like privacy.

"I remain with you because someone wishes you ill. And because that ill-will may have something to do with me."

"It could be coincidence, my lord."

"I do not believe in coincidence. I have been reading papers left by Major James who had been my confidential man of business. They suggest reasons *I* might be in danger, but I cannot fathom any connection to you. At least not yet. But I do not wish you unaccompanied until I get to the bottom of it all."

"Thank you, my lord. I confess I have been frightened."

Hastings smiled. "So you should be. Your life is not insured, is it?"

"What?"

The smile grew broader. "The best thing that could happen to my creditors would be my sudden death."

Vanessa shook her head. "I have no creditors, my lord."

"Then this must be something to do with mine. Is your pistol at hand?"

Vanessa nodded.

"You must promise me that for the next week you will take every precaution. Write to me before you return to London and I shall have the footman who handed you up this morning meet your coach. Accompany no-one but him."

"But I am expected in Bath!"

Hastings shook his head. "Unless you have protection there, do not return. This will all resolve in the next few days." His voice softened. "I do apologize, my dear. Call me overzealous, but I am persuaded I am the cause of your difficulties. I insist on providing what assistance I may."

He looked up, and Vanessa followed his gaze. Two men were approaching the phaeton, seeming to admire the horses.

"It is time to rejoin the children. And" – he pointed towards the inn – "that is surely your coach." He handed her the portmanteau. "Forgive me if I do not accompany you, but I shall watch until you board. Stay on this side, where I may see you."

Vanessa nodded, taking her case and curtseying. She raised an arm to wave at the children and hurried towards the coach. She glanced back once, seeing the two men retreat as Lord Hastings approached. Then she was inside, taking the last, cramped, backwards-facing seat, just as the coachman shouted "Last call."

CHAPTER XXX
1823

The first thirty miles on the coach seemed endless. Vanessa's seat was between two portly passengers, neither of whom had recently bathed. She wasn't sure whether the unadulterated body odor of the man on her right was worse than the cheap perfume of the woman on her left, but the combination could, she thought, become lethal. On this increasingly hot summer's morning she could see perspiration starting to stain both their clothes. How long will I last? she wondered.

To her relief those two alighted at Guildford, and only one passenger, a young and slender woman, came aboard. None of those opposite cared to change to the now-spacious rear-facing seat: Vanessa and the young woman had it to themselves. And she was a reader, her book already in hand, so Vanessa didn't have to demonstrate all over again, as she had to the passengers opposite, that she did not want conversation.

As the coach left Farnham for the last ten miles to Alton, Vanessa began to think seriously about the walk from the coaching inn to Chawton House. At little more than a mile it was short enough, even with her case, but she could not help thinking of the tree-shaded stretch where Lonsdale had killed a man.

Lonsdale was still in Hampshire – indeed he had promised to come to her performance tomorrow evening – but he would not be there to protect her this afternoon. She tried to tell herself she wasn't worth another kidnapping attempt. And if she was, wouldn't they know she might just as well return to Bath as to Chawton?

No. Her engagement tomorrow was public; handbills were all over the county. Vanessa looked around, uneasy. Two of the passengers opposite were talking quietly. The third was asleep, and the young woman next to her was engrossed in her novel. She finished the volume as Vanessa watched, rummaging in her reticule for the next.

She felt Vanessa's eyes on her and smiled. "Five volumes, can you believe it?"

"Is it worth the bother?"

"I think not. It's called *Guilty or not Guilty; or, a Lesson for Husbands*. I conceived that lessons for husbands could easily fill five volumes, but I was wrong. It is sadly repetitive. If I had the first volume with me I should offer it to you, but I'd room for only these last two."

"Thank you," Vanessa replied. "But I am about to alight at Alton. Are you travelling far?"

"Portsmouth. My husband is in the navy."

"Active?" asked Vanessa.

The young woman smiled again. "Yes. One of the lucky ones."

Vanessa nodded and looked away. The young woman took the hint and returned to her book. Somehow the short conversation had allowed Vanessa to make a decision. Those who wished her harm could be anywhere. She would spend what was needed to hire a carriage to Chawton.

Alton was quiet, and she was the only passenger to disembark. A coachman at the inn was eager for her business. Ten minutes later she was with Martha at Chawton House.

"Lord, my dear. You've never arrived in a private carriage before. Have you become so grand? Will you convey us all to Winchester tomorrow?"

Vanessa laughed. "So I might, if it wouldn't cost more than my evening's pay."

Martha smiled. "Charles and Frank are as determined to hear you as I am. Edward has sent his barouche to take the ladies to Kent next week and we may use it tomorrow. There will be room for us all, even old Mrs. Austen should she choose to come.

"And," Martha continued, holding out an envelope. "You have a letter."

Vanessa tore it open as the maidservant came to take her case.

"It's from Captain Lonsdale," said Vanessa. "He's coming to hear my music too. He says he'll drive me here afterwards, and go on to stay with his cousin at Selborne."

Martha clapped her hands. "Perhaps he'll be in Winchester early enough to dine with us."

The maidservant was waiting for them inside.

"You are in the same room as last visit, Miss Horwood," she said, bobbing a curtsey to Vanessa. "You've a little time before dinner should you care to go up."

Vanessa could feel the tension in the dining room as soon as she entered, and was glad to have had those few minutes to collect her thoughts. She had expected to see Henry, her previous antagonist, but he was not present. Instead it was Cassandra who pointedly looked the other direction as Charles held Vanessa's chair.

Vanessa did her best to ignore the snub, turning to speak to Frank. Both he and Charles were still in uniform, returned from another fruitless day in Portsmouth.

"We have worn out our welcome for now," said Frank, in answer to Vanessa's question. "Which is just as well, as we are determined to hear you play. Mary sends her regrets – as indeed she does for this evening. She says she is too heavy to travel, too heavy even to come downstairs. But she insists that I go, that the baby will not come for another week."

"We shall deliver you to Winchester whenever you choose," said Charles. He turned to Cassandra. "There is room for two more in the barouche."

"We have spoke of this already," declared Cassandra. "I certainly shall not attend. Nor will Henry. He and his wife have engaged themselves to come from Farnham tomorrow, to keep company with our mother."

"You disrespect our guest, sister," said Frank quietly.

Once again Cassandra refused to look at Vanessa, but she met her brother's eyes defiantly.

"I should never have believed a musician for hire would *become* our guest."

Martha raised her head, gazing around the table.

"I have heard Vanessa play, as indeed has Frank," she said slowly. "The very first morning she appeared in my life, and a happy morning it was, she played for Jane and me at the cottage. I remarked to Jane afterwards that I wondered if Vanessa might play the piano-forte in public, and Jane declared that the public would be fortunate if it were so."

Vanessa winced at Cassandra's reply.

"Jane would never have countenanced such vulgar display within her own family."

"Not so," countered Martha. "I remember Jane's very words: 'Not every woman is so blessed as to have the father and brothers I do. Were it not for them I should have had to make the London booksellers' rounds myself.'"

"That is not the same thing," insisted Cassandra.

"Writing and music may not be the same," said Charles. "But the *principle* is the same. The victory in this argument goes to our departed sister, God rest her soul."

"We shall not expect your company, Cassandra," said Frank, in a tone that concluded the discussion. "Our mother will be grateful for your presence."

The conversation that followed was, not surprisingly, strained. Vanessa was grateful when Martha pleaded fatigue on Vanessa's behalf, and accompanied her upstairs.

Vanessa's plan of practicing for tomorrow's recital had vanished. She'd have to hope that her skill at sight-reading would not desert her and embarrass her fellow-musicians. At least she'd have *some* time with them before the program began.

Martha spoke once they had reached Vanessa's bedroom.

"Cassandra is slow to love, my dear, but she loves deeply when she is moved. I regret extremely that she was not present when you first met Jane. That would have made all the difference."

"Ought I to stay in Winchester tomorrow night, and return directly to London?"

"Certainly not. We shall leave together for Winchester tomorrow morning. I shall join Charles and Frank on a visit to the Cathedral and a walk round the city. If Captain Lonsdale fails to come, we shall drive you home after your recital as well. Either way I shall have you all to myself the next day."

Vanessa took both of Martha's hands. "Thank you, love."

"And now to bed," said Martha. She leaned forward, kissing Vanessa's cheek. "Do you have a basin and a glass of water?"

Vanessa smiled. "I have everything I need, and am in no hurry to rise in the morning. But I'll do my best to breakfast and be gone before Cassandra and her mother arrive."

"Yes," said Martha. "We shall walk in the orchard together, before we go to Winchester."

CHAPTER XXXI
1823

Martha's plans for a walk were spoiled by morning rain, but it gave way to misty clouds and occasional shafts of sunlight as the barouche made its way down the highway. They dropped Vanessa at the recital hall before noon, and she was able to spend an hour tuning the pianoforte before the other two musicians arrived.

Vanessa knew them well: brothers who played violin and cello. The violinist had caused some previous difficulty by declaring an undying love for Vanessa, followed by a proposal of marriage. The cellist later told Vanessa that his brother had only given over when he realized they were about to lose the best pianist they'd ever engaged.

The recital hall was in St. John's House, on the north side of Winchester's High Street. The building itself was ancient, its public room in grand Elizabethan style with a ceiling at least twenty-five feet high. Fortunately it had some more modern fittings, courtesy of a colonel whose portrait hung on one side of the room opposite a larger portrait of King Charles the Second.

Well over a hundred chairs were set out. Vanessa couldn't imagine they'd all be filled. She said as much to her fellow-musicians, but they were both confident.

"It is advertised throughout the county as the musical event of the season," said the violinist.

His brother smiled. "The handbills say we are "that incomparable fraternal duo, accompanied by the renowned Canadian pianist Miss V. Horwood, now resident in London and Bath.""

Vanessa winced. It was the same handbill that Mr. Shuffleton the bank-teller had seen in Alton. Anyone paying the slightest attention would know exactly where to find her this evening. Assuming, of course, that Lord Hastings was right, and more people were on her trail. She felt a burst of anger. What can they possibly want from me?

Her worries abated as they worked through the program. The brothers were fully rehearsed, and it only remained for Vanessa to become acquainted with their latest interpretations of the music, its structure and tempi.

The first piece on the agenda was a sonata for piano and violin by George Frederick Pinto, an English composer who'd died young fifteen or so years earlier. The piano part was dominant, at times brilliant, but emotionally flat. She was much happier with the piece that closed the first half of the recital: Mozart's B-flat Major Trio. The brothers gave the opening allegro just the right, not quite rollicking, pace, in contrast to the slow larghetto movement. They ran through the larghetto twice more, then broke for tea.

"The third movement will send them out happy," said the cellist. "And ready for Beethoven. The more happy because we gave them an Englishman at the beginning."

Vanessa smiled. She knew English audiences loved their own composers, but one of the reasons she so enjoyed playing with the two brothers was their unerring choice of what she considered to be great music. They pandered to their audiences' preferences as little as possible, and always chose at least one composition that challenged all three performers.

In this case it was Beethoven's *Archduke* Trio, which she'd played with the brothers twice before. She discovered as they rehearsed that they wanted more this time, to dig to the music's core, especially in the slow movement.

They went through several passages repeatedly, and the afternoon was almost gone before the three of them adjourned for dinner.

"Two hours before we begin," declared the violinist. "And I am altogether wrung out."

"Your fault for wanting everything just so," said the cellist.

"Thank you," Vanessa put in. "It was worth it. If we can manage the Beethoven this will be our best evening so far."

Both brothers beamed. "We've a private dining-room at the hotel opposite," said the violinist. "We may dine without speaking to anyone, even ourselves."

They checked the tuning of their instruments one last time and took a light dinner in silence. Afterwards they avoided the small crowd at the public entrance, passing along the High Street towards an alley leading to the back door. Even so the first person Vanessa saw was someone who recognized her.

Aeneas Shuffleton was directly in her path, heading towards the public entrance. He bowed, beaming.

"I am all anticipation, Miss Horwood. May I assume these are your fellow musicians?"

Vanessa hated small talk before a performance. But she managed introductions and farewells in a short time, and without leaving Mr. Shuffleton feeling he'd been cut. Soon the three musicians were out of sight in the alley, and backstage where they could hear the murmurs of the audience.

There was a curtained door that led to the raised platform where they would play. Vanessa opened the door and peeked at the audience, just as Martha entered with the Austen captains, splendid in their dress uniforms. Lonsdale had joined them, fully their match in his own bright red. Poor Martha, by contrast, seemed a little dowdy in her dark woolen dress. Its square décolletage was long out of fashion, but at least its unadorned deep burgundy nicely set off the topaz cross around her neck.

There were still ten minutes to go before the performance and already the room was nearly full. The Austens had to settle a dozen rows back in order to have four seats together. What they did not see, though Vanessa did, was Mr. Shuffleton's entrance just after. He was now flanked by two other men, both – as almost any man would be – taller than he, and one of them tall by any standard.

Vanessa recognized the slighter of the two, one of Shuffleton's fellow-employees at Hoare's bank in Alton. But the other man looked nothing like a banker, and decidedly not the sort of man one would expect to see in a chamber-music audience. There was scar-tissue around his eyes, his hair was lanky and heavily-pomaded, and his shoulders nearly burst from the seams of his ill-fitting frock-coat.

Shuffleton cast a sidelong glance at this man. The bank teller was obviously afraid of his companion, but Vanessa could see the smaller man's determination to compose himself as he turned his attention towards the piano-forte.

By now the room was altogether full, with only a few stragglers coming through the doors. Vanessa looked towards the cellist, who in turn looked at the house manager.

"Two minutes," said the last, looking at the watch in his hand. "We allow late-comers that much and no more."

The applause was polite as the musicians entered, and all but a few voices quieted as they began. Vanessa expected attention to wander as they worked their way through the Pinto sonata, and it did. But the audience was properly hushed during the Mozart larghetto, and the rousing last movement brought loud clapping and even a few cheers.

Vanessa liked to do one of two things during an interval, she never knew which beforehand. The first was pacing, the second finding an overstuffed chair in which she could sprawl. There was no chair tonight, so she began to walk.

The last thing she wanted was to speak to anyone. Her fellow-musicians knew this, and tried to deflect the house manager as he approached her. But the man insisted.

"A gentleman threatens to become unpleasant if you will not meet him after the performance."

"All the more reason I should decline to do so," said Vanessa.

"I beg you will allow me to offer more encouragement than that."

"Tell him I regret that I am driving home with friends, and must depart immediately the performance is over."

The manager nodded, but a moment later Shuffleton's burly companion forced his way through the curtain, followed by the other two. Shuffleton was trying both to protest and apologize at the same time.

Almost immediately the curtain opened again. This time the intruders were Lonsdale and the two Austens.

Charles looked embarrassed, but Frank spoke with the ease of long command.

"You seem to have an unwelcome guest."

Vanessa looked at Lonsdale. His eyes were on the big intruder, and he was clearly ready for a fight. The intruder sensed as much, turning and giving a bellicose smile.

"Stand down, Captain Lonsdale," said Frank. "And you too, sir," to the intruder.

Both took a step backwards. Frank turned to Shuffleton.

"Had you something urgent to convey, Mr. Shuffleton?"

Shuffleton's face was bright red. "I cannot tell you how much I regret the imposition, Miss Horwood."

Vanessa forced a smile. "I do not believe you are responsible, sir."

Frank's voice remained matter-of-fact. "Are both your companions leaving the building now, Mr. Shuffleton, or" – Frank smiled – "just the larger of them?"

"I'm going nowhere," muttered the big man, coming closer to peer at Vanessa.

In an instant Lonsdale was between them. Shuffleton's eyes darted around the room before returning to Frank.

"Perhaps we should all go, Captain Austen."

Charles spoke for the first time. "No indeed, Mr. Shuffleton. You must join our party for the last of the music." He smiled at Vanessa. "It is much too good to miss."

Shuffleton's fellow-banker spoke for the first time. "You may stay, Shuffleton. You will find the two of us at the Wyckham Arms after the performance."

"I'm going nowhere," repeated the big man. "Get this lobster out of my way."

Vanessa glanced at the house manager, who appeared close to panic. Frank nodded to him. "There's a rear entrance for performers, I expect."

The manager pointed and in the same instant the big man darted around Lonsdale, pushing his face close to Vanessa's.

"Quick, gentlemen," said Frank.

Before the big man could react Charles and Lonsdale each slipped an arm along his side, encircling him under his armpits and securing their hands on his neck. In an instant the big man was hunched over and forcibly marched, roaring his protests, to the back entrance.

"Perhaps you could open the door?" Frank suggested to the house manager.

"I have it," the banker replied quickly, and a few seconds later both banker and intruder were outside, the larger with a little more help from the two officers.

The manager closed and bolted the door, as Frank spoke once more.

"You might bolt the front entrance as well, sir. Your visitor's temper may need some time to cool."

The manager went through the curtain at a run, returning a moment later with a sigh of relief.

"It's done," he said.

By now Charles and Lonsdale had rejoined Frank, tugging their uniform jackets into position. The two Austens promised not to leave until they had seen Vanessa and Lonsdale safely on the road after the concert. Then they rejoined Martha in the audience.

Lonsdale, his eyes on Vanessa, said, "Perhaps it's time to finish the music." Then he smiled, rather wolfishly Vanessa thought, and followed the Austens through the curtain.

CHAPTER XXXII
1823

As the musicians returned to the stage Vanessa could see Shuffleton behind the Austens, an empty seat either side. He'd extracted a small writing case from his pocket and was scribbling a note, nervously looking up and around the room at intervals. She determinedly put him out of her mind, and took her seat at the piano.

But she soon realized that her fellow-musicians were more disturbed by the intrusion than she was. The violinist's hands were shaking as he picked up his instrument.

"Do you suppose there might be a bottle of brandy close by?"

"No," declared the cellist. "Brandy will see you through the first movement but not the second. Take your cue from Miss Horwood, who appears untroubled."

Vanessa shook her head. "Not true. But the music will settle us."

"Yes," said the cellist. "It's time to play."

Unfortunately for them all, the first movement of Beethoven's *Archduke* Trio was measured and deliberative, just the kind of music where uneven nerves were likely to be exposed. But Vanessa managed the opening piano solo without incident, and when the violin missed a beat on its entrance the cello was there to set it right.

She glanced at the two brothers. The cellist responded with a reassuring smile, and soon they were lost in their performance.

The audience rose to its feet at the end. Vanessa was especially touched to see Mr. Shuffleton's applauding hands held above the heads of those in front; the rest of the man was invisible. The Austen captains were clapping as well, and when Charles leaned over and murmured to his brother, Frank grinned and, in a voice that filled the room, called 'brava.' Martha might have had tears in her eyes – Vanessa wasn't sure at such a distance – but next to her Lonsdale, often demonstrative in an audience, appeared distracted.

Vanessa was relieved that no-one suggested an encore. Performances usually lifted Vanessa's spirits, but tonight's left her drained and melancholy. Part of the problem, of course, was the intrusion during the interval, but there was more to it than that. Rehearsing and performing had taken her mind off Cassandra's outburst the night before, but now her words – "musician for hire" – returned in full force. Vanessa knew that Martha's defense had not dented the armor of Cassandra's disapproval.

After most of the audience had dispersed Lonsdale came forward to conduct Vanessa to his curricle. Martha and the Austens had waited to see them on their way, true to Frank's promise.

It was beginning to rain as they approached the stables. Lonsdale took Charles to one side and spoke quietly, out of Vanessa's earshot. Charles looked her way during this exchange, raising an eyebrow but saying nothing. Then Martha kissed Vanessa goodbye, murmuring how proud she was of the performance, and both Charles and Frank bowed as Lonsdale handed Vanessa into the carriage. Vanessa looked back as Lonsdale drove away, seeing Frank take Martha's arm as they returned to the stable-yard to collect their barouche.

The hostler had pulled up the hood of the Lonsdale's curricle against the rain, but so far it was little more than a mist, not so wet as to make the roads muddy. Lonsdale still hadn't spoken to Vanessa, but he looked happy, doubtless anticipating another reckless drive. She'd known him do as much as fifteen miles in an hour – they would likely reach Chawton well ahead of the Austen carriage. Earlier in the day she'd looked forward to the drive back, thinking it would be the perfect outlet for post-performance nerves. Now, after the events of the evening, she'd lost her enthusiasm.

She leaned back against the seat, grateful for the leather padding. For all his addiction to speed, Lonsdale was an expert driver. He'd given her some lessons on the high ground above Bath and she knew how much effort went into controlling the kind of high-spirited horses that drew a curricle.

The curricle took them back along the high street, passing St. John's House. There was enough light from its open doors for Vanessa to see Lonsdale's expression. There was something beyond driving there, but she couldn't tell what it was.

"Well?" she demanded.

He shook his head. "You look tired. I've never seen you like this after a performance."

"I'll be all right," she said. "The room was too small for the audience. They never opened a window, and I didn't need that oaf to force his way in during the interval. A little fresh air will see me right."

Lonsdale nodded, flicking his whip above the horses. They turned east out of the High Street and as they came onto the highway outside Winchester the horses moved from a trot to a steady, perfectly-paced canter. Five minutes later they had the road to themselves.

The horses were undaunted by the mist and Lonsdale gave them their heads. They cantered along Temple Valley, scarcely slowing as they passed through the little village of Ovington. Another quarter hour saw them to the outskirts of Alresford, and to Vanessa's surprise Lonsdale pulled back on the reins, slowing the horses back to a trot and taking the turn towards the centre of what was still called the new town. A moment later he pulled them to a walk.

"What are you doing?" Vanessa asked.

He turned to her, his face inscrutable. "I've taken a room at the George in Broad Street. I should not wish the horses to be overheated when we go in."

At first she missed the point.

"Why didn't you tell me sooner so I could have gone with the Austens? Will there be another room for me?"

His voice became hard. "We have trifled too long, Vanessa. We arrive at the George as man and wife."

"No, sir," Vanessa replied instantly. "We do not."

"By God we do," said Lonsdale. They passed a single gas-lamp, which illuminated his angry flush as he continued.

"No man could be as patient as I, nor given you so much opportunity. But you've played the coquette at every turn. No more. I am making the change easy for you."

"Stop the horses," she said coldly.

He ignored her. She opened her reticule, pulling out Lord Hastings's pistol.

"Look at me, Will."

He glanced her way, then froze. She'd leveled the pistol directly at his chest.

"You may stop the horses and let me out, or I shall shoot. I am quite good with this, but I cannot be certain I shall not damage you more than I might wish."

His jaw clenched. Vanessa knew he was both fast and fearless. She had to keep him away from her.

"Pull up the reins with both hands," she said. "Away from me. If you move any other muscle I shall shoot."

Suddenly, unexpectedly, Lonsdale grinned. "By God, Vanessa, you're good."

He followed her orders, and Vanessa slid out onto the road.

"I wish I could say I thought you were good too, but I can't. Now drive on."

"Vanessa, no!" His face was serious now. "I cannot abandon you on the highway in the middle of the night."

"You've already abandoned me."

"It's not too late. We'll get you a separate room. Or I'll drive you to Chawton."

"Drive on," Vanessa repeated. But her voice broke halfway and her eyes filled with tears. "Damn you, Will. Get away or I'll shoot, if only to make you stop talking."

Lonsdale began to slide towards her, but Vanessa lifted the little pistol again, holding it with both hands. Their eyes met, and she surprised herself by looking steadily at him, even through her tears.

After a moment he moved back to the driver's position, lifting the reins. The horses moved on cue, and Lonsdale kept his eyes forward. She could still see the carriage as it turned off the main road.

Vanessa lifted the strap of her reticule over her shoulders, pulled her bonnet down and her shawl more tightly around her. Then she began the long walk to Chawton. She kept her pistol under her shawl, taking no chance that Lonsdale or anyone else might come after and find her unprepared.

Her tears were gone, and she calculated she could reach Chawton House in three hours or less, barring highwaymen or other incidents. There was no hope of the Austens' carriage overtaking her. It would have followed the main highway along Tichborne Down and be halfway to Chawton by the time she was in its way. It was well before midnight and less than ten miles to Chawton. She'd rather defend herself against a highwayman than see Lonsdale again, or be anywhere near him.

A few stars were becoming visible and a waning moon was starting to glow behind a pale cloud. She knew the Winchester to Chawton road better than she wished. She'd first travelled in the opposite direction, in a police constable's cart on her way to gaol six years earlier.

CHAPTER XXXIII
1823

It was after two in the morning when Vanessa finally reached the house; she'd heard the church-bell chime the hour as she approached. Martha had waited up for her, sitting close to the front door where she could hear a knock. She took Vanessa in her arms as she staggered inside.

"You poor poppet," said Martha, holding her candle aloft as she looked down at Vanessa's muddy boots. "I never believed Charles when he said you were staying the night with Captain Lonsdale."

"I was a fool," said Vanessa, trying to stop her tears from coming again.

"Cassandra declared herself certain that he'd already seduced you."

Vanessa gave a small laugh, but it turned into a sniffle.

"I put her right," continued Martha. "I told her he'd been trying for months, and that he would never succeed."

"This time he tried in earnest. I had to walk from Alresford."

"Lord, child. I shall get you a hot drink and a bedpan and put you to bed. And if all this weren't bad enough, I have a note for you from Mr. Shuffleton. He asked if you were likely to attend matins tomorrow."

Vanessa's smile was genuine this time. "And you told him I was a heathen and a foreigner."

"No, love. He was so much in earnest that I told him we should certainly be at St. Nicholas's every morning until you chose to return to London."

Vanessa's shoulders slumped. "Including tomorrow."

Martha put an arm around her, turning towards the stairs.

"Especially tomorrow. Now you are to go upstairs and get out of those damp clothes, whilst I draw some coals from the fire for your bedpan. I shall be with you in a moment."

Vanessa sighed with gratitude. "Thank you, Martha."

Ten minutes later, with the comfort of Martha's parting kiss and the warmth of brandy and bedpan meeting somewhere in her middle, Vanessa fell sound asleep.

Martha had to shake her awake the next morning, notwithstanding the un-drawn curtains and the bright sunlight streaming through the window. She hand-ed Vanessa Mr. Shuffleton's note, which confirmed his intent.

Miss Horwood,
I implore you to meet me in the cemetery of St. Nicholas's Church before matins. It is a matter of the gravest urgency.
      Yrs. &c.
        A. Shuffleton
Please forgive the unpardonable incident in W'chestr this evng.

"*Before* matins," cried Vanessa. "What time is it now?"

"Time enough," said Martha. "But not for breakfast."

Vanessa realized she was ravenous, but she could not fail to meet Mr. Shuffleton. Something important was afoot, something that mattered to her and that he was afraid of. 'Gravest urgency' was not, she suspected, a term he would use lightly.

Mr. Shuffleton was waiting as promised, in the shadow of the old church's tower. At a distance Vanessa could see him trying to smile at the few parishioners who ventured beyond the church's entrance, but as she and Martha drew closer it became obvious how forced those smiles were, and how much his nerves were on edge.

When he spotted Vanessa he looked carefully around, noting everyone else approaching. Then, seemingly satisfied, he stepped out, greeted her and Martha with a bow, and suggested they continue to walk through the cemetery, away from the entrance.

As they rounded the front wall he began to speak quietly.

"I believe, Miss Horwood, that you and Miss Lloyd are sufficiently close that you may rely on her discretion?"

"Yes, sir."

He stopped among the tombstones, out of sight of the road and in the shadow of the long wall of the church. Candles from inside brightened the stained glass of the window above him.

He dropped his voice, so low it was little more than a whisper.

"This pertains in no small part to the Austen family, but it is Miss Horwood whom I believe to be in danger. Will you swear to me that what I tell you goes no further?"

Martha shook her head. "I owe my entire felicity to the Austens. If they are imperiled and I have information that could save them, I must disclose it."

Shuffleton nodded. "I agree. But in this case their safety lies in *not* knowing the information I am about to impart."

"Very well," said Martha. "But I must be the final judge of that."

Shuffleton nodded again, gathering his thoughts.

"The two men who joined me at the recital last night."

"One of them," said Vanessa, "was from your own bank, was he not?"

"Yes," Shuffleton confirmed. "You may have noticed he was as discomfited as I."

Vanessa nodded. "The other man was not a banker."

Shuffleton gave a wan smile. "He was, after a fashion. He was said to represent the Marquess of Hastings."

He turned to Martha. "You are aware, Miss Lloyd, that until its failure in 1815 I was employed by Mr. Henry Austen's bank, Austen, Gray & Vincent, and that its successor, Messrs. Hoare, was afterwards kind enough to retain me."

"Indeed," said Martha. "And you were kind enough after the failure to allow the Misses Austen an advance of five guineas, without security, until Miss Jane Austen was able to exchange one of her navy bonds."

Mr. Shuffleton bowed. "I did not tell you it was my own money. Mr. Gray emptied the bank of all but sixteen shillings the day before it closed."

Martha looked startled, but Shuffleton raised a hand to forestall her speaking.

"For the last eight years I have wished to know what caused the failure of my employers' bank, and afterwards the collapse of Mr. Austen's bank in London. Both had a number of large notes drawn upon the credit of the Earl of Moira – the present Marquess of Hastings. It appears the Earl failed to discharge these obligations when they came due and that Mr. Austen was unable to persuade his own creditors to accept them. Some of these notes were acquired by Hoare's at a substantial discount when it purchased the few remaining assets of the Alton bank."

Vanessa turned to Martha. "Do you remember what Henry said when he first learned I'd visited Lord Hastings?"

"Yes," replied Martha. "Especially as I had heard the same language before. Henry described the Marquess's actions as 'unexampled treachery.' These notes must have been what he meant."

"Say no more," said Shuffleton. "I must make haste. It will not surprise you that it is the large man you have to fear. He said that several more banks were in danger of going the way of Mr. Austen's."

"I cannot understand what this has to do with me," said Vanessa. "Lord Hastings told me it took years for him to repay his debts to the Austen bank, but that he did repay them."

Shuffleton shook his head. "I cannot speak to that. But I overheard the Marquess's man last night. He said you must be taken out of the picture. Those were his very words: 'out of the picture.'"

Martha gasped. "Would he kidnap her?"

Vanessa gave a quiet laugh. "If that was his intent last night I have little to worry about. He could scarcely have been clumsier."

Shuffleton did not smile. "Do not underestimate these people, Miss Horwood. My advice is that you absent yourself from this neighborhood at once. And do not tell me where. I must be entirely ignorant if I am questioned by my employers."

During the course of this exchange Shuffleton had progressively lowered both his voice and his head, to the point where he now seemed to be whispering to one of the tombstones. Abruptly he looked up, scanning the surrounding area as though – Vanessa almost laughed at the idea – he was scouting for enemy troops.

Her amusement vanished as she realized how much Shuffleton endangered himself by giving her this information. In his own way, she realized, this tiny man in his threadbare frock coat, with wispy hair and watery eyes, was every bit as brave as any soldier.

Shuffleton took a step backwards, bowing.

"I hear the organ, ladies. We must end our communion with the dead and rejoin the living." Then he whispered. "Give me a few moments to enter the church."

As he rounded the corner Martha began to look faint. Vanessa took her arm.

"Let me walk you to a pew. Will Henry be there?"

Martha nodded. "He and Cassandra will see me home. But what of you?"

"Better not to know. I shall be gone by the time you return."

"May the lord protect you, my dear. And do not fail to write."

By now they were inside the church. Martha had recovered enough to take her usual place in the pew next to Cassandra and old Mrs. Austen. Vanessa turned quickly away, not wanting to speak to anyone. She curtseyed to Henry as he entered the church in his black curate's cassock, his wife at his side, and then she was outside, running as soon as she felt unobserved. Two minutes later she was in her room, packing her small bag.

CHAPTER XXXIV
1823

B ut Vanessa's plans for flight ended with a cry from the floor below. She dropped her bag and started down, just as the cry turned into a scream of pain.

Mary Austen was half out of her bed, the bedding and floorboards soaked with a mixture of blood and water. Vanessa caught her before she fell, pulling the bedclothes aside as she pushed Mary back up. As Mary's legs were lifted she gave another cry of pain.

"Bear with it a moment," Vanessa said, as calmly as she could. "I'll send for the midwife and bring you what I can. Then I'll stay with you."

"Frank. . ." Mary whispered.

"Is he here?" asked Vanessa.

Mary shook her head. "Portsmouth with Charles," she croaked. "Left early, told me to rest."

"We'll send for him."

Vanessa ran down the two flights to the kitchen, shouting for help as she entered. One of the maids hurried to the stables to send a boy for the midwife, as the housekeeper heated water.

"I'll send the maid up wi' it, Miss, and a rider to Portsmouth for the captain soon as the boy returns. Will I go to the church for the ladies?"

Vanessa shook her head. "I'll stay with Mrs. Austen till they come. It cannot be long."

Vanessa took a jug of cold water, a glass and a cloth. When she reached the bedroom Mary was in mid-contraction, white with the effort of it. She seemed already exhausted.

But she smiled as she looked up. "You've never done this, have you?"

Vanessa shook her head, pulling a chair close to the bed. "Save your strength."

There was hair in Mary's eyes, but as she reached up to brush it away another contraction hit. "Oh!" she cried, reaching for the bedframe as she tried to raise herself in order to bear down.

When it was over Vanessa helped her resettle.

"Would you rather stand?"

Mary slumped against her pillows.

"I've had so many babies by now they should come easily," she whispered.

Another contraction came and went. Mary tried to smile again.

"It's wicked of nature to make us forget the pain. Each time I swear I shall never, ever, forget, and then a few months later I say to Frank 'I'm ready for another.'"

Vanessa smiled, feeling the tears in her eyes as she stroked Mary's damp hair. She'd been ready to rage against the injustice of the male-dominated society that forced women to bear child after child. But now Mary had exploded Vanessa's indignation in one little phrase: "I'm ready for another. . . ."

Another contraction came. But this one became a convulsion of Mary's entire body as she screamed, unable to push. Vanessa stood by, helpless.

As the convulsion shuddered to its end the maid entered with clean linens over one arm, a hot kettle in one hand and a basin in the other. The housekeeper followed, hurrying to Mary's side.

Mary's eyelids began to flutter. "Stay with us, madam," cried the housekeeper. And then, more softly to Vanessa. "This is not good."

"Who's there?" came a new, female voice from below.

"Thank God," whispered the housekeeper, stepping out into the hallway. She leaned over the rail. "Here! Mrs. Frank cannot keep her eyes open."

To Vanessa's relief the midwife bustled in, all Scottish energy and reassurance.

"Ach," she said happily. "'Tis the sensible one. Wake up, ma'am, we've done this before."

Mary's voice was faint. "I need your help this time."

"We'll get'un out." The midwife placed a hand near the top of Mary's belly and pushed. Mary sat bolt upright, shrieking with pain.

The midwife glanced at the housekeeper, nodded, and pushed Mary back against the pillows. "We'll wait it out, love, and let the bairn come in its own time."

But the baby didn't come, and the ensuing three hours saw progressively weaker contractions. Martha and Cassandra came and went, and even Henry made a brief appearance, promising to stay in the house until the baby could be baptized.

Vanessa never left the room. Three hours extended to four, and then five, with Mary repeatedly losing consciousness. The midwife beckoned Vanessa into the hallway.

"Wait," whispered Vanessa. "Let me fetch the others."

When Martha and Cassandra arrived the midwife spoke formally, her Scottish accent all but gone.

"I believe the head is wrong placed, perhaps sideways. I have tried to get the baby to turn in the womb, but. . . ." The midwife shrugged. "I must ask while she may still speak at what point she wishes me to cut."

Vanessa winced, turning away. But Mary had overheard.

"Now," she said in a clear voice. All four women came close as Mary continued. "Fetch the wet-nurse and cut as soon as she arrives. The baby will be tired and need feeding, whether or not I'm here to do it."

"Aye," said the midwife. "That it will."

Vanessa went down to send the stable-boy for a wet-nurse, only to discover that one of the maids had already fetched her. The boy himself had long since ridden to Portsmouth in search of the Austen captains, but there was no word of them yet.

Vanessa took another hot kettle upstairs, and another basin of fresh cloths. She dreaded what was coming next, and she could tell from Martha's and Cassandra's faces that they did too. Mary seemed too tired to care, and when the midwife made the incision Mary scarcely winced.

But the blood came in a flood as the midwife reached in to extract the baby. Vanessa joined the others in trying to stanch the flow, but it was no use. The baby boy gave his first cry in the same instant his mother breathed her last. The midwife cut the umbilical cord, called for the wet-nurse, and closed Mary's eyes.

"She was a good woman. Pity her husband didn'a get home in time to say goodbye."

The midwife handed the newborn to the wet-nurse, who retired upstairs. Then she washed and dried her instruments.

"The reverend's downstairs, I believe. I'll send 'im up afore I go."

Then she was gone, leaving behind three women and a corpse.

CHAPTER XXXV
1823

Martha was first to speak. "Is there enough water for you both to wash?" Vanessa nodded. There was a cake of soap by one of the water-basins. She picked it up, mechanically going through the motions of getting Mary's blood off her hands and arms. But it was on her dress as well; she felt it would never entirely leave her.

Martha went downstairs as Cassandra immersed her blood-stained hands in the second basin, looking at the far wall, away from Vanessa.

As the echo of Martha's footsteps on the staircase began to fade Cassandra spoke, eyes still on the wall.

"Martha declares that outside our families you are the person most dear to her in the world. And she says although your acquaintance with my sister was short, that Jane loved you as well."

Vanessa fell backwards into her chair, so exhausted she could scarcely keep her balance. Her arms hung by her side, away from her dress as though her hands were still bloody even after their scrubbing. She remained silent. If Cassandra had more to say, she would get to it in her own time.

It took several minutes of soap and water before Cassandra spoke again.

"No-one shall know the truth of this hereafter. I have destroyed every letter from that time that Jane ever sent me. Even Martha never knew."

Vanessa felt a burst of anger. She wanted to shake Cassandra, to scream 'Knew what?' She raised an arm to push herself out of the chair, but the arm refused to respond. She met Cassandra's eyes and quickly dropped her own, realizing that Cassandra would never continue to speak unless Vanessa remained passive.

Cassandra turned her eyes back to the bloody basin, her voice dull. "The Marquess of Hastings betrayed Jane. For nearly two years they were privately engaged and Jane was the happiest woman in the world. He promised to sell his estates and discharge his debts, to escape London and the Prince of Wales. He promised her a new life in the country."

"What happened?" Vanessa whispered.

"He wrote asking her to come to town, and she expected they would finally declare themselves. I accompanied her, all anticipation, and we stayed as usual with Henry in Upper Berkeley Street. The morning after we arrived Henry was ill and asked Jane to take a letter to his office on her way to his lordship's house. His lordship's man intercepted her, to tell her why they must not marry, and that his master was leaving town at once."

"And then?"

"Jane was inconsolable. But she had the presence of mind to find a hackney carriage and came directly back to me. Jane had never told Henry of her engagement, knowing that Henry would never be able to keep the news from his wife and that if he breathed one word to her the story would be all over town. I heard Jane's cries as she entered the house. She had kept the carriage waiting outside, and I had us both back in it almost at once. But the necessity of restraint the rest of that day upset Jane all the more afterwards."

Cassandra lifted her head at last, staring across the room at Mary's corpse. A faint wail came from upstairs.

"Henry is performing the baptismal rite. The baby won't last long, poor thing."

Tears came to Vanessa's eyes at last, whether for Jane, the dead mother, or her bruised and battered child she could not tell. She started to speak, but could not.

Finally she asked, "Where did you go?"

"To our brother Edward's house in Godmersham. There was an express out of Ludgate Hill direct to Canterbury. We reached Edward that evening and swore him to secrecy. I learned then that Lord Moira himself had called at the house earlier, but I dared not tell Jane. Edward ordered the servants to say that neither Jane nor I was at home to anyone."

"Why wouldn't *you* speak to Lord Moira?"

"Jane was adamant she could not marry him under any circumstances."

As she spoke Cassandra buried her face in her hands. Vanessa heard a stifled sob, and then Cassandra met her eyes for the first time.

"I shall never know if I did right. Lord Moira can only have called at Godmersham to attempt a reconciliation. Edward and I could have seen him at his inn – Edward suggested as much, and I forbade it. Jane had seemed so happy in Devonshire that first summer that I told her and his lordship they should marry at once, but afterwards I heard from Henry how stained his lordship's reputation was, how ruinous his finances. . . ."

Vanessa stifled her outrage as best she could. What use now to accuse Cassandra of robbing Jane of her chance for happiness?

Cassandra seemed to sense Vanessa's anger, and was quick to continue.

"Edward, bless him, gave Jane the quietest room in the furthest corner of the house. I nursed her for a week before she rose from her bed. A few days later we went to Hampshire, to stay with Alethea and Catherine Bigg at Manydown Park. It was at that time their brother Harris conceived an affection for my sister, which led to that dreadful event two months later."

Vanessa started to speak, but once again Cassandra hurried on.

"Then we returned to Bath."

Cassandra rose, tugging Vanessa from her seat.

"Come. Martha told me your story. If you are in danger from the Marquess we must hear from Henry as well."

"Wait," Vanessa cried, pulling Cassandra to a halt. In her own time Vanessa had read of Jane's accepting another suitor, then breaking the engagement the next day, but she had to be certain.

"What was the dreadful event at Manydown Park."

A spot of color rose in Cassandra's ashen cheeks. "Harris Bigg-Wither proposed to my sister that December. She was still too wounded to know how to reply. He insisted, and she acquiesced. When we retired that night she was beside herself."

A ghost of a smile crossed her mouth. "He was utterly unlike Lord Moira, graceless and clumsy, and unkind to his sisters. The first thing Jane said after she stopped crying was 'How may I accept a bear when I have loved a lion?'"

"And?"

"She retracted the next morning and we fled."

"And now," Cassandra continued, her grip firm on Vanessa's arm. "We shall find Henry."

Henry's story, thought Vanessa. The image of Henry in Portsmouth came to her mind's eye, the evasive, even surly expression on his face when his brothers had asked about Vanessa's accident on the rope ladder at the *Royal George*. What else did Henry know that he had so far concealed?

"Come quickly," said Cassandra. "Henry will have finished baptizing the child. He'll leave for Farnham as soon as he may. He always runs when there is grief in a house."

She flung open the bedroom door and they entered the hallway. Henry was above, halfway down the stairs from the upper floor. Even though Vanessa had seen him a few hours ago, she almost didn't recognize him. His cassock and collar gave him away, but he looked bone-weary and old, closer to seventy than fifty. When he saw his sister's determined face, he winced.

"You will sit with us, Henry, next to poor Mary's body. And in the name of the Lord you profess to serve, you will tell us the entire truth of your dealings with the Marquess of Hastings."

"Lord Hastings has no place in this house," muttered Henry as he came downstairs.

"Hold the door for us, Vanessa," said Cassandra, taking his arm.

Henry tried to withdraw, but Cassandra held on. A moment later the three of them were back on the straight wooden chairs by Mary Austen's deathbed, Henry closest to the corpse. Cassandra had turned that chair towards the other two, and now the women were side by side, facing him, with Mary a silent witness to the proceedings.

"Miss Horwood has reason to believe her life is in danger, and that you or the Marquess – or both of you – may be implicated."

"I?" replied Henry indignantly.

"Stop this, Henry," said Cassandra firmly. "You may wear the collar, but your authority is divine, not your own. No more hypocrisy."

Henry heaved a sigh. His whole demeanor changed, from arrogance to humility. He met Vanessa's eyes for an instant, and looked away.

"Did you cause the man to attack me on the path from Alton?" asked Vanessa.

"Certainly not," said Henry. "He threatened us both, and I had never seen him before."

"You had certainly seen him," Vanessa replied, "as he was on the fringes of the cricket match throughout the evening. But I accept your denial. What of the ladder on the *Royal George*?"

"I am at fault," said Henry quietly. "An evil impulse which has haunted me ever since."

"She could have been killed," cried Cassandra.

"I did not believe so," said Henry. "I wished her injury – I do not deny it – but I felt certain a fall would do no more than prevent her returning to the Marquess and delivering Edward's letter."

"Which returns us where we started, brother," replied Cassandra. "Your dealings with the Marquess may be of great consequence."

"Very well," said Henry. He sighed. "Would that Lord Moira had never been born. His man – the Marquess was Lord Moira then – came to me in 1813 with a proposal. I asked why his lordship had not sent Major James, with whom I had previously dealt. The man said there were particular reasons his lordship wanted to favor me, reasons to which James was not privy. When I told him I had no idea what he meant he said I should enquire no further."

"What was the proposal?" asked Vanessa.

"Lord Moira had accepted the governor-generalship of India and wanted to consolidate his debts. I was told he had authorized whatever compounded interest was necessary, and I was offered a brokerage fee on every new note I could place. I could even further compound upon the stated rates, and pocket the difference in addition to my fee."

"And?"

"I refused, of course. It would have been a fraud upon his lordship."

Henry gave a faint smile, apparently cheered by the recollection. "I believe they thought me so desperate that I should have agreed to anything."

"If you refused to participate, what are you afraid of?" asked Vanessa.

"I did not refuse to participate. I refused to participate in the *fraud*. I placed the notes on the best possible terms and accepted the brokerage fees."

"Which you spent," said Cassandra.

Henry's head went up. "Bankers must keep up appearances, sister. And my remittances as Receiver of Taxes for Oxfordshire were past due."

"What went wrong?" asked Vanessa.

"I held earlier notes of Lord Moira's to the amount of £6,500. Moira's man promised that these need not be compounded and would be repaid as they came due. But they were not. In the absence of their proceeds I had to withdraw from the Alton bank and assume some of its debts. By then my obligation to the Crown to remit the Oxfordshire taxes was pressing. I wrote to Major James, begging for something – anything - on account, but another man returned the letter to my office, a dangerous-looking man I had never seen before. He offered to redeem the notes I held at eight shillings in the pound."

"Surely there is nothing in that to shame *you*," said Cassandra.

Henry sighed. "I have not yet been entirely truthful. In the years before Lord Moira went to India I took advantage of his embarrassment to purchase bills at discounts far above the legal rate. Moira's man said his lordship would consider accounts settled if I accepted the offer at eight shillings, and that otherwise his lordship would charge me with usury. I protested I could not accept eight shillings in the pound, that so small a return would insure my bankruptcy. The man laughed in my face. Then he said if I ever tried to collect on the notes his lordship would see me dead."

Vanessa nodded. "And you believed that if I delivered Edward Knight's letter to Lord Hastings he would assume that meant you were trying to collect."

"Just so," Henry replied. He paused, eyes downcast. "I have come to believe that my bankruptcy was divine punishment, and that afterwards through God's mercy I was able to take holy orders. Perhaps I must now accept that my punishment is not yet complete." ·

"Do not presume to construe God's plan, Henry," said Cassandra. "Finish your story, and let Miss Horwood go."

"After my bankruptcy proceedings the Exchequer Court released his lordship's obligation for my notes on the ground that the discounts were indeed usurious. Thus my sureties – Edward and our uncle Leigh-Parrot – had to assume the debts and make the Crown whole. At that point the notes became Edward's, out of my control."

Henry's face had grown more animated as he spoke of his time as banker. Now it fell back into lines of worry and fatigue.

"And you dared not take Edward into your confidence," said Cassandra.

Henry nodded. "As long as the Marquess was in India I knew Edward would not attempt to collect. When I heard a fortnight ago that the Marquess was in London I thought once more of confiding in Edward, but the same report had his lordship leaving for the Continent in a matter of days."

Cassandra's face was grim. "And you instead prayed that Edward would not hear the news of the Marquess's return."

Henry raised his eyes to his sister's. "I should not have said that prayer."

"No," said Cassandra, rising and gesturing for Vanessa to do the same. "You should not."

CHAPTER XXXVI
1823

Vanessa caught the three o'clock coach from Alton, emerging at Charing Cross exhausted in mind and body. Throughout her journey she'd stared out the window, seldom seeing anything but visions of Mary Austen dying and her battered baby writhing in distress. Mary's screams and the baby's plaintive wails echoed in her mind.

When she'd tried to force her mind elsewhere it ended in one of two places: Will Lonsdale or the Marquess of Hastings. The more she thought of Lonsdale and what had happened in his carriage, the less she blamed him. She'd certainly led him on. She was as much at fault as he.

And then there was Lord Hastings. Had he betrayed her? If so, that seemed the worst of all. She knew she'd felt some kind of attachment to him, old as he was. A substitute father? That was part of it, but there'd been something more, on his side as well as hers.

In view of what Cassandra and Henry had told her there could be little doubt that Hastings had been behind her attempted abductions – or were they attempted murders? But why? And how could anyone – politician or otherwise – seem so honorable and at the same time be so duplicitous? Was there some clue to the Marquess's character in Henry's account of the 1816 bank collapse?

It was a relief to be able to get out of the coach at Charing Cross, to stretch her arms and legs, however discreetly. She lifted the shoulder strap of her reticule over her head to secure it, and accepted her portmanteau from the coachman. A light drizzle had begun to fall and what was left of the evening light was gloomy.

She'd been looking forward to the half-hour's walk to St. Paul's and the Bell Inn, but she wasn't sure she could face it in the rain.

It was only fifty yards to a hackney stand, but there appeared to be none waiting. When a voice behind her called "Carriage, ma'am?" she turned to accept.

Three men seized her. One clapped a hand to Vanessa's mouth to stifle any cry for help. Their carriage, a large landau, was alongside, both hoods up. As the men bundled her inside, she could see two more men on the driver's platform. Dark-skinned, handsome. She shuddered.

"What about her case?" called one of them.

"Leave it," said a voice Vanessa recognized. "She won't need it."

She managed to twist her head, and recognized the man who'd forced his way backstage at Winchester. His two companions were Indian. More of Lord Hastings's men.

The big man seemed even larger and more intimidating now, his smile frightening.

"Your lads thought themselves quite the bullies marching me out of that hall. What they didn't know was that all I needed was a close look at you, so's I could tell my mates what to watch for."

"But you could see me from the audience," said Vanessa, momentarily distracted.

The smile grew wider. "Not with these eyes," he replied, pointing to the layers of scar tissue around them.

"Where are you taking me?"

"Hush," said the man. "Almost there now, an' you'll find out."

The carriage pulled up outside a house that could have been anywhere. A man from the driver's platform jumped down and ran to the door. A moment later he returned with a companion, this one with a cape hiding his face. He climbed into the carriage, opposite Vanessa. Then he dropped the cape, leveling a pistol at Vanessa's chest.

"Keep her hands away from the shoulder-bag," he commanded.

It was Sir William Clifton.

Vanessa was so angry she almost spat at him. "I should have known. Lord Hastings has to finish whatever he starts, doesn't he?"

"Be quiet," said Clifton. He gestured to the big man.

"Get the bag off her shoulder and over here," said Clifton. "She has a gun in it."

Vanessa slumped in her seat as the big man pulled the bag away.

"Now will you say where you're taking me?" she asked him.

Clifton interrupted. "You need to answer some questions, my dear." The last two words were sarcastic, imitating the deep Irish voice of his employer.

"I don't know why I should," said Vanessa. "You're going to kill me anyway."

"You needn't die," said Clifton. "There's an East-Indiaman leaving the docks on the morning tide. You can be aboard, with enough money in your purse to live in Calcutta until Captain Lonsdale arrives."

Vanessa shook her head. "You wouldn't have thrown away my case if that were true."

With the hoods up and the window-shades down it was dark in the landau. The darkness matched her spirits. How could she have been so wrong about Hastings? She wanted to weep, but at the same time she was so angry she was tempted to attack her captors. She knew Hastings would never let her go to India. She might as well die fighting.

Clifton sensed something.

"Take one of her arms, each of you," he snapped at the men either side of her. Each linked an arm in hers, just above the elbow. It was like a parody of an arm-in-arm promenade, except that as the two men folded their own arms across their laps Vanessa's were drawn painfully tight.

She had no idea where they were going, or even in what direction. She tried to keep track of time but could not. She only knew that when the coach finally stopped it was fully dark outside. Moonlight gave her a glimpse of masts and she caught a whiff of fish and sewage. Then she was bundled into a warehouse.

"Upstairs," said Clifton.

Her two captors pushed her up a narrow staircase and into a small, bare office, slamming and bolting the door. She could hear descending footsteps and muffled voices, and then nothing at all. A dirty window allowed a murky view of a wasteland of worn-out and broken naval stores, but the window was nailed shut from the outside.

The ships she'd glimpsed a moment earlier were at least two hundred yards away, out of earshot even had the window been open. It was unlikely anyone might be closer, nor was there any way out of the office other than the door she'd come through.

Just as well the office is empty, she thought, wearily taking a seat on the floorboards. If there'd been a chair I'd probably try to break it over someone's head.

After a while her anger started to cool. He wants me to worry. He wants something from me, but I don't know what it is.

As Vanessa's worry edged towards despair Clifton finally entered, carrying a small chair in one hand and his pistol in the other. He stationed the big Englishman outside the office and took a seat, well clear of Vanessa and close to the door. He gazed imperiously down at her.

"This doesn't have to be difficult. I merely need to know exactly what you have told Lord Hastings."

"About what?" asked Vanessa.

"Don't be coy," Clifton snapped. "For all he tried to do for them, his lordship has had no communication with the Austens for nearly ten years. I made certain of that. But they've said something to you, and you've passed it along to his lordship. I need to know what it was."

Vanessa shook her head. "Lord Hastings betrayed them. He betrayed Jane, and if that wasn't enough he cheated Henry so badly that Henry went bankrupt. What could I possibly say to his lordship?"

Clifton sat up straighter, smiling in triumph.

"Did you know he was about to marry that useless jezebel? He was ready to give up everything and live on his estate in Wales. He told James it was the fondest wish of his heart." His smile twisted into something else, something close to rage. "But James, always a fool, told me."

Vanessa's stomach knotted. For a moment she was afraid she might be sick. Then she felt a surge of relief and even something close to triumph.

Clifton wasn't acting on behalf of Lord Hastings. He'd *betrayed* Hastings all those years ago when he was ready to marry Jane. And been betraying him ever since.

It was Clifton, not Hastings, who didn't intend to let her live. Clifton's expression was rapt. She looked out the window to keep from watching him, but some kind of spring coiled inside her had finally unwound. Her tears began to flow as he continued.

"I got to the hussy first. I knew she wouldn't believe any ill of his lordship, so I asked if she appreciated that his marrying her would entail financial ruin and the end of his political career. She defied me at first, but I shouted her down. When she gave way I told her she must leave London and that if she ever spoke a word about his lordship we would sue for defamation and destroy whatever reputation she and her family might pretend to. She was sobbing by then, or I might have said more."

"Surely that was enough," Vanessa whispered, staring at the floor.

"Yes," Clifton answered. "That was enough."

There was a noise of footsteps from below, a shout, and then silence.

"See what that is," called Clifton to the man at the door. "Report back."

A moment later Vanessa could hear returning footsteps. This time it was one of the Indians.

"All's well, sir. Someone at the wrong warehouse."

Clifton darted another glance at Vanessa. She had an intuition that he didn't want to see her, that in his mind she was already dead and disposed of. She tried to think rationally, to control her shivering body. She'd have managed it, if only she'd been able to stop her tears. They were dripping onto the floorboards now. She tried once more to control them, and shamed herself further by starting to sniffle.

Clifton's tone became reminiscent. "That fool of an Austen banker was my greatest success, at least until India."

"I don't know what you're talking about," said Vanessa.

"You don't need to know."

But Clifton couldn't resist. After a moment he continued.

"My wife was his lordship's ward. When I married her I discovered his lordship had mortgaged every penny of her inheritance. When he got the Indian appointment I promised him I would consolidate his debts, get him better terms and fewer creditors."

Vanessa tugged at her sleeve, trying like a child to wipe her nose on it.

"Look at me!" cried Clifton.

Vanessa said nothing, defiantly turning her head further towards the window. Clifton pulled his chair round, cutting off her view, his pistol aimed at her all the while.

"Listen carefully, Miss Horwood. This is how clever your friend Henry Austen is. When I approached him with an offer to make him the broker in refinancing his lordship's debts, he embraced it. He never asked a single question, not even about the ruinous discounts. He refused an offer to further compound the notes to his own advantage, and seemed to think this made him the paragon of all bankers. By the time I was finished with him I'd cleared twenty thousand, and set aside another fifty thousand in bearer notes which I could place upon our return from India."

Vanessa stole a glance at Clifton. His face was a mirror of conflicting emotions. Pride and self-satisfaction, certainly. But he was frightened as well. Was he talking to keep the fear at bay?

"His lordship was another fool," Clifton continued. "He'd sign anything, even notes for thousands, without looking. James spoiled him."

A deep voice from the doorway interrupted.

"That is one way to put it, Master Clifton."

Clifton whipped his pistol around but Lord Hastings was faster, shooting it out of his hand. With a cry of pain Clifton grasped his wrist, blood oozing through his fingers.

The deep voice softened. "Would you collect his weapon, Miss Horwood?"

Vanessa scurried on hands and knees to do so. When she looked up Hastings's face was like iron, his pistol firmly trained on Clifton.

"I should say that Major James was honest, as I now know you are not. And it was truly ungentlemanlike not to offer Miss Horwood a handkerchief for her tears."

"Damn you," choked Clifton.

Hastings pulled a large cloth from his pocket and held it out to Vanessa, keeping his distance from Clifton as she took it.

"I think you had better tie off his arm so he doesn't bleed to death. At least not till we have the rest of his story."

"Get away from me," spat Clifton as Vanessa approached. And then, to Hastings, "How did you find me? And where are my men?"

"*Your* men?" said Hastings. "Did you think any of them would oppose me? From the moment Miss Horwood left my house they were under instructions to report any orders they received from you."

He bowed to Vanessa, but his eyes remained on Clifton.

"I am sorry, my dear, that we did not prevent your abduction. Once I became aware of Clifton's activities I gambled, quite inexcusably, that he would boast to my men of his purposes before bringing you to any harm."

Vanessa answered for the first time, her voice breaking. "I forgive you."

Hastings addressed Clifton, his voice cold. "You will sit still and pull back your sleeve for Miss Horwood. Miss Horwood is to keep her body well clear, so that if you make a single untoward move I shall have a clear shot at your heart."

Vanessa followed orders, rolling up the handkerchief and tying a tourniquet on Clifton's forearm. Then she backed away, keeping her distance from both men.

"And now," continued Hastings, more mildly. "We shall have the rest of this most interesting tale."

"I've nothing to say," muttered Clifton.

"Oh, but you have. I believe I have you entirely to thank for leaving India in disgrace. And only this morning I finally learned that my debts, which you had me believe I was paying down these last ten years, are treble the amount they were then. You may count it an article of my affection for your wife that I do not leave your dead body out there amongst the rest of the waste."

Clifton sneered. "You would never do so."

"Do not count on it, sir," snapped Hastings. "Continue!"

Clifton started to shrug, then winced as the movement reached his arm.

"There's little enough to tell. Once you trusted me it was the easiest thing in the world to co-opt your debts to my own ends. But I could not negotiate notes from India. As long as James was alive he redeemed them in strict order of issue. This was my only chance."

"For what?"

Clifton didn't answer, and after a moment Vanessa spoke.

"He told me he had fifty thousand pounds in notes you signed, my lord, ready to sell."

"Does he now?" said Hastings. "No doubt he will be pleased to return them to me."

Clifton raised his head. "They are nowhere you can touch them."

Hastings shook his head. "Then they will be no use to you either."

"But they will," Clifton insisted. "You were Governor-General of India for ten years. You must get an award from the King and a pension from the East India Company. As long as these are in prospect your promissory notes are worth at least twelve shillings in the pound."

"Ah," said Hastings.

There was a long silence, which Clifton finally broke.

"Well?"

Hastings smiled. "I owe you no reply, sir."

He backed towards the door, still covering Clifton with his pistol. Vanessa knew he was about to call to his men below and then the rest of the truth would be lost.

"Wait!" she cried.

Hastings paused.

"There is more to his story than your debts, my lord," she said.

"Surely not," replied Hastings.

"You had not arrived when he told me he was responsible for ending your engagement to Jane Austen."

For a moment she thought Hastings would break down. His hand on the pistol shook, and when she glanced at Clifton she saw cold calculation in the man's eyes. She tightened her grip on Clifton's gun.

"What of this, sir?" said Hastings, his voice hoarse. And then, more evenly. "I perceive what you are thinking. Do not presume to move even a finger, or you are a dead man."

Clifton licked his lips, eyes darting around the room. He opened his mouth to speak, but Hastings cut him off.

"No. I shall not hear you speak of Jane Austen. Even her name in your mouth would offend me. But this banking business affects my wife and children. I shall have the rest of it."

Clifton repeated, "I've nothing more to say."

Vanessa jumped as Hastings's pistol discharged. Clifton cringed, then – evidently realizing he had not been hit – rose to his feet.

"Hold, sir," said Hastings, taking a step back. "I assure you my weapon is not discharged."

Vanessa had raised Clifton's pistol, ready to shoot if necessary. It was a single-shot, not much larger than her own. But Hastings was holding the gun he'd talked about at Manton's shop, the one with the rotating chamber. Clifton saw that too, and his face was pale as he resumed his seat, once again clutching his wounded wrist.

Hastings continued. "You abducted Miss Horwood to further your own schemes. I have every confidence she would have refused to speak even had she anything you needed, which I doubt."

He paused. "But you, sir, will speak, or my next bullet will splinter your leg. I shall not kill you, but when I am finished you will wish I had."

Vanessa shuddered at the cold rage in his voice. Evidently it had its effect, because Clifton began to chatter.

"All I had to do was change a few amounts and rates on your promissory notes to allow myself the difference. I made twenty thousand then and you signed new notes for me for another fifty. Austen acted as broker so my name never came into it."

"I signed no notes for Austen," said Hastings.

"You did," said Clifton, "but they had other men's names on them."

"So you retired debts upon which I was paying eight and nine percent, and substituted notes at twelve."

Clifton's smile came and went, like a nervous tic. "More than twelve. But Austen and a few others kept some older notes, believing they would collect in 1814 and 1815."

"This I remember. I sent money to James, with direct orders to settle them."

Clifton's smile was back. "I intercepted those orders, and the money. My agent offered Austen and the others eight shillings in the pound. They refused."

"Your agent," said Hastings. "Presumably the colossus we've taken below."

Clifton said nothing. Vanessa backed against the wall, needing its support before she could speak. She held Clifton's pistol tight, with both hands.

"*You* were Lord Hastings's man Henry spoke of." She turned to Hastings. "Henry Austen confirms this story. He called the offer in 1816 'unexampled treachery.'"

"And so it was," said Hastings. "But none of my own."

His eyes returned to Clifton. "I have heard enough, except one particular. You have embezzled notes as well as money which is neither yours nor mine. Where is it now?"

Clifton clamped his mouth shut, and Hastings leveled his pistol. Clifton looked up, meeting Hastings's eyes for an instant before turning his head away. He seemed to sag in his chair, and the defiance in his voice was gone when he answered.

"Here in London."

"How much in all?"

Clifton kept his eyes on the far wall. "Fifty or sixty thousand, including your notes."

"Which?" Hastings snapped.

"Sixty."

"And how much were you paid to blind me to your fraud in India?"

"I shared in the profit."

"Where is that?"

"What's left is in Calcutta."

"Was Major James ever part of these frauds?"

"No. I knew he would never participate."

Hastings raised his voice, calling to his men below. As they mounted the stairs Hastings spoke once more to Clifton, slumped in his chair.

"You will deliver my notes, which we shall destroy as they have no value. And we shall transfer the other ten thousand to my solicitor, along with authority over and the precise whereabouts of your accounts in Calcutta. Some of that money will support your wife and children. The rest goes to my creditors.

"In the meantime you will empty your pockets for Miss Horwood. I am told your man abandoned her entire equipage at Charing Cross. She will need replacements."

Clifton hesitated. "Empty them, sir," repeated Hastings. "Inside out."

Hastings's eyebrows went up as more than five hundred pounds of banknotes emerged.

"I cannot take all this, my lord," cried Vanessa.

Hastings smiled. "Perhaps not. Shall we share it equally, as we did that note of Captain Lonsdale's at White's?"

"It is still too much."

By now three of Hastings's men were entering the room, and it was easier for Vanessa to give in than continue her protests.

When she surveyed the new arrivals she saw that one was the very image of the young Indian man who'd confronted her and died in Alton. She recoiled in surprise.

The young man bowed. When he spoke he had the same indeterminate accent as the dead man.

"I am sorry if I frighten you, Miss. May I ask why?"

"Do you have a brother?"

"I do."

Hastings turned. "Your assailant?"

Vanessa nodded.

Hastings's voice was matter-of-fact. "Lonsdale did well to take him."

He took the young man's arm and walked him to the doorway, speaking quietly. The man tensed for a moment, and then crossed the room to Clifton.

"You sent my brother without his lordship's authority."

Clifton didn't look up.

The young man turned to Hastings. "May I kill him?"

Hastings shook his head. "He will live if he does as he's told. I shall not deprive my ward of her children's father. But you may go with him when he returns to India, and if he fails to produce his money you may kill him then."

"Very well, my lord."

"And if he fails to co-operate in the meantime you may damage him as you see fit."

The man bowed. "Thank you, my lord."

At a nudge from his captor Clifton shuffled downstairs, Hastings and his men close behind. Vanessa, realizing she was about to be left alone, quickly followed.

Hastings was already interrogating Clifton's big accomplice, having retrieved Vanessa's reticule in the process.

He turned to her. "If we give him to the constables you will have to testify that he kidnapped you."

Vanessa shook her head. "He never harmed me."

"He says he has taken none of your belongings."

Vanessa nodded. "And I'm sure he abandoned my valise on Clifton's orders."

Clifton's barouche was still outside the warehouse, along with Hastings's old phaeton. The men who had been among Vanessa's kidnappers were there too, looking uncomfortable. Hastings ordered them all into the barouche.

"The phaeton is ours," said Hastings. "Try to make yourself comfortable for a moment longer."

Even though the carriage was Hastings's familiar phaeton, Vanessa wasn't ready to climb into it alone, especially not with its hood up and interior dark. She stayed where she was, as Hastings turned to the dead man's brother.

"Do not let Clifton out of your sight until you are at sea. He will work his passage when his arm heals. You and two others will have a cabin. There and back again. When you are safely gone I shall speak to Lady Clifton."

The young man bowed again, and Hastings took Vanessa's arm.

"Come, child," he said. "It has been a long and unpleasant day. The Marchioness will be glad of your company."

A coachman rode postillion on the lead horse, giving the two passengers privacy during the drive from the east London docks to Campden Hill. It wasn't long before Vanessa's questions overpowered her.

"What made you suspect Clifton?"

Hastings stretched his long legs, pushing himself into a corner of the seat where he could look at her only half sideways.

"James never liked him. That should have been enough, but it wasn't, even though I had my own doubts.

"It was ill manners that betrayed him. Clifton should have been with us for supper the night you were attacked near my house. In twenty years I had never known him fail to attend upon an invitation he'd accepted. He had to have been desperate."

His face settled into repose, its lines deep and melancholy. They passed the next few minutes in silence, but as they approached the ancient Tower of London Hastings spoke again.

"You must wonder what happened after Clifton committed his first act of treachery. In 1802, when he spoke those abominable lies to Jane."

"Yes," said Vanessa. "Please tell me."

Vanessa knew Lord Hastings was about to revisit events he might have spent twenty years trying to forget. From then on she knew better than to interrupt.

CHAPTER XXXVII
1802

Moira had struggled to break free of the mob, to reach Jane before the hackney-carriage drove her away. But he'd seen bottles passing from hand to hand and knew from long experience that such a crowd could turn violent at any time.

Most of it was still in Pall Mall, jostling to make the right turn into St. James's Street. As Jane's carriage pulled away towards Piccadilly, Moira knew it was now or never for his escape. If the crowd reached St. James's Place, blocking the way from Moira House, he would never get his horse past them. And without a horse he would never catch Jane.

He edged past the vanguard, turning to raise both arms.

"Hear me!"

To his relief those directly in front of him stopped. Gradually the crowd settled.

"Thank you lads and" – he spotted an overdressed and gaily-painted woman among them, caught her eye, and bowed – "and ladies. I shall not forget your hospitality this morning. Nor" – he raised his voice – "nor shall the government."

A roar of approval came in reply.

"But now," Moira shouted. "Let us disperse. We've been up all night."

Three or four men had already shown themselves leaders, and it was one of these who'd recognized Moira as he emerged from the Palace. Moira gestured to him, digging in his pocket for money.

"It won't go far," he said, handing it over. "But buy what bread you can and see it fairly dispersed, would you?"

The man nodded. "It'll do, my lord." Then he grinned. "It's a start." He turned away, raising his arms in the same gesture Moira had used a moment earlier.

"Let's go! Lord Moira is buying us breakfast."

In the ragged cheer that followed Moira rounded the corner towards his house. Once he knew he was out of sight he began to run. Soon he was on his horse, galloping across Piccadilly and through Mayfair towards Henry Austen's house the far side of Oxford Street.

A maidservant answered the door.

"Tell Miss Jane Austen that Lord Moira begs an audience."

The woman bobbed a curtsey. "This way, please, your lordship."

"I shall find my own way. You find Miss Austen."

There was a dining room on one side of the entry hall and a small drawing room opposite. Moira chose the latter, impatiently striking his boot with his riding crop as he paced the floor.

It was nearly ten minutes before a small, middle-aged woman entered. She was overdressed in the latest French style and positively simpering.

"My lord Moira," she declared. *"C'est vraiment un honneur."*

Moira would have none of it. "You are Mrs. Henry Austen?"

She curtseyed again. "Yes, my lord. Please forgive my husband. He is in bed, *avec un mal de tête.*"

"Speak English, woman," Moira roared. "Where is his sister?"

Mrs. Austen seemed about to cry. "I thought she was with *your* sister, my lord."

The maidservant came to Mrs. Austen's rescue.

"Begging your lordship's pardon. Cook tells me that both Miss Jane and Miss Cassandra left, not ten minutes since. They gave her this letter."

Moira snatched it from her hand. It was addressed to Lady Charlotte Rawdon. In his heart he knew it was for him, but he could not open it in front of these people.

"Did the cook see them go?"

"Yes, your lordship."

"Get her."

According to the cook Jane had kept the hackney-coach waiting when she arrived at the house. She'd run to the upstairs sitting-room, sobbing, the cook believed. Five minutes later she and Cassandra departed, each holding a portmanteau and with Cassandra's free arm supporting Jane, who had covered her face.

"Did they say where they were going?"

"No, your lordship."

Moira glared down at Mrs. Austen. "Will your husband know?"

She shook her head. "He's seen no-one all morning, my lord."

She looked so much like a beaten puppy that Moira took pity.

"I beg you will forgive my manners, ma'am. I have been in the Lords all night, and I. . . and my sister had counted on spending the morning with Miss Austen."

Mrs. Austen's face lit up, as though a world of gossip lay before her.

"You are here on your sister's account solely, my lord?"

Moira did his best. He had no time for more games.

"My sister is fond of Miss Jane Austen. If you would be kind enough to give me her direction, my sister will write to her."

"They spoke of visiting another brother. But I do not believe they said which one."

Moira was about to explode. Every passing minute put Jane closer to a coaching inn. But where?

"Is it more likely Hampshire, or Kent?"

"Indeed, my lord. It must be one or the other. I know that *I* should choose Kent."

In itself this was almost enough for Moira to choose Hampshire, but from what he knew of Jane's travels Kent did seem the more logical choice. Would Mrs. Austen have a coach timetable? Moira decided against asking. He'd already shown too much of his own interest to this scatterbrained woman.

He bowed. "Thank you, ma'am. Please convey to your husband my hopes for a speedy recovery."

Mrs. Austen gave a deep and elegant curtsey. "It is I who thank your lordship. I know Mr. Austen will appreciate your kindness and condescension."

Moira knew that the most likely coaching inn for East Kent was the Swan with Two Necks, in Cheapside. Its coaches went all directions; indeed it had been his point of departure for Exeter the year before.

He'd have to ride hard to have a hope of reaching the inn before Jane's hackney carriage, but he must read her letter first. He tore it open as he stood close to his horse, its familiar animal scent soothing his nerves.

His intuition had been right: the enclosure was addressed to him. There were spots of moisture where the paper was still damp from her tears, and in one or two places the ink had run.

My Lord, (it read)

I have these past several months anticipated a conclusion to yr. Affairs that would enable yr. Ldshp. to accomplish the Object of our Accord – I shall not say of yr. Promise. I attribute yr. Ldshp.'s disinclination to wound me the reason you have not yrself explained to me the impossibility of this Object.

I beg you will consult yr. Ldshp.'s own understanding for the reasons of my Departure.

Do not doubt my lasting Affection, or that I shall remain,
Eternally, yr. Ldshp.'s sincere Well-wisher,
J. Austen

All too soon Moira learned there'd been no sign of two young ladies at the Swan with Two Necks, and that the only coach for East Kent had departed two hours since.

But by now his heart was firm in its conviction that Jane was headed for her brother Edward's house in Godmersham. He hired a rider to return his horse to Moira House and rode post for the southeast, changing mounts in Rochester and Sittingbourne. He approached her brother's village in the late afternoon.

The main road to Godmersham House curved past small clusters of trees. In the distance the house was larger and handsomer than Moira had expected: red brick, an older three-storey centre flanked by matching two-storey additions.

The fifty-mile ride had left him bone-tired and feeling like a fool. His horse was as tired as he and he finally let her walk at her own pace. Jane could not possibly have arrived, even if she had climbed aboard an express directly from her hackney carriage. Edward Austen was not at home either: training with his militia near Ashford, said his servants. As far as they knew his sisters were not expected, but they were, of course, welcome at any time.

Moira asked directions to an inn and left a note for Jane begging her to send for him. The innkeeper evicted a man and wife from his best room, found a hostler to take Moira's horse, and ordered dinner brought to his room. Moira fell into bed soon after dark.

But he could not sleep. 'Consult your own understanding,' Jane had written. 'Do not doubt my lasting affection, or that I shall remain, eternally, your sincere well-wisher.' The last part was her way of saying farewell, but he tortured himself with the first.

For the past year he'd been distracted by his own vanity, by the role he'd played in the peace settlement with France and in the subsequent negotiations with the ministry. All the while he'd continued to hope that the Prince's debts would somehow be repaid.

By now he was out of bed and pacing. He should have known a Tory ministry would find a way to keep Whig peers hamstrung. Even more astute was the way the ministry managed to show its disapproval of those who helped the Prince keep to his dissolute ways. 'Value presumed received upon endorsement' meant that every wealthy man who'd lent the Prince money would never see a penny of it returned.

What Jane had called Moira's 'understanding' had been his own mean self-service. She'd been patient for a year and a half. He should never have asked more of her.

Had he missed signs that her patience was at an end? Only yesterday she'd seen him give James instructions to start selling estates and pay off his creditors. This final betrayal over the Prince's debts had given Moira, irrevocably, the courage to leave London and abandon all his pretensions. He and Jane would become modest country dwellers. He'd serve his country as a soldier or parliamentarian no further than it demanded.

And now she'd left him. He was not surprised when a letter came to the inn the next afternoon, stating that Miss Jane Austen was not at home. Nor were his subsequent letters answered.

CHAPTER XXXVIII
1823

Vanessa opened her eyes. She'd been absorbed in the rich strains of Lord Hastings's voice as he recounted the story of Jane Austen's lost romance. He was watching her, smiling. It was a wistful smile, but she could tell he was more at peace with himself.

"Now I know what happened," he said. His tone was different, less ruminative and more decisive. Vanessa knew if she had any more questions she must ask them now. Once they reached Hastings's family it would be too late. And once he left England she would never see him again.

"Where is Major James now?"

"Dead. Poor James! Some of my suspicions lingered after Clifton's accusations. In my heart I knew James was loyal, but my mind – my treacherous mind – continued to doubt."

He sighed. "When I finally accepted that Jane was gone I told James I wished to further the interests of her family in every way I could. From that day on I believe he never accepted a commission from the Austen bank, and it was James who gave me news of Jane's sailor brothers, one of whose careers, at least, I was able to advance.

"Nor did I ever pay James what I owed him myself, taking Clifton's word that he was compensated elsewhere. After a time I got him promoted, and my solicitor sent odd sums for the benefit of his family while I was in India. But it was never enough, and now he is gone."

Hastings lapsed into silence. The carriage was approaching Knightsbridge when he abruptly straightened.

"I am a selfish old man."

"No," said Vanessa firmly. "You are not."

"Indeed I am," he replied. "I should be calculating how best to repair my fortunes for the benefit of my wife and children. Instead I find myself thinking of what I lost twenty years ago."

"You still love her, don't you?"

"More than I can say. She waited longer than she ought, and Clifton struck at the precise moment I was ready to marry and retire to Wales."

"Why did he have to know your plans? He said James told him everything."

"James acted upon my instruction." He shook his head. "I cannot imagine what Clifton said to her."

"He told me," said Vanessa. "He said the marriage would ruin your finances and destroy your political career."

For an instant a gas streetlamp illuminated the carriage. Hastings's eyes were blazing.

"It could only have been that. He appealed to the one thing that could possibly have driven her away, her generosity of spirit. No wonder she never replied to my letters."

Vanessa felt a sympathetic anger. "I'm surprised you let him live."

Hastings smiled. "I am not your Captain Lonsdale, my dear. What purpose is served by Clifton's death? He returns to India without a patron and, I trust, penniless. Let him die in obscurity, just as I shall."

"What of the award he mentioned? And the pension?"

"There will be nothing of the kind. The King and the East India Company have spoken. I shall take my family to Germany next week, out of reach of my creditors. Including, I regret to say, Jane's brother Mr. Edward Knight. He will be too far down the list at my solicitor's office to receive anything but a pittance.

"At some point I expect the ministry will be embarrassed enough to offer me a sinecure somewhere, but my career, indeed my life, is over."

His face once again settled into its sorrowful lines, but after a moment he turned back to her.

"I am impertinent to ask, my dear, but will you marry Lonsdale?"

Vanessa shook her head. "I am finished with him, my lord."

"Please accept my congratulations. I admire him greatly, but you deserve someone more kind."

Vanessa tried to smile, but could not. She thought she had no more tears, but her eyes filled.

"Someone like you, my lord."

Hastings waved a hand in dismissal, turning his head to look at the shops along the pavement. Were there tears in his eyes too?

He reached into his sleeve, then recalled himself.

"I wasted my handkerchief on that villain, and now I have need of it."

They had turned into the lane to Campden Hill when he spoke again.

"You remind me of Jane more than I can say, Miss Horwood. You are more fierce, as befits the frontierswoman you are. And you are nothing alike in looks. But there is something. . . ."

"You need not say it, my lord."

He smiled. "Do you suppose she modeled that improvident baronet on me, in her last novel?"

"Sir Walter Elliot in *Persuasion*," she replied. "Never believe it. I see your character only in her heroes. And I'm certain she did too, however painfully things ended for you both."

"I suppose if she had married she would never have turned to writing."

"We'll never know," said Vanessa. She smiled back at him, but Lord Hastings had turned away.

HISTORICAL AFTERWARD

The initial inspiration for this novel came from reading Brian Southam's *Jane Austen and the Navy*. Southam quotes a letter from Admiral Lord Nelson responding to the Earl of Moira's request that command of a frigate be given to a little-known junior captain named Francis Austen, son of a Hampshire clergyman.

Moira's letter does not survive, and nothing came of his request. Nelson's reply, dated 30 March 1805, is in the Hastings archive at the Huntington Library. It is carefully and diplomatically evasive, too good not to quote:

> A frigate would have been better calculated to have given Capt.
> Austin *{sic.}* a fortune out of the Medn. than coming under my
> command, where nothing is to be got except the French fleet. . . .

It goes on to treat of other matters and then, in a postscript, returns to Francis:

> You may rely upon all attention in my power to Capt. Austin. I
> hope to see him alongside a French 80 gun ship and he cannot
> be better placed than in the *Canopus*. . . . Capt. A. I knew a lit-
> tle of before; he is an excellent young man.

What connection could there have been between Jane Austen's sailor brother and a celebrity like Moira? In the end, as is often the way of such things, the answer to that question became little more than a footnote to my story. There were richer areas of historical uncertainty, involving Jane Austen and Lord Moira themselves.

Jane Austen moved with her family to Bath in the spring of 1801. She attended balls at the Assembly Rooms and began to make friends, notably with a Mrs. Chamberlayne with whom she went on long walks. For about three weeks in May, Jane's letters teased her sister Cassandra with tales of a dalliance with one Mr. Evelyn. In the final passage of the last surviving letter from this period, Jane reports that Mr. Evelyn took her for an "Airing in the very bewitching Phaeton & four. . . to the top of Kingsdown." Within a few days of this airing, at the beginning of June 1801, to quote Jane's biographer David Nokes, "Jane Austen went missing." (*Jane Austen*, 1995, p. 239).

Jane's family destroyed all her correspondence for the next three-and-a-half years. All we get are a couple of secondhand sightings. The Austen family, as Deirdre LeFay puts it (*Jane Austen: A Family Record*, 2004, p. 135) "had been thinking of going to Sidmouth in the coming summer [*i.e.* 1801], and in the absence of any evidence to the contrary they presumably fulfilled this plan."

It was during this Sidmouth visit, according to a family tradition supposed to be based on a story told by Cassandra, that Jane was observed to be in love. The first scholarly appraisal of this possible love affair was offered by the pioneering Jane Austen scholar R.W. Chapman (*Facts and Problems*, 1948). More recent treatments are Park Honan's (*Jane Austen: Her Life*, 1996, pp. 185-186), and David Nokes's (pp. 242-245), the last of these suggesting that Cassandra's account is not to be relied upon. I have, therefore, made my own use of it.

It is also worth noting that in December 1802 Jane first accepted and then retracted her acceptance of an offer of marriage by Harris Bigg-Wither, of a Hampshire family Jane had known since childhood. There are any number of reasons Jane might have behaved as she did, and in the absence of historical evidence I suggest one possibility.

Could Jane herself have played a role in Lord Moira's determination to advance the interests of her two sailor brothers, for whom he wrote letters in 1803, 1804, and 1805? And could Moira's connections with the Austen family have somehow affected his own later career?

It is, of course, monstrously improbable that Moira-in-disguise went to Bath's Assembly Rooms in 1801 and fell in love with Jane Austen. But however farfetched such a romance might seem – between a poor, Tory clergyman's daughter and a famous Whig peer – the history of the English Regency is filled with even stranger romances, and indeed marriages.

Deirdre Le Faye, in the biographical index to her edition of Jane Austen's *Letters* (1995, p. 521), states that the real owner of the phaeton Jane rode in that spring was William-Glanvill Evelyn (1734-1813), sometime sheriff of Kent. This Mr. Evelyn was well-known as an equestrian – a 1799 letter by Jane declares he "has all his life thought more of Horses than anything else" – but in 1801 he was approaching seventy and notably infirm. Perhaps he had the energy to take a young woman out in a sporty four-horse carriage. I chose to believe he did not.

Le Faye cites another Mr. Evelyn more to my purpose, a John Evelyn of Marlborough Buildings, Bath. There was an earlier, more famous John Evelyn as well, contemporary of Samuel Pepys, who published enough books that the educated and urbane Moira might well have had some in his substantial library, perhaps even the 1661 *Fumifugium: or, the Inconveniencie of the Aer and Smoak of London Dissipated.*

If Jane's connection to Moira is fanciful, which I do not dispute, her brother Henry's connection to Moira was genuine and long-lasting. Henry, as Brian Southam suggests, was the "likely route" to Moira's patronage for Jane's two sailor brothers. By 1801 or thereabouts Henry was "established as an Army and Navy Agent and on his way to becoming an established banker." (Southam, p. 93).

Early on Henry became one of Moira's many lenders, and continued so until the latter left for India. The correspondence of Moira's confidential man of business Charles James, also in the Hastings archive at the Huntington Library, documents the banking relationship and also shows that in addition to the unproductive letter to Lord Nelson on behalf of Francis Austen, Moira more successfully intervened with the Navy on behalf of Jane's younger brother Charles, who in 1804 received his first command, a sloop out of Bermuda, thanks to Moira's efforts.

In 1816 Henry's bank collapsed and he became personally bankrupt, blaming much of his trouble on what he called the "unexampled treachery" of Lord Moira. It appears, however, that Moira's debt to the Austen bank at the time of its failure amounted to no more than £6,500. By my reckoning £6,500 in 1816 is equivalent to something around £450,000 in modern money – a very large sum, but one unlikely to make or break a bank unless that bank was already in trouble, as the historical record shows Henry's to have been. It is also recorded that Moira partly paid down this debt by sending a £2,000 draft from India in 1819.

Henry Austen's high life and subsequent bankruptcy prompted different views among his family. Southam (p.333) quotes some affectionate reminiscences by nieces, but adds that later generations of Austens

> examined [Henry] through a less rosy glass, discerning an 'almost exasperating buoyancy of spirits which no misfortunes could depress and

no failures damp. . .' a 'sanguiness' which must have been particularly galling to those of the family whose savings went down with him, not least his uncle James Leigh-Parrot who lost £10,000 and his brother Edward, who lost twice that sum.

I confess that I too find Henry exasperating, but I should add that although my account of his bank failures and personal bankruptcy is strictly historical, there is *no* historical evidence that he ever took brokerage fees for placing Moira's debt, or was threatened by Moira's agents, or behaved anything less than gallantly towards women.

Nevertheless I believe Henry's character deserves a more cold-blooded assessment than it has generally received. One modern writer, Robert Bearman, in "Henry Austen and the Cubbington Living," remarks that some of Henry's post-bankruptcy correspondence "is worldly and opportunist and certainly could not have been penned by one of his sister's fictional heroes." (*Persuasions* 10 (1988), p. 22). I agree, and would only add that there *is* one Jane Austen character of whom this correspondence of Henry puts me in mind: Mr. Collins, from *Pride and Prejudice*.

Jane Austen's own character is much-debated, but well enough documented in her novels and letters as well as by many biographers that I need not elaborate upon it here. I have given my own impression of her in this novel, and can only say that I tried to be as faithful as I was able, using her and other historical characters' own words whenever context allowed. For readers who recall her dedication of *Emma* to the Prince Regent I note that only a couple of years earlier, in a letter to Martha Lloyd, Jane wrote that "I hate [him]" and that she could "hardly forgive" the Princess of Wales "for calling herself 'attached & affectionate' to a Man whom she must detest." (*Letters*, p. 208). But both sister Cassandra and brother Henry opined that the "permission" Jane received to dedicate *Emma* to the Prince "must," as David Nokes puts it, "be considered as a form of command." (Nokes, p. 468). Reluctantly, Jane acquiesced.

I also tried to be true to the personalities and whereabouts of the rest of her family. All her brothers spent time at Chawton House in the early 1820s, and Edward was certainly visiting from Godmersham at the time I put him there. His letter to Lord Hastings, quoted in my story, is genuine and dated from Chawton House. It survives in two copies in the Hastings archive at the Huntington, the second copy containing a cover note surmising that Hastings must not have received the first.

Mary Austen, Francis's first wife, died in childbirth in July 1823 at the age of 39, not, according to the *Hampshire Chronicle*, at Chawton where I put her, but at Government House, Gosport. Her obituary read, in part: "Her sweetness of temper, gentle manners, and affectionate disposition had endeared her to all who knew her." Her infant son Cholmeley clung to life until early 1824.

Francis Rawdon-Hastings, ultimately Marquess of Hastings and Earl of Rawdon in the British peerage as well as Earl of Moira in the Irish, died in office as governor of Malta in 1826, the sinecure he anticipated at the end of my story. He attracted many contradictory assessments during his lifetime. I accurately quote an 1803 letter from the Prince of Wales, afterwards Prince Regent and (from January 1820) King George IV, calling Moira the friend "to whom I have ever through a long series of years unveiled the most secret thoughts of my heart and soul." I am equally accurate in the Prince's treatment of his friend. The Prince borrowed at least a hundred thousand pounds from Moira, repaying not a penny, and consistently subverted Moira's legislative and political efforts. Although the Regent responded to the chorus of praise following Moira's successful campaigns in the Nepalese Wars of 1814-1816 by elevating him to become Marquess of Hastings, once the Regent became King he denied Hastings further recognition and financial reward, essentially hanging him out to dry at the conclusion of his long and arduous service in India.

By the time I have Moira meet Jane in 1801 he had already contracted debts above and beyond his massive liabilities on account of the Prince. Not least of these came from the blank checks he left at his country estate, Donington Park in Leicestershire, for the use of aristocratic French émigrés who were refugees from Robespierre's Terror and its guillotine.

Moira is bound to have hoped that steps taken by Parliament to alleviate the Prince's debts would result in at least some repayments. None came, but I cannot prove my story's allegation that this was a result of maneuvering by a Tory ministry in order to deprive Whig lenders of their just deserts.

I am probably unfair to Flora, Countess of Loudoun and Marchioness of Hastings, in imagining her husband to have been in love with Jane Austen before his marriage in 1804. Moira was by all accounts a loyal and devoted husband, but it is reasonable to point out that the Countess of Loudoun was rich when she married Moira, and that the most Moira's sole modern biographer can say of the marriage is that "the two lived together in peace and amity." (Nelson, *Francis Rawdon-Hastings*, 2005, p. 133). In his last year in Malta, Moira – he was Lord Hastings by then, of course – left instructions that upon his death his right hand should be severed so it could be buried with his wife in England. She outlived him by nearly twenty years.

Moira's debts were so large by the time of his marriage that his wife's wealth could do little to alleviate them. Although he knew in 1813 that he was going into a kind of exile as Governor General of India and Commander-in-Chief of its armed forces, he hoped he would at least gain the wealth of his predecessors in those posts. Things went wrong from the beginning when the Prince Regent characteristically betrayed Moira by declining to insist on the latter's receiving the pay for both positions. Parliament did, however, vote him £60,000 when he became hero of the hour after his successful military campaigns in the Nepalese Wars, and – significantly – Parliament made this award off-limits to the newly-elevated Marquess of Hastings's creditors.

But that was all he got, even after further successes in the Third Anglo-Maratha War, the annexation of Singapore in 1819, and initiating highly-successful educational and public works improvements in Delhi, Calcutta, and elsewhere. These last, which greatly improved the lot of the Indian population at large, were the achievements which gave the Marquess the greatest pride.

Hastings left the Governor-Generalship of India under a cloud at the end of 1822, his reputation tainted by apparent involvement in a series of fraudulent banking transactions perpetrated by Palmer and Co. on the Nizam of Hyderabad. This bank had an active partner in Lord Hastings's protégé, Sir William Rumbold, who was characterized in an early edition of Debrett's *Peerage* as Hastings's "chamberlain." I have extrapolated from this event in Rumbold's life to fashion my fictional character Sir William Clifton, but I do not impute any of Clifton's traits or actions here to the historical Rumbold.

In 1809 Rumbold married Lord Moira's ward, Harriet Elizabeth Parkyns. I have borrowed Harriet's first name and the fact that her trust fund went into Moira's keeping upon her father's death. Everything else about her is my own invention.

The fraud perpetrated by Palmer and Co. left the Nizam of Hyderabad a million pounds in debt at a colossal annual interest rate: various sources suggest either eighteen or twenty-five percent. Something similar must have happened to Hastings's own finances. He consistently wrote of his relative frugality in Calcutta and his remittances from earnings to pay down his debts in England. But he left England in 1813 some two hundred thousand pounds in debt, and upon his return ten years later owed, according to his biographer, as much as the Nizam: nearly a million pounds. (Nelson, pp. 169-170.) The Marquess of Hastings's return to England was unique in the annals of British governors of India. He came home poorer than he'd left.

I have also done my best to be true to the peripheral aspects of Moira's life in London, from his residences in St. James's and Campden Hill, to the old soldiers he helped and the merchants with whom he dealt. My reference to Thomas Dermody is roughly accurate: no one is quite sure where he lived in the summer of 1801, but he had previously lodged with another Bond Street bookseller. And Cooper's millinery shop at 113 New Bond Street, for example, is drawn from one of the many creditors' letters sent to Lord Hastings when his return to England in 1823 became known. Cooper's bill was for items purchased by Moira's wife ten years earlier ("Check silk dresses £8-0-0, 11yds. India Muslin £3-17-0," etc.)

Not surprisingly the Marquess was remembered by different people in different ways. Christopher Hibbert, the biographer of George IV and Lord Nelson, describes Lord Moira in the latter work as "stately and courtly, inconsistent and extravagant," and a "severe martinet," this last with no authority cited. (see *Nelson*, pp. 348-349). Roland Thorne in the *Oxford Dictionary of National Biography* (online, citation taken 1 Sept. 2010) summarizes Moira as "overconfident of his nurtured abilities. . . encounter[ing] a series of fiascos, military and political, and thwarted ambitions. He was therefore jealous of the professional triumphs of Cornwallis and Wellington, and was outmatched by the political nerve of Pitt, Grenville, Grey, and Canning."

Anyone who has read this far must know that my own estimate of Moira is higher. I close with the account which influenced me most, by Jane Austen's exact contemporary and fellow-novelist Lady Charlotte Bury. Like Jane, Lady Charlotte was born in 1775. She published her first novel, *Self-Indulgence*, in 1812, a year after Jane Austen's *Sense and Sensibility*. In 1810 Lady Charlotte became lady-in-waiting to Princess Caroline, estranged wife of the Prince of Wales, and would have closely observed Lord Moira in the years immediately preceding his departure for India. Here's what she wrote on that occasion (*The Diary of a Lady-in-Waiting*, ed. A. Francis Steuart, 1908, Vol. I, pp. 55-56):

> Lord Moira is sent off to India; - I call it being sent off, for it is evident the [Prince] Regent cannot bear to have him near his person. How few people, in any rank of life, have sufficient nobility of soul to love those to whom they stand indebted! Would you lose a friend, oblige him - not in the minor circumstances of life; but let the obligation be vast, and it crushes friendship to death. Lord Moira has accepted this honorable banishment, because he cannot help himself, and is ruined. But

who ruined him? He lent uncounted sums of money in former years, of which no note whatever was taken, and of which he never will see one farthing in return. Yet no one pities or feels for this man. Why? - because he is of nobler stuff than the common herd. Vanity and ambition were his only flaws, if flaws they be; but his attachment, or rather devotion; to the Regent was sincere, chivalric; and of a romantic kind, such as the world neither believes in nor understands; it was a kind of affection which amounted even to a passion of the mind, and, like all passions, led him into one or two acts beneath the "chevalier sans peur et sans reproche." But nevertheless, he is a noble creature upon the whole; and what can poor human nature ever be more? Formed to live in another day than the present, some men seem born too late, and some men too soon. . . .

Made in the USA
Middletown, DE
21 July 2017